VERRAZZANO'S HORIZON

A Tale of Discovery

Roger M. McCoy

NewWorldExploration.com

Cover design: Sue McCoy

Cover photo: Michael D. McCoy

Book layout by www.ebooklaunch.com

ISBN 978-1-5323-2383-6

Other Books by Roger M. McCoy:

Ending in Ice: The Revolutionary Idea and Tragic Expedition of Alfred Wegener (Oxford)

On the Edge: Mapping the Coastlines of North America (Oxford)

Field Methods in Remote Sensing (Guilford)

Translator's Preface

It has been my good fortune to discover this unknown journal written by Gerolamo Verrazzano, brother of the explorer Giovanni Verrazzano. It provides many new details and insights to the meager information available to us about the first exploration of the east coast of the United States. Gerolamo discusses many events that occurred during the voyage that were omitted from Giovanni's account. He also records his own conversations with knowledgable men of the early sixteenth century, and we see their thoughts on current trends in the culture of the time: the upheaval caused by Martin Luther and others in the beginning years of the Reformation, the rise of humanism, developments in medicine, and the expanding European perception of the world. All these changes were in early stages of development and Gerolamo's journal often reflects the wonderment of those living in a time of rapid transition.

Translation of ancient documents is extremely tedious and filled with many decisions regarding meaning and intent of the writer. Insofar as possible I have tried to maintain Gerolamo's sixteenth century style of writing without his ponderous and laborious sentences that sound unnatural today. Also I have added snippets of historical background throughout to provide more context for events that Gerolamo describes. I hope the reader will forgive the inclusion of a journal of my own experiences during this translation.

This was a momentous voyage of discovery and a first detailed account of European contact with indigenous people on the east coast of North America. Gerolamo has done a great service in showing us the character of the men who made this adventure. Maps of Verrazzano's voyage up the east coast of North America and Dieppe, France in 1600 are on the last pages.

Ross Turner
New York City, 2011

I, Gerolamo da Verrazzano, here begin my account regarding events related to the voyage completed in the year of our Lord 1524 in the name of His Royal Highness Francis I of France and commanded by my beloved brother, Giovanni da Verrazzano. It is my great honor to join this journey as assistant navigator and primary cartographer.

Chapter 1

March 3, 1523 Dieppe, France

Today I heard the shout, "*Il viaggio è approvato!*" and knew immediately we would soon sail on a voyage of discovery.

Giovanni burst into the dimly lit dining room of the inn, repeating his good news, babbling a mixture of Italian and French beyond comprehension. I had never seen him show such exuberance, but I knew all this incoherent talk must mean that Giovanni had just received the approval of the king.

My brother grabbed my hands and danced among the bewildered diners in Le Marin. He could not calm himself enough to give me a coherent account of his news, giving me instead a flood of disconnected details from the king's letter. He blurted something about the king allowing four ships to make the voyage. He told us the king would not pay for any ships, then added that the king would provide one from his navy. He felt sure our family connections in Lyon will provide all the money we need. Then he babbled about hiring crews, outfitting ships with provisions, and possible starting dates. He said something about getting some ships from his employer, Viscount Ango. Many times he repeated how interested the king had been in his New World adventure. He was chattering out bits of his thoughts as fast as they entered his mind. Poor Giovanni was talking in circles.

When his excitement subsided a little, he explained the most important details in the letters patent. The document from the king declared that my brother, Giovanni da Verrazzano, was to be in command of the expedition, and was to represent the interests of our good King Francis I in the unknown lands of the west. That one provision would make Giovanni a wealthy and powerful man when his discoveries turned into vital ports with important cities and abundant resources under his governance. All profitable trade from the new land would enrich Giovanni beyond imagination.

Underlying this decree from the king is the expectation that Giovanni will be the discoverer of a water passage to the Orient. Little wonder he is so exuberant—this letter will make Giovanni famous among those few, lucky adventurers who are opening up a new and unknown world. Most importantly it fulfills his dream of exploring new lands beyond the western horizon.

Sleep this night was out of the question, we could not rest until a plan was worked out in our heads. We spent most of the night at a candle-lit table in Le Marin planning

Giovanni's presentation to our bankers of Lyon—how to make the expedition sound potentially profitable, how much time and money will be needed to outfit four ships for six months of exploration, and hundreds of other details. These bankers have mounds of money, and are eager to make investments that will strengthen their share of trade with the Orient. As added benefit, a trip to Lyon is always welcome so we can visit our aging parents, and Giovanni also can visit his beautiful young wife, Beatriz. He is at sea so much under the employ of Jean Ango that he seldom sees Beatriz. Incidentally, it is this same employer, wealthy ship owner Jean Ango, Viscount of Dieppe, from whom we expect to borrow three ships, and will of course make it of substantial benefit for him to do so. There is so much to do.

August 14, 2010   Rouen, France

When I first read those words in that fragile manuscript, I knew I had made a real and vital discovery. Gerolamo da Verrazzano, brother of the well-known explorer, had indeed written an extensive journal chronicling their voyages. I long hoped that Gerolamo left something of note besides his famous map. Finally there it was before me, in a library not far from the former home port of the Verrazzano brothers. Already I had learned that they were living in Dieppe and probably originally came from Lyon rather than Florence. Conventional wisdom has always considered them to be Florentine by birth. Now I face the task of ferreting out their connection to the Verrazzano family in Florence. There clearly is a connection.

Their voyage in 1524 completed the first eyewitness-defined map for the central portion of eastern North America and the first description of its inhabitants, but surprisingly many people today have never heard of Giovanni Verrazzano. Some know about a bridge by that name in New York City, but can't say why it has that name. Maybe his brother's journal will bring him the recognition he deserves.

This lucky find came after a week of working with little result in the Villon library in Rouen. Then today I happened to meet the archivist, a tall, blond, smartly dressed woman with an ID tag reading Nicole Duval. That's when I realized it's time to get some help from a librarian. "Hello," I opened, "my name is Ross Turner, and I'm here on leave from my university in New York. I am researching the spread of the Renaissance in France, and looking for related documents. I've studied the artists and craftsmen who came north from Florence, but I want to learn more about the Italian navigators. Particularly I want to know more about the explorer Giovanni Verrazzano. I know he sailed from the Normandy port of Dieppe, and I thought the Villon might be a likely place for any documents. Do you know of any such materials?"

Her eyebrows arched in surprise as she said, "What a coincidence, Mr. Turner. Just recently we received a donation of papers for that time period from a local estate. In the letter of transfer the name Verrazzano appears and suggests that something of his is included. Come, and we will have a quick look at those boxes." I followed with anticipation as she walked toward a stairway to the basement.

Nicole opened a locked storeroom that smelled a bit like my grandmother's attic. "Here they are," she said pointing to their newly arrived manuscripts. As we came to the shelves holding these forgotten treasures, I spotted an aged wooden crate labelled 1500-1550, and my hand reached impulsively for the shelf. Nicole cleared a work space on the table. With great anticipation we opened the box and began examining and sorting its contents. There it was: a musty packet of leather bound, yellowing manuscripts written on vellum in Italian with

Gerolamo's signature on the first sheet! I never dreamed I would find such a windfall.

"Ms. Duval," I said excitedly,"how, or where, will I be able to examine these papers? This document is obviously a diary written by none other than the brother of Giovanni da Verrazzano. I would like to have access to these documents for several months to read and translate all this. Must I wait for them to be cataloged?" To my surprise, she seemed just as pleased about this discovery. "This could be a great discovery for our library, too," she said excitedly, "I will see what I can do."

Nicole soon arranged with the library administration for me to have a pass card providing regular access to a work table in the archive room, and thus began my months of tedious translation. This will be a task with white gloves and magnifying glass, bending for hours over Gerolamo's sixteenth century, barely legible, handwritten Italian manuscripts on discolored and corroded pages. It is the chance of my lifetime. I came to the Villon because of its reputation as a research library that specializes in the heritage of the Normandy region, and now I know I came to the right place.

I was far too excited to sit down and start working so I insisted on taking Nicole to lunch any place she liked. "Good idea," she said, and took us to a small bistro near the library where we had a simple but sumptuous meal of onion soup and salmon quiche. I had never tasted such soup. The onions had been thoroughly caramelized to bring out their full sweetness, which happily was enhanced by a layer of melted Gruyère cheese. The quiche, too, was utterly perfect, as was the bottle of chilled Sauvignon Blanc. The two-hour lunch gave me a chance to get acquainted with Nicole. We talked the whole time about our jobs and interests, and we both seemed to enjoy a meal and easy conversation. Nevertheless, by now I was itching to get back to the library and start working. Our lunch ended with an agreement that she would show me another of her favorite eateries soon. We walked together back to the library, and I settled down to a more thorough examination of Gerolamo's journal.

This evening I made a phone call to my longtime friend and amour, Lorena Guzman, to let her know about my discovery of the Verrazzano manuscript. We have always shared our triumphs and disappointments, so as I expected, she was pleased to hear my good news. She had recently been promoted to associate professor, so she also had some excitement of her own. I miss her, especially at times like this when we share good news with each other.

Lorena and I knew each other as undergraduates, then reconnected when we each happened to take jobs at the same university, she in anthropology and me in history. In our renewed friendship we found that we still enjoyed sharing daily successes and disappointments, cooking dinner together, and taking trips. Before long our friendship became a love affair with a shared apartment. Now in our mid-thirties, neither of us has much interest in marriage and family, and we both are quite content with the arrangement. Most of the time we are at home, but my research sometimes requires travel to work in the archives of distant libraries. Her work in the ancient cultures of Central America is equally engaging and also requires occasional long absences. Fortunately communication is easy these days and we can always stay in touch.

I told Lorena about meeting Nicole and how she had cleared the way for me to begin work immediately. Lorena said she expects regular updates on my progress. When I told her about the delicious onion soup, quiche, and wine she made some comment about my eating too well, but I know she would have loved it too.

March 4, 1523 Dieppe

When Giovanni arrived in Dieppe yesterday, the happy news spread like a flash of lightning around the city. In our premier port city any news affecting shipping is of utmost importance. This particular news caused an added stir of excitement because it involves exploration of an undiscovered part of the New World.

A new expedition means employment for the experienced seamen that call Dieppe their home port. Merchants, chandlers, rope makers, shipbuilders, and sailcloth weavers all feel a surge of business when ships are outfitted for a voyage. Much of my job will be to help oversee all these details, making sure the ships are prepared for a voyage lasting up to a year.

Before I proceed further, however, I think I should record some detail of Giovanni's stay in Lyon where his hope for this voyage became a reality. Happily for me, I also attended the meeting and recorded its proceedings. King Francis the First had moved his entire court to Lyon for a few weeks while he met and bargained with the Florentine bankers for money to finance his endless war with the Spanish King, Charles V, also Emperor of the Holy Roman Empire. While in Lyon I learned about the immense task of moving the king's court to Lyon. This move required 12,000 horses to move courtiers, knights, tents, food, and all the luggage needed by nobility. The retinue stopped at the end of each day of travel to stay in the chateau of a nobleman, where the group may linger for several days absorbing the poor beleaguered nobleman's hospitality and resources.

In Lyon the king summoned bankers to express his need for more war funds, but he also revealed his interest in entering the lucrative game played by Spain and Portugal in the New World. The king made it clear that he should share in the wealth enjoyed by those Iberian kings, and naturally the bankers of Lyon would enjoy a handsome profit as well.

Giovanni Verrazzano is well-known among the Florentine community in Lyon from his days of sailing as a merchant seaman out of Venice and later from Dieppe, when he became a captain and trader for the wealthy shipowner Jean Ango. As captain of one of Ango's ships, Giovanni has circulated among Ango's collection of artists, philosophers, and scientists who lived and worked in his home, providing stimulating dinner conversations at his manor on the harbor in Dieppe. Most importantly, Viscount Ango himself is among a small group that Francis the First counts as personal friends, and he was also the one who proposed Giovanni as the best choice to command the expedition. We regard this important man as our greatest ally in this venture, and I am certain he will be of great help in our preparations. It is not too much to say that our success depends on the support of this man. His influence will facilitate the ambitions of two men: Giovanni da Verrazzano and Francis I, King of France.

My brother is a big man, strongly built, with a personality to match. When he enters a room he takes command by his mere presence, his resonating voice, his full, black beard, and his congeniality. I am certain his air of confidence was reassuring to the king. Giovanni is a well-liked man with few enemies and many powerful friends. He is accustomed to commanding a ship and expects subordinates to act quickly when he speaks. These traits surely served him well in his presentation to the king.

Giovanni and I look somewhat alike outwardly, although I am slightly smaller in size. But our personalities differ greatly. I am quieter than he and more inclined toward study. I enjoy a few friends, but easily feel crowded when I am around many people. I enjoy my studies and have become a capable mariner, navigator, and cartographer. Perhaps one of our greatest differences is my willingness to become acquainted with ordinary shipboard subordinates and learn about their special skills and beliefs. This trait may not be the way to command a ship, but I find that it helps morale among the crew and keeps me abreast of murmurs of discontent among them.

Giovanni received notice to come before the king to present his case for making a voyage to the New World under the aegis of France. He truly loves this sort of thing, and thrives on association with people of power. He does it so smoothly and graciously. Bankers and rich merchants attended the presentation in abundance. Giovanni was especially pleased that his friend and employer, Viscount Jean Ango, was present to lend support. He hoped to speak to Ango about providing three nefs to supplement the one offered by the king. Financial supporters from several Lyon banks were there, including our mother's gracious brother Thomassin Gadagne, who had made all the arrangements and contacts for Giovanni's audience with the king. How fortunate for us to have this influential relative as a banker. The bankers, merchants, several members of the royal court, Giovanni and I were assembled in the great hall of the host's chateau when the King entered. The long room with its high ceiling and stained glass windows offered a perfect venue for this regal meeting.

Translator's Note: A nef is a ship larger than a caravel and commonly used by the Genoese, Spanish, Portugese, French, and English in the late fifteenth and early sixteenth centuries. Its name varied from caracca or nao in Genoa and Spain, nau in Portugal, caraque or nef in France, and carrack in England. They had a large aftercastle, a smaller forecastle, and ample room for storing everything needed for long voyages. The overall length of the Dauphine *was about 115 feet.*

I was impressed by the youthfulness and physical vitality displayed by the king as he strode the full length of the hall along a broad aisle to the raised dais. All present made a sweeping bow as the king passed. As he seated himself on the dais at one end of the hall, he nodded to the First Secretary of the Council to begin the proceedings. This was my first audience with a king, and I was struck with awe at the grand appearance and his commanding presence. It immediately became clear, however, why he was known as "Francis of the Big Nose." In truth, despite his handsome appearance, the nose became the focus of my attention.

Our king is also known among his subjects as the "Warrior King," for his inclination to don his armor and lead the fight in battles. Taking personal charge of a battle places the king in a very dangerous situation—dangerous for France as well as his personal safety. But this king is proud of his daring behavior and his strength. The people admire him for it. He is physically well built, and I have heard he loves to engage in many kinds of sport, such as tennis, wrestling, hunting and jousting. I can well imagine that he easily wins in any contest.

A lesser known side of him however, is his love of the arts. The king has been largely responsible for bringing the culture of Florence to France. He has brought architects to design grand palaces, and artists like the great da Vinci and Cellini. This admiration for anything Florentine certainly accounts for the banker's selection of Giovanni as the navigator most likely to attract the king's interest. French mariners must feel slighted to have a foreigner selected for this lucrative position.

Giovanni looked impressive in his finest blue doublet as he stepped forward to face the king. He started his presentation with a summary of the great advances in knowledge of the world that have been made since the discovery of new continents. He told the king that since the New World's discovery in 1492, the world has changed faster than in any period in history. More than half the known world has been discovered by men still living. The pace is fast, new lands are rapidly being discovered, and their riches are being claimed by other kings in Spain, Portugal, and England. Giovanni's speech grew stronger as he progressed and the king was visibly mesmerized by the prospect of expanding his domain and enriching his treasury. Of course, the well-educated king already knew much about voyages to the New World, but made no effort to interrupt Giovanni.

Giovanni then changed course, speaking to the king about the benefits that would come to France by finding a passage to the Orient. The silk merchants of Lyon would be able to avoid the long and complicated trade routes involving many points of exchange along the way. By the time raw silk reaches Lyon, it has been through so many other traders that the price is extremely high. If France becomes the nation to secure a direct trade route to the Orient uncluttered by numerous agents and traders, then profits for the merchants of Lyon would soar, and the king's share of this lucrative business would benefit as well. As Giovanni described the potential wealth, I heard a murmur of approval pass among the bankers. Throughout the presentation the king leaned forward in his chair, his gaze fixed intently on Giovanni.

Next the king asked Giovanni a surprising question, "Good sir, what is it that makes you an explorer?"

Giovanni's response was one of the most self-revealing statements I have ever heard. "Your Highness, can you imagine crossing an ocean? For weeks you see nothing but a perfect, empty horizon. You are only a small point at the center of an immense circle. This inspires awe, but it also inspires fear. Fear of storms. Fear of isolation. Fear of fatal sickness. Even fear of the immensity itself. An explorer of the unknown must drive those fears deep into his belly. He must study the stars, and watch the compass. He prays for a fair wind and he hopes for success."

"Then he sees a faint haze on the horizon. He watches a day and the haze turns to a shadow on the far rim of the world. The dark stain on the horizon slowly spreads and you begin to let yourself believe. At night you see a light in the far distance from a nameless being unknowingly setting a beacon. In the morning you dare to utter the word…LAND! Land means life. Land means rescue from the fearful immensity. Land means restoration and deliverance. The explorer comes out of the immensity into a new life never before experienced. That is what it is like to sail beyond the horizon to unknown places and that is the essence of the New World, Your Highness. That is what makes an explorer."

With only a moment's hesitation the king gave an insightful response. "Verrazzano, I like your hope and rescue. You create an image of man redeemed, I think in your discovery of a New World you will discover yourself as well."

"Truly spoken, Your Highness. You speak with the mind of a true explorer."

I think it is possible that Giovanni won the king's heart at that moment. When Giovanni finished his lengthy and eloquent proposal he could see that the king desired to become a part of this exciting new world. Then to our surprise the king suddenly dismissed Giovanni and all the others without so much as a word of his intent.

This sudden change of mood dashed Giovanni's enthusiasm and the attendees to the audience left the room in a subdued hush. A murmur of surprise passed among the courtiers present. What had happened to cause the king to turn cool so suddenly and end the meeting? Clearly everything had gone well. Nothing had been said that would offend the king. Giovanni returned to our parents' house full of misgivings and began for the first time to imagine his dream collapsing. At that time I returned to Dieppe, and Giovanni stayed in Lyon to await the king's decision and to confer with the bankers. Later I learned of the events that occurred after my departure.

Two restless days passed with no word from the king's secretary. During those awful two days Giovanni paced the floor by day and never slept at night. He had given his best effort to persuade the king of the value of the ultimate voyage of his imagination. He anticipated giving up his dream of exploration and returning to his life as a merchant seaman. With Jean Ango's ships Giovanni had sailed the Mediterranean to markets of the Levant, and over the Atlantic Ocean to rich fishing waters off Cabot's Newfoundland. This gave him a foretaste of new lands, but for Giovanni the life of fishermen and traders lacked the dream. As his dream of exploration emerged, Giovanni had created a muse for all explorers that he calls *Orizontas*, the seductress awaiting an explorer just beyond the horizon. Orizontas urges explorers to sail beyond the horizon to find new lands filled with the seeds of wealth or destruction. Now the dream seemed to be fading.

At last the king summoned Giovanni to a second audience. Others who had been present to support Giovanni in the first meeting were not invited to the second audience. The king's friend, Jean Ango, had already returned to Dieppe and the Lyon merchants were not present. This seemed ominous and sent a chill through Giovanni. Worse still, he had to wait until the next day for the answer. Giovanni's meeting was not an audience at all, but merely a meeting with one of the king's ministers. Much to his relief, the purpose was to sign agreements defining the terms of the king's support for Giovanni's dream expedition. At that moment Giovanni became the man who would establish France in the New World! The king left instructions for Giovanni to contact Viscount

Ango and Admiral de Bonnivet of Normandy, who is also a friend of the king. These two powerful men were directed by the king to help with the outfitting and provisioning of ships. Their influence will be of utmost importance to the success of the expedition.

Giovanni went to each of the bankers and merchants in Lyon who had attended the first audience, thanked them for their generous support, and made promises to tell them as soon as possible the details of his financial needs. They were all as pleased as Giovanni to see this important voyage become a reality. He especially expressed special thanks to our uncle Thomassin for his great help in arranging this audience and for advising him on his presentation to the king. Then Giovanni set off on his six day journey over muddy roads to Dieppe, where he arrived just yesterday in a state of high excitement and danced around the normally quiet dining room of Le Marin.

I finally had a chance to read the letters patent and saw that the king had agreed to provide the nef, *Dauphine*, from his navy but no money. He also granted authorization for three additional ships, which we must find and acquire on our own. Also we must raise enough money to cover all expenses of the voyage. However, the most important part is that the king gave permission to make the expedition. Without his sanction we could not begin.

The exquisitely penned document gave Giovanni certain rights to whatever discoveries and income resulted from the voyage. These rights were based largely on the assumption that we would be successful in finding a passage through this new continent, which the Spanish claim in the south and the English in the north. We feel certain that the twenty degrees of latitude between those north and south points must surely contain a connection by sea to Cathay and the lands of spices and silks. Some place in those 700 leagues there must be a passage to the Orient.

The agreement states further that Giovanni will claim for the king of France all new discoveries of lands not already ruled by a Christian monarch. Giovanni will become governor of those new lands and keep a tenth part of all the gold, silver, gems, spices, and other goods exported from them. He, or his appointed agent, will adjudicate any disputes or crimes committed in the new possessions. Although I am not mentioned in the king's letters patent, Giovanni pointedly told of me, "You, my dear brother, may rest assured that you will also benefit enormously from the success of this event. We may both anticipate the adventure as well as the potential wealth and acclaim." My brother loves to speak in a generous manner, but he is a shrewd man when it comes to the details. We shall see.

Our family has provided an ample income for each of us and we live comfortably. Greater wealth, therefore, is not an important goal for me. My own expectation for this voyage is to become the first cartographer to complete the map of this great unknown part of the New World. Mine will be the first such map drawn by a cartographer who actually visited the New World and determined locations for himself. This will be a tremendous opportunity for me and a fitting legacy to pass to the future. Such a map will be a wonderful tribute to my mentors, Ruysch and Vespucci. Ruysch's beautiful map of the world was made just sixteen years ago, showing the islands discovered by Columbus and the Newfoundland discovered by the Italian Caboto, when he sailed for King Henry VII of England. Ruysch's map connects the two known areas with a continuous shoreline that is wholly imaginary. When I was his assistant, he expressed the wish that someone would soon sail along that unknown land and provide much needed information for that faraway coast. I think my beloved mentor will be very proud that one of his own protégés fulfilled that wish. If only I could travel to Cologne to break the news to him myself.

Chapter 2

March 7, 1523 Dieppe

In a few days Giovanni must return to Lyon to consult with the bankers about financial support for the expedition and to show them his estimate of our needs. Bankers and silk merchants see a great opportunity for making money on their investment and are eager for action, but they must hear from Giovanni about details of costs and conditions. This will require a great amount of preparation from Giovanni before he can assure the investors their money will be well spent. They already know Giovanni's reputation as a navigator and trader and feel comfortable that he is the right man for the job, so the battle is half won. But they will want to see detailed estimates for all expected expenditures, along with assurances that Viscount Ango will be able to furnish three additional ships.

Most of Giovanni's preparation for the meeting with bankers will take place in a meeting with Viscount Ango. To that end Giovanni and I have been invited for an extended visit in the Ango household here in Dieppe. A visit to the Ango home is much more than an evening party. Visitors are expected to stay for several days and the array of guests makes the event exceedingly memorable. Giovanni has already made one such enchanting visit to

Ango's home, but this will be my first. One can never be sure until arrival what other illustrious guests may be present. Some of them come, as we will, to use Ango's extensive library, which contains many of the books, maps, and globes created by the most brilliant minds from antiquity to the present time. One can study astronomy, mathematics, philosophy, cosmography, and navigation within the walls of this fascinating home. Equally important, one may have discussions with the other guests, perhaps ship's pilots who know routes to Newfoundland fisheries or to Brazil for loads of brazilwood and exotic birds. We could meet mapmakers from the Dieppe school of cartographers, captains such as Jean Parmentier, a native of Dieppe who has sailed the coasts of Africa and beyond to Calicut, the city of spices. A man of many parts, Parmentier is not only a navigator and cartographer of great repute, he also excels in his first love, writing poetry.

At Ango's spacious home, we expect to spend time in the library or in engrossing conversation at anytime, but especially during dinner which is attended by all guests. The very name of his house, *Pensée,* or Thought, shows what the viscount expects to occur within this fine home. Needless to say Giovanni and I are eager to begin.

Later in the afternoon we walked the short distance from Le Marin to Ango's home. The chill of March was still in the air as the sea breeze filled the city. I always feel a certain pleasure just walking the street facing Dieppe harbor, passing by ships from the Levant unloading their aromatic spices, the pungent odor of fishing vessels, and the shouts of sailors to one another as they work on their daily tasks of cleaning, caulking, and repairing their ship's rigging and sails. The raucous din of seagulls squabbling, especially near the fishing ships, creates a ceaseless commotion. Merely to be amid the lively activity of a major seaport like Dieppe gives me a chill of excitement. But today more than ever we both felt great elation and confidence.

Very soon we came to Ango's home on the main quayside street. The front side of the house faces inward toward the port and the opposite side turns outward toward the beach and the sea. This orientation of the house exactly expresses Ango's two sides. He is both the most prominent man in Dieppe and its primary adventurer into the world. As I approached the facade facing the port I saw carved wooden friezes depicting scenes of exotic places, scenes of battles between the Normans and the English, and scenes from Aesop's fables.

The main entry was not on the street, but on the side of the house opening into a walled garden. We rang a bell at an ornate door in the wall and a footman let us into a beautifully designed garden that was totally concealed from the street. Before entering the house I glanced briefly around the garden marveling at its beauty. This exquisite courtyard has a sculpted fountain, several small flower beds, and a small, white gazebo. I could gladly spend the rest of the day in the enjoyment of this inviting retreat.

As the footman escorted us into the ornate foyer of the house, we were greeted by another servant and led up a broad staircase to our rooms. Unlike the entryway, my room was simple, but elegant. The furnishings consisted of a four-post bed of carved, stained wood, oak table with a stool, and a washstand. There were tapestries on the walls and heavy, draped velvet cloth at the window. It was comfortable, but clearly guests were not expected to spend much time in their rooms.

I left the room and before finding Giovanni, I took a short walk through a few of the hallways. I was immediately struck by the exceptional beauty of this elegant house within our city. The house provides views of the ocean, the port, the sea cliffs along the beach, and the beautiful valley of the Arques River. Furniture of fine design is found throughout. The halls are lined with wonderful masterpieces by Italian sculptors and painters. Italian tiles cover the floor. This house is truly worthy of a princely owner. Ango may have named this house Pensée after one of his father's ships, but the name just as well suggests a place of thoughtful solitude frequented by fine craftsmen and scholars. One long hallway was decorated with large wall paintings depicting ancient mythologies. I especially noticed one painting portraying Bacchus with nymphs and satyrs in a garden. I later learned that a Flemish painter created them on a commission for Ango.

In a short time I heard a bell summoning us to vespers in the chapel. The group gathered in the chapel appeared to be family members along with other invited guests in addition to Giovanni and me. Inside the chapel I noticed the exquisite stained glasswork in the windows and the finely carved seats. Everything about this house reflects work by the finest craftsmen employed to carry out Ango's tastes. My own family in Lyon lives quite well, but we have fewer commissioned artistic works.

The prayers were those you might expect from a seafaring family. We heard special prayers for each of the crews presently sailing in Ango's ships, then said together the 21st to the 30th verses of the 107th Psalm, the sailors' psalm, followed by the *Salve Regina.* There was a special prayer for the success of our coming voyage. To this one I gave a heartfelt, "Amen." After prayers we moved into a small oak-beamed and paneled dining room used only by the Ango family and perhaps a few guests. Today only guests were present.

Ango himself greeted each of us in turn, radiating his warmth of personality. Around his shoulders he wore the heavy golden chain of honor, bestowed by the king in recognition of his appointment two years ago as Viscount of Dieppe. A large gold pendant engraved with the Ango coat of arms hung from the chain for all to see. Ango stands out as a man of great wealth and authority with his gold chain and a black velvet doublet with paned sleeves revealing a white satin jerkin.

As Ango continued to greet the guests, I strolled briefly around the room to better absorb its detail. One wall was lined with buffets made of an exotic black wood called ebony, which I have heard of but have never seen. The walls were hung with pictorial tapestries from India and Turkey. Ango appreciates the creative products of a wide variety of craftsmen, as well as the creative minds of philosophers, composers, writers, and exceptional people in all fields of endeavor. My gaze stopped at two striking portraits of Viscount Ango and his wife.

The Viscount noticed my interest in the portraits and came to my side for a private conversation about them. "When the king bestowed the title of viscount on me," Ango said, "he also ordered one of his court painters, Jean Clouet, to make these portraits of me and my wife, Anne. This man Clouet has developed great skill in the use of chalks to produce the most lifelike portraits I have ever seen." Ango seemed eager to inform my attentive ears. "I am told that Clouet is working on a new portrait of the king that will surpass anything done before."

As he continued my private tutoring, he asked if I had seen the painting of Bacchus in the hallway near my room. "That painting was made by a different Flemish painter," he said, "and is another example of the inventiveness of those northern painters. They have learned to mix their paints in a new way by combining powdered pigments with linseed and nut oils rather than egg yolk, thus making the color mixtures smooth and easily blended. The result is a remarkable brilliance of color, light, and shadow. Clouet himself taught me these details about Flemish painters when he resided here making our portraits."

I could see the truth in Ango's explanation of the paintings. Certainly the picture of the viscount wearing the heavy necklace of his high office and holding the astrolabe and compass of a seafaring man showed more expression and feeling in the face than other portraits. The same was true of the portrait of his wife. Clouet had captured her beauty perfectly with his chalks and portrayed her beside a coat of arms symbolizing her noble Guilbert family origins in Normandy. The ever gracious host, Ango said, "I can see you are interested in paintings. I hope I can show you others in my collection soon. Please take another close look at the one of Bacchus and notice the quality of the paint." Then he turned to tend other guests.

As I continued my survey of the room I stood at the window where I could look down on the traffic of ships moving in and out of Dieppe harbor and the bustle of activity on the quayside street. The room was filled with the sounds and fragrance of crackling logs in the fireplace and the chatter of several conversations as guests gathered in the room. I think I have never experienced such delight as being surrounded by the aura of possibilities that I sensed in that beautiful, intimate room.

The Viscount gestured each guest to his place around a large oval-shaped oaken table, choosing for Giovanni and me a place at his right. Then he offered a short prayer and we were seated. Viscount Ango mentioned to the group that the oval table and cushioned chairs had been designed to ensure comfort for a long evening of eating, drinking, and discussion. Indeed, each place had a comfortable straight-back chair, rather than the stools found in many homes. Ango's own chair was wider with a velvet cushion, and arms at the sides. The hanging chandelier above the table shed soft candle light, adding to the warm feeling within the room. The table was set with silver pieces, the finest porcelain plates, and etched glass goblets. Porcelain is an innovation new to this region, and I always admire its delicate beauty. Each plate held the usual round of bread, with a white linen napkin atop. A sharp carving knife, a two-tined fork, and a silver spoon were placed beside each plate. This sort of tableware setting is also used by our own family in Lyon, as the custom originated in Florence and other parts of Italy years ago.

The oval table was covered with three cloths: the undercloth was a heavy tapestry, over which was laid a heavy green cloth, and the top cloth was the usual white linen. The centerpiece was an elegant oval silver basin filled with fragrant flowers. At one end of the table was Ango's silver nef, a container crafted in the shape of a sailing vessel to hold his personal eating utensils. Instead of a large salt basin, smaller salts were placed within reach of each person. The carved oaken sideboard held a large silver ewer and basin, which we each used for rinsing our hands upon entering the dining hall. The washing is rather ceremonial, and typical for such an elegant household, as no one would want to begin such an important event with dirty hands.

Waiters began bringing in the steaming hot dishes in a grand procession: roasted mutton, duck, and fried cod, with potatoes, lentils, and fresh bread, all on porcelain platters. The food was taken to the sideboard where the meat was carved. We were each offered selections of the meats by servants. Also on the sideboard were Venetian crystal glasses for the wine, which was cooled in a large vessel of water. With each new course, the platters of food on the sideboards were changed, and servings were brought to us on new plates.

Footmen kept our goblets filled and conversation soon began to flow as freely as the wine. As we dined, our plates were removed and clean plates brought in for new courses that included delicacies of shrimp, oysters, fruits, and cheeses. Ango's kitchen also presented four different soups for our enjoyment, a new epicurean delight. The meal was thus enjoyed slowly, with each new dish as rich and pleasing as the conversation.

After the meat, fish, soups, and other dishes were finished, servants cleared the table entirely, removing the white linen cloth, and placed before each guest a small glass dish, a small fruit knife, and clean wine glasses. The sweet dishes, fruits, and nuts, were then brought to the table on a large silver tray for our personal selection. Crystal cruets of sweet wines were placed on the green cloth as well. This appeared to be the signal that our light conversation would turn to other subjects.

Ango began with an account of a journey he took three years ago with our king to meet with Henry VIII of England near Calais. He explained, "The purpose of the visit concerned negotiations which our king hoped would lead to an alliance against their mutual enemy, Emperor Charles V, who seems to think the Holy Roman Empire should expand into England and parts of France."

It soon became clear that Ango had little respect for the Emperor and even less for the King of England. The years of conflict between England and France could possibly be forgiven, however, if the two countries could form a pact to unite themselves in opposition to the mutually despised emperor.

Viscount Ango's story continued, "This gala event lasted for three weeks in June of 1520, and was a spectacle of such extravagance that even I, who am accustomed to the excesses of royal courts, was amazed. Prior to the meeting, the English built an authentic appearing castle of wood at the outer edge of the Pale of Calais, that small, English-owned piece of France. Just beyond the Pale, the

French built a similar structure to accommodate banqueting and diplomatic meetings. Surrounding these wooden castles was a great city of 400 tents to accommodate all the courtiers, cooks, sporting groups, and the multitude of people needed to support a three-week long event."

Ango paused while a waiter filled his glass, then continued, "Colorful pennants flew from each tent creating a beautiful sight over the area that came to be called the 'Field of the Cloth of Gold' because many of the pavilions were covered by cloth with real filaments of gold woven through the fibers! This was just one example of the extreme extravagance exerted by the rival kings in an intense effort of each to outspend the other. The days were filled with games and competitions of skill, pitting English and French courtiers against one another. In truth, the competitive spending spree of the two kings nearly bankrupted both of them."

Viscount Ango reiterated his low regard for the English king, and described him as a "vain and arrogant bull."

"The English king was so convinced of his physical prowess," Ango continued, "that he challenged our King Francis to a wrestling match. Our king rose to the challenge reluctantly, but given the intense rivalry between these men, there was no way to avoid the match. As it happened, however, Francis quickly threw Henry to the ground to the startled gasps of onlookers. The defeated Henry tried to be gracious in his loss, but it was obvious that his enormous pride had been badly damaged. Needless to say, the feasting and games ended that day, the alliance between France and England against the Emperor Charles V never happened, and Henry returned to his role as an adversary of France." The viscount obviously enjoyed telling us his account of the event as much as he had enjoyed being close to men of power.

Ango entertained us with other stories of life among the English royal courtiers, hundreds of whom had accompanied King Henry to Calais. For the most part, Ango considered the English lacking in any refinement whatsoever and he enjoyed joking about the crude manners he encountered while among them.

Ango next turned to a more pertinent subject and opened the discussion that was foremost on his mind. "Jean Parmentier," he began, "what do you think about the possibility of finding a passage to the Orient by sailing due west from France?"

It seemed that everyone at the table had some opinion on this matter, and the discussion became very lively. Parmentier, one of Dieppe's own navigators and cartographers, enlightened us about the return of the remains of Magellan's small fleet just last September, unfortunately without the famous Magellan. That voyage showed conclusively that a route existed far to the south at fifty-four degrees. This had been a dangerous passage and required an extremely long voyage. Parmentier finished by saying, "All logic supports the presence of another passage in the northern hemisphere. It is simply too large an area to imagine that no break exists with a water passage through the land." Everyone at the table nodded in agreement.

Giovanni noted to our group that Columbus insisted for some time that he had indeed reached the Orient, but soon conceded that he had instead found a new and unknown continent. Columbus, however, was unsuccessful in finding a way through this obstructing mass of land. Giovanni continued telling of the English efforts in the New World, "John Cabot, sailing for the merchants of Bristol, had not truly found a passage. He located Newfoundland, marvelous amounts of cod, and what he supposed was a passage to the Orient. But rather than pursue the passage, Cabot returned to England with glowing optimism and persuaded his investors to send him back with more ships and provisions. Unfortunately, his ships were lost and exploration for a passage in the northern latitudes ended. The only outcome was that fishermen from England and France began making regular voyages to Newfoundland to fill their ships with cod." This summary by Parmentier and Giovanni was not news for most of us, but it provided an excellent opening for Giovanni to expand on his own views.

As this conversation continued, servants quietly cleared the table of plates and utensils, while all guests gave rapt attention to the conversation with occasional exclamations of approval at appropriate moments. The servants left the goblets on the table and kept them well supplied with wine through the evening.

Giovanni said he had heard the French ambassador to Spain tell of a voyage to the New World by Ponce de León, who sailed up the east coast of an area called Florida to thirty degrees latitude and found no water passage. Also Lucas Vasquez de Ayllón sailed even farther north to thirty-three degrees with no sign of a passage. Giovanni observed that it would be pointless to sail where those Spanish ships had already gone to no avail. Therefore the starting point should be at thirty-three degrees north latitude. Viscount Ango spoke to the other obvious reason for starting at thirty-three degrees, "We have no knowledge if the Spanish established a presence at thirty-three degrees or not. The worst thing that could befall this enterprise is to encounter hostile Spanish ships in territory they seek to defend from intruders."

Giovanni agreed that he had no taste for turning an exploration expedition into a sea battle. "I have no plans," he said, "to carry heavy cannon, and my poor ships would probably be captured or sunk. To be sure, I am not a warrior but a mariner and trader."

"No one has returned to search the latitudes north of lands found by the Spanish," Giovanni continued. "This vast stretch of unknown land from thirty-three degrees to fifty degrees north of the equator is the place that excites my imagination as it would any true explorer. I agree with Jean Parmentier that somewhere in the 700 leagues covered by this mysterious region must lie an opening through the continent. The temptress Orizontas beckons me to these unknown latitudes with her irresistible lure."

Giovanni explained his idea of an explorer's muse named Orizontas, and everyone at the table must have sensed that Giovanni was an inspired man of great vision and the right one to embark on a quest to find the passage in those middle latitudes. This appealing topic so dominated the conversation for the rest of the evening that nothing else was discussed.

Wine continued to flow during the night, and each man grew more eloquent with his advice, suggestions, or warnings about the undertaking. The first question on everyone's mind was the decree made by Pope Alexander VI just two years after Columbus's first voyage. This treaty between Spain and Portugal, made at Tordesillas, Spain, was unilaterally imposed upon all Christian countries under the pope's domain. All newly discovered lands west of a meridian 370 leagues west of the Cape Verde islands would belong to Spain. Lands east of the line would go to Portugal. France and England were not even consulted, although they are both naval powers in Europe. The problem in many minds was that this treaty had the authority of the pope behind it, and ignoring a papal bull could have dire results.

One of the guests opined that the king should not claim land in defiance of the treaty. Viscount Ango, a strong supporter of the king and frequent plunderer of Spanish ships himself, said that King Francis knew very well that his approval of Giovanni's voyage would violate the bull, but apparently was unconcerned. Ango continued with visible emotion, "The treaty should not have been made without the knowledge and consent of France. The only reason Spain and Portugal could behave in such an arrogant way was that the kings of France and England were out of favor with the pope for various reasons." Ango expressed his great revulsion over the infamous treaty. "This treaty is invalid, and I swear that neither Spain, Portugal, nor the pope would act against any country that ignores the treaty. Henry VII displayed the same attitude when he approved John Cabot's voyages. These kings are resolved to test the limits of Spain's willingness to enforce this unfair division of the world. When God created the sea, He never expected it to become the property of a particular nation."

Giovanni, who had sailed Ango's ships to the fishing areas near Newfoundland, said, "Nothing happened to Henry VII for sending Cabot to the New World. After some minor protest to England, King Manuel I of Portugal sent Corte-Real to Newfoundland to establish a Portuguese presence in the area, but in the eighteen years since they have not explored the area again. The English also have not yet returned to the New World, but they firmly consider Newfoundland and all the lands beyond to be theirs."

Giovanni continued, "Now is the best, and maybe the last, chance for France to acquire New World land and claim its wealth. The time is right, and I am extremely grateful that our benevolent King Francis has shown his trust in me to be the right man for the task."

Captain Laurent Hebert, one of Ango's captains, had spoken little so far, but at this point he related tales about the New World that sailors passed among themselves. No one knows how much of their lore is true, but such tales provide both intriguing potential of untold riches, and cautions about headhunters, cannibals, and dangerously shallow waters with growths of seaweed that can entangle ships. Hebert told of unimaginably strong and long-lasting winds that appear in certain latitudes in the summer season. Ships hit by one of these storms seldom survive. Another annoying problem that Hebert spoke about is the steady change of the compass as a ship sails westward on the Atlantic, and a vigilant pilot must make regular corrections. While the compass corrections are not difficult, it is mysterious and disturbing to have the compass change while the position of the Pole star stays constant. It makes a pilot question the reliability of his instrument, and every mariner knows that voyages on the big oceans require a trustworthy compass, without which it is uncertain if a ship could ever return to home port.

Hebert continued, "On a long voyage these tales of the unknown mysteries lead to doubts among the crew. When their imaginations play on these doubts they often become restive. The wise captain will be on his guard for such problems, and they can begin with such simple things as an erratic compass." Giovanni replied that he, too, had sailed as far as Newfoundland fisheries with sailors who had experienced some of these mysteries, "The sailor's fears and superstitions do indeed need to be controlled or they can disrupt the voyage."

After standing for a final toast to the honor of our host, the guests prepared to leave the dining room. Viscount Ango motioned for Giovanni to stay behind for a word in private. Giovanni later told me Ango knew that the king directed Admiral Bonnivet of Dieppe to oversee the preparation for the voyage, and he assured Giovanni that this appointment will be helpful in easing the preparations. The admiral is highly respected in France, especially here in Dieppe. Much could be done on his authority alone. But it could become difficult if the admiral were to be personally involved in these preparations. It would take a little diplomacy to persuade him to delegate this task directly to Giovanni, otherwise many details could be overlooked in preparing for an exploration expedition by a man whose main experience was warfare. Viscount Ango offered to speak to Admiral Bonnivet as a friend and learn of his intention.

"Even more serious," Giovanni continued, "Admiral Bonnivet's favorite sea captain is a man named Antoine Conflans, who happens at present to be captain of the *Dauphine*, one of the ships allocated to my expedition. Ango gave me a word of warning about Captain Conflans. He is an exceedingly imperious man who works well only when he controls everything. He is also arrogant and overbearing. These traits have made him an effective commander in naval battles, and he is the most highly regarded captain in the French navy."

Giovanni said, "I felt the hair on my neck rise at the thought of anyone but myself presuming to command this expedition. Yet I know that Captain Conflans will easily have the attention of the admiral who could quickly turn to the king if necessary. The power of the navy and the throne stands with Conflans."

Ango had offered a shred of hope to Giovanni, who just happens to be his favorite captain and sea trader, "Giovanni," Ango told him, "you must do nothing to aggravate the situation until we see Conflans' intentions. Perhaps the good captain will surprise us. In the meantime, your utmost tact and diplomacy is needed." Giovanni vowed to me, "I will crush that arrogant captain if he interferes with my expedition."

March 8, 1523 Dieppe

After a sound night's sleep following the long dinner and conversation, Giovanni and I had a quick breakfast of bread and butter with cider and spent the day in Viscount

Ango's library. There we found a trove of information about the cost of voyages made by Ango's ships. We found valuable accounts about the optimal rigging for Atlantic voyages, and the size and needed skills of crews. We found ships' logs made by captains sailing the North Atlantic, with details of the winds and sea conditions they encountered. Most importantly, we found a wonderful supply of maps, many of which are the only existing copies. We will be busy with this information for one or two more days, preparing as thoroughly as possible for a successful voyage of at least six months with four ships. Although we know the voyage will last about six months, that will be possible only if no serious mishaps occurred. So we must plan provisions and equipment for at least a year and consider the potential for damages from storms or groundings.

Our list of needs includes: food for up to 200 men for one year, spare masts and spars for four ships, spare sails, rope, barrels of water, wine, and cider, and plenty of caulking material. Although we will not be armed sufficiently to defend against attacks by hostile ships, we must carry light weapons to hunt and to protect the ship from unwanted boarding parties. To this purpose we will carry forty each of crossbows and arquebuses, with ample kegs of powder and balls. Small-bore falconets mounted on swivels on the gunwales will be our only type of artillery. These can aid in signaling other boats or frightening possible intruders, but have no real value in warfare. We plan to have no military men on board as our objective is strictly exploration, not conquest.

We found everything necessary to present a budget of costs to the bankers and merchants of Lyon. If we move quickly to obtain their funds, the voyage could begin by the start of summer. Also we will soon begin contacting merchants and ship suppliers in the local area to be certain they have the necessary goods available. Fortunately the king's agents have already issued a decree to all suppliers in Normandy alerting them to our project. The message informs merchants that our expedition has the king's sanction and that they are to make any goods we need available at the regular price. It contains a strong warning that any attempt at profiteering will be considered a crime against the crown.

March 9, 1523 Dieppe

After gathering information for the past two days, we finally have an account of money required for our voyage. Our best estimate, with some contingency padding included, is that we will need at least 1,800 *ecu d'oro soleil.*

Translator's Note: There is a great deal of uncertainty involved in translating monetary amounts from the 16th century to the present, but the best estimate is that this would be about $250,000 in 2010 U. S. dollars.)

Now Giovanni is ready to return to Lyon for a meeting with his intended investors. The weather has been very wet this spring, so it will be a slow trip on muddy roads. He plans to stay with our parents in Lyon and visit his young wife, Beatriz. She lives with our parents when Giovanni is away, which is most of the time. Beatriz is dearly loved by our parents and helps them in many ways. Giovanni leaves tomorrow morning.

March 10, 1523 Dieppe

There is much for me to do while Giovanni is in Lyon. I am staying on at the Ango villa to study the logs and diaries of captains of the Ango fleet. As pilot for the voyage, I hope to ascertain the best route for us to cross the Atlantic. Captain Hebert has sailed the northern route to Newfoundland along the 48th parallel. He described slow progress on the outward voyage due to westerly winds, but the return was much quicker. He suggested we use the northern route because it is better known. I am almost certain that the southern route would be better for our needs. It is well-known that Columbus found good following winds for his entire crossing and found westerlies for his return. No one knows the limits for each of these winds, but we certainly will test them.

August 27, 2010 Rouen

I've spent the past weeks poring over the Verrazzano papers. This has been the most exhilarating time of my professional life. For a historian it simply cannot get much better than this. I have newly-discovered original source materials and I can also visit the sites where most of these events occurred. Thankfully this is only the beginning of my sabbatical leave. The grant gives me living expenses for another six months for translations and travel to places of interest to the Verrazzano study. When I'm through here I'll need to return home for a few days to catch up with work on campus. Then comes the long tedious job of editing and annotating all I've done.

I'm eager to finish the translations, so exciting, yet so slow and sometimes tiresome. When I'm desperate for a break from the library basement, I'll visit Dieppe to get some feeling for how it might have been to live there in the 16th century.

Nicole sat down with me today and said, "Ross, I want to hear more about your findings in Gerolamo's journal." I was surprised that she had used my first name but very pleased that she was interested. We spent nearly an hour talking about it. She frequently broke in with insightful questions on points I will need to research in the future.

August 29, 2010 Rouen

Nicole invited me to come to her apartment for dinner yesterday. She said she loves to cook and needs to practice. Her meal, however, was that of an accomplished chef who has had plenty of practice. She casually said, "Ross, I hope you like a good beef stew." Whereupon she proceeded to serve a beef bourguignon beyond any I had ever eaten. The mingling of flavors from beef, bacon, and wine with onion, garlic, and thyme provided my finest meal since coming to France. We finished a bottle of burgundy during dinner and talked on into the night over a second bottle. As the evening progressed our conversation turned from small talk about our jobs to the successes and disappointments in our lives. Soon we felt talked out, and suddenly we locked in an embrace that felt like a long awaited gift for both of us. We were starving people satisfying a hunger.

I awoke this fine Sunday morning with cathedral bells jolting my cotton-filled, wine-soaked head. Would they never stop ringing? The dinner, wine, and love-making left me almost immobile. Nicole gave me a sweet smile, a kiss on the cheek and offered to cook us a breakfast, but that sounded like more than I could handle. What a night! After sharing morning coffee, croissants and more conversation with Nicole, I went for a long walk to clear my head and returned to my hotel.

March 23, 1523 Dieppe

Giovanni returned from Lyon yesterday with a letter of credit to be taken to the bank in Rouen. The investors provided everything we requested within a few hours after Giovanni's presentation. The letter names each investor with their amounts and contains the seal of the Lyonnaise Bank. One of the investors, of course, is our mother's brother Thomassino Guadagni, one of the wealthiest men in Europe. When he talks, people hear only his money speaking. Another big contributor is Francois Bautier who is perhaps the wealthiest silk merchant in Lyon, and also happens to be Thomassino's brother-in-law. This is the wonder of being born into a wealthy family. There are eight investors now supporting this expedition for a total outlay of 1,800 *ecu d'oro soliel.*

The king himself contributed nothing in cash, but provided other valuable assets for the expedition. He assigned the naval ship, *Dauphine*, along with its famous captain, Antoine Conflans, in command. That ship, followed by three others, will lead this expedition in a grand style.

Giovanni is elated, but has a thorn in his neck over this Captain Conflans. The implication in the king's letters patent is that Captain Conflans will command the *Dauphine*, which is to be the flagship of the expedition. This means that Giovanni could find himself in a subordinate role on the same ship, or worse, on one of the smaller ships. This is no insignificant matter. I have not yet met this Captain

Conflans, but I know my brother very well, and Giovanni, like most captains, will never again be a subordinate on a ship. He has had too many years of meritorious experience, not in warfare as Conflans, but as a navigator and trader, which is the primary purpose of this voyage. The command of a ship and an expedition must be clear and undivided, so I am certain that Giovanni will find a way to resolve this matter. Two men of a dominating nature simply cannot share such an important command.

Chapter 3

March 30, 1523 Dieppe

Today Giovanni and I made another visit to Viscount Ango. His magnificent manor by the harbor is always a pleasure to experience after our small rooms in Le Marin. Today I felt a touch a spring in the air with wonderful balmy air and warm sunshine on our faces. Gone was the chilling of the sea breeze. The fields are greening, the birds are chattering, our souls are restored from the unending gray days of winter. Our only intention on this visit was to confirm to Viscount Ango that we had secured the money for the voyage and that we are now ready to begin preparing ships.

Ango received us graciously, as always, and motioned for us to make ourselves comfortable in his private work room where he had a large table with maps and papers scattered about. He had obviously been working there when we arrived, as he had a large book of accounts open before his cushioned chair.

"I trust you had a successful trip to Lyon and are fully rested," the viscount began. We exchanged a few minutes of friendly banter, then Giovanni said, "The funds are now guaranteed, and we are ready to begin outfitting ships for the voyage. We need to make an agreement about which of your ships will be available and settle the financial arrangements with you."

Ango leafed through some papers on his table, and said, "The *Normande* is making a training voyage along the coast to Havre d'Grâce and should return to Dieppe within a week. Several other ships would arrive soon afterward. Two of those other ships along with the *Normande* will be assigned to your voyage of exploration."

Ango brought up the matter of his charges for our use of three ships. Instead of the usual amount for fees, Ango proposed a one-tenth share of profits resulting from trade during this and subsequent voyages. One-tenth was not unreasonable, but Giovanni had allowed only one-twelfth in his estimates. His investor group expected a one-half portion of the profit, and the king demanded one quarter. Giovanni explained to the viscount about the division of interests in the voyage, and Ango then agreed to accept one-twelfth, but with additional fees for use of the ships. This was much more agreeable to Giovanni, as he can make savings in the expense of provisions to accommodate greater usage fees. Viscount Ango had his assistant write the agreement; we signed the document, toasted the event with a glass of wine, and my brother and I returned to the streets of Dieppe in a jovial mood. Now the endless details of preparation lie ahead, and we are confident we have ample money from Giovanni's investors for the expense of hiring crews, rigging the ships, and provisioning the ships.

April 15, 1523 Dieppe

All four ships are now in port, and we went to the docks to assess their condition. Le Marin is only a short distance from the waterfront and we hurried through the bustle of workers and vendors on the street. There at the main pier lay the nef *Dauphine*, the slightly larger *Normande* and two other ships waiting to be unloaded after their voyages to distant ports in the Levant. The *Dauphine* is a new ship built only five years ago in the port of Le Havre and named in honor of the king's newborn son, François Dauphine of France, and has seen action as a naval ship since construction. She has three masts and a bowsprit. The mainmast and foremast are rigged with square sails and mizzenmast with a lateen sail. The large aftcastle and smaller forecastle provide room for crew and storage.

It was obvious even as we approached that the sail rigging would need to be refurbished. All four of the ships are similar to the *Dauphine*, but the rigging shows signs of wear or damage. We will replace damaged sails and spars, especially the main mast on the *Dauphine*. It split badly during a recent storm.

The ships' supply of barrels, spare masts, sails, spars, rope, caulking, and many other things is almost depleted. We will need to contact merchants for these items immediately. Hiring crews will not be difficult as there is a large reserve of able seamen in Dieppe. Seamen from other nearby Norman ports, Havre d'Grâce and Fécamp, will also show up as soon as word goes around that a long voyage is about to begin. Many of the crew for the *Dauphine* are permanently with that ship, so most of the hiring will be for the *Normande* and the two smaller ships, the *Intrépide* and the *Égyptien*.

As we approached the *Dauphine*, we realized that we were about to meet Captain Conflans for the first time.

Giovanni took the initiative to introduce himself to the famous naval captain. Conflans is a rather broad man for his height, has an engaging friendly manner, and a thick growth of red hair on his head and chin. He immediately offered to show us around his *Dauphine* and point out items that needed attention before undertaking another voyage. His comment that caught us most unaware was, "My preference, of course, is for naval duty, but Admiral Bonnivet obviously felt my experience was needed for this particular exploration voyage. I suppose his reasons are sound."

Giovanni well understood the innuendo. The navy, as usual, felt that anything of importance on the sea required its guidance. But Giovanni ignored the slight and responded with grace, as Viscount Ango had suggested. "Well, esteemed captain, we shall look forward to the benefit of your expertise." I was frankly rather surprised that Giovanni answered with such reserve. He can be tactful when needed, but diplomacy is not easy for him. I knew I would hear more of this later, and it was not long in coming. Captain Conflans spent a few minutes with us on the main deck, then took leave for some imaginary appointment of great importance—probably he was in a rush to find a mirror. I am certain he owns at least one of those expensive metal-coated looking glasses.

"Either Captain Conflans will be subordinated or Giovanni Verrazzano will not be going on this voyage," my brother whispered after Conflans had turned his back and walked away. "And if he sails with us, it certainly will not be as commander of the flagship, *Dauphine.* I do not yet know how, but I will deal with this arrogant louse. I have read his

Treatise on Navigation and find it seriously lacking in depth, just as I find his character deficient. I will have my way in this matter."

Giovanni's dark eyes fixed intently on the retreating figure of Captain Conflans, and his reddened cheeks revealed his sudden anger at the insult to his abilities. My brother is not a man to ignore such belittling of his reputation. His navigational skills equal or exceed those of any captain in France, and he is extremely sensitive to the least show of disregard for his abilities. He also knows, however, he must not push too openly against a prominent man like Antoine Conflans, with his connections to Admiral Bonnivet, or the whole expedition could be in peril. Conflans has the ability to prevent this voyage. Clearly Giovanni's euphoria from a few weeks ago has given way to anxiety about Conflans and the stress of the day-to-day routine of countless details. He is so intent on his objectives that he no longer participates in light conversation. I am seeing a different side of my brother.

April 16, 1523 Dieppe

Today we began in earnest with the arrangements for re-rigging and buying stores and provisions for the ships. This is no small task, and to begin we paid a call to Admiral Bonnivet, a close boyhood friend to the king and now the designated overseer for all preparations. The admiral could not see us until mid-afternoon, so much of the day was spent planning how the carpenters should expand the officers' quarters on the *Dauphine*. We must include additional sleeping quarters me and for a surgeon, a position not usually found on ships. Caring for ill and injured is usually assigned to a seaman who happens to have some skills as a barber. Giovanni's thinking is quite modern in this regard. He says that our venture into the unknown, far from civilization, demands that our limited crew be protected by the most recent advances in medicine.

As our meeting hour arrived we walked to Bonnivet's home near the waterfront. We were shown into a well-furnished room that seemed to be a work room with tables and cabinets for maps. The servant said that the admiral would arrive soon. After letting us sit for a suitable time, Admiral Bonnivet walked into the room and sat in a straight backed arm chair that was much too small for his girth. He was bedecked with the trappings of his rank, although I could see the nacre buttons on his gray doublet were under great strain, and his hose were stressed from his thick legs. I think the admiral has been living a life of great ease. He motioned us to be seated, made some idle comments about the constant demands put on him, then moved directly to the subject of interest.

"I am greatly interested in the success of your venture to the New World," the admiral said as soon as we met him. "The high reputation of Giovanni Verrazzano is well-known among naval officers, and we are confident you are the perfect commander for this voyage. The outcome is bound to be good for France." I could see that Giovanni was almost afire with pride at this recognition from the admiral.

"I am very pleased to see such unexpected enthusiasm for our venture," Giovanni replied. "I detected much less interest from Captain Conflans recently."

"Of course, you will find Captain Conflans is a proud man with a high regard for his own reputation," the admiral said. "Since his navigation book received such high acclaim, his self-regard has blossomed. But he is truly a skilled mariner and valued naval warrior, and I would hate to see our navy without him. He will be a valuable asset to your coming voyage, I am sure. With this voyage France will show just how she feels about the horrible decree the pope made when he divided the undiscovered world between those Iberian usurpers. What a travesty!"

We had not expected the admiral to show such support for our expedition. On the contrary, Bonnivet had obviously caught the king's enthusiasm for seeing France acquire new lands and wealth in the New World. The outcome could only enrich France and this, of course, would be good for the admiral's navy.

Admiral Bonnivet said, "About your preparations, I have already designated a manager from my staff, Lieutenant Fournier, to handle the purchase of stores and provisions. Another good man, Ensign First Class Bonnet, will oversee whatever changes the ships' rigging might need. Captain Verrazzano, you should contact each of these able men to begin the job of refitting the ships."

This is very good news for us. These men will have ready access to all the providers and craftsmen in the area, as their jobs keep them in constant touch with such sources.

To our dismay, Admiral Bonnivet added one piece of bad news. "Captain Verrazzano, I have ordered Lieutenant Fournier and Ensign First Class Bonnet to report directly both to you and to Captain Conflans."

"I would have preferred to have sole responsibility, Admiral Bonnivet," said Giovanni, "but I will certainly follow your wishes. Your interest in our venture is most important to us and duly appreciated."

Giovanni shot a look in my direction at the news that Conflans would also have a part in these vital preparations. Again, to my surprise, he said nothing in opposition to Bonnivet's plan. Admiral Bonnivet is clearly a big asset for us and a dutiful servant to the king's wishes, but Giovanni is showing great caution with him. We thanked the Admiral for his time and for his great support for our endeavor, and took our leave.

"What has changed you, my brother, to make you behave so reservedly regarding Conflans? I expected you to reveal your feelings to Admiral Bonnivet, but you did not."

"It is quite simple," Giovanni replied, "I think Admiral Bonnivet is not easily swayed by men he considers subordinate. I intend to adhere to Viscount Ango's advice and let him be the one to cajole our admiral. Ango can speak with him as an equal and will find a subtle and clever way to make Bonnivet see a benefit to himself by a reassignment of Conflans. In the meantime we must be careful not to lose Bonnivet's good will.

April 17, 1523 Dieppe

This morning we had a short meeting with Lieutenant Fornier to let him know our needs and to confirm the names of ships that needed supplies. We told him that each ship will require provisions for up to fifty men for a year. The lieutenant already had prepared lists of stores and supplies needed for ships of various sizes having crews of prescribed numbers. This is a routine task for the lieutenant and he will keep us informed, along with Captain Conflans, of his progress. We could not possibly suggest to the Lieutenant that he bypass Conflans, though Giovanni confessed to me that he considered it.

April 18, 1523 Dieppe

Today we met with Ensign First Class Bonnet regarding rigging the sails of our four ships. This meeting took a sour turn when Bonnet announced, "Captain Verrazzano, I have already spoken with Captain Conflans on the matter, and the matter of rigging for the ships is settled."

Giovanni's face suddenly reddened as he spoke, "What is it exactly, may I ask, that has been settled between you and Captain Conflans?"

"Sir, Captain Conflans wants the normal replenishment of damaged sails, masts, and spars, but he said I should report to him as work progresses. I assumed, sir, that he was in command."

Giovanni's response came strong and fast. "Ensign First Class Bonnet, you were mistaken to make such as assumption, and in the future I admonish you to consult me directly before completing your tasks. You may proceed with restocking as needed, but you must do nothing about refurbishing the rigging until I have worked out an understanding with Captain Conflans."

Being a naval man, the Ensign perhaps had not realized that Giovanni was the primary person in this expedition. But Giovanni's jaw tightened as he leaned toward Bonnet's face to put that fact firmly into his mind, "Ensign First Class Bonnet, I am the one who conceived this voyage, I am the one who raised the finances for this voyage, and I am the one who will see it to success. You, therefore, will take care not to bypass my authority even though you may receive counter orders from Captain Conflans. Is this clear?"

Bonnet gave a subdued "Yes, Sir, Captain Verrazzano," and we immediately left. Surely Conflans will soon hear of this outburst.

I think Ensign Bonnet is a capable man and knows his job well. Once everyone understands that Giovanni is not a subordinate in this expedition, things will move along smoothly. Giovanni has never had to work so closely with naval men, so it is a new experience for him. I know he will have these arrangements go according to his wishes, or there will be a serious clash between these two headstrong captains. As it happened, an unexpected meeting with Conflans took place as we were leaving the supply storage where we had talked with Bonnet.

After a cordial greeting among the three of us, Giovanni raised the issue of sail rigging. "Captain Conflans," began Giovanni, "it has come to my attention that you think you have assumed command our coming voyage of exploration. Would you please enlighten me as to your reason for this mistaken idea?"

Conflans responded in the manner of instructing a midshipman. "Captain Verrazzano, I am obviously the one with greater experience and skill. It therefore follows that I should lead the expedition. Also I am already commander of the *Normande* and I do not relish the idea of ceding that to you."

Giovanni responded with a fiery repeat of the lecture he had thrown at poor Ensign Bonnet, but added information that he planned to lead the expedition along a southerly route five of six degrees north of the route Columbus had taken.

Conflans listened attentively, then responded, "But surely, Captain Verrazzano, you do not intend to sail south and west as Columbus did. If so, you will sail right into the teeth of the Spanish warships and your expedition will be blown to tiny pieces. No matter how well you arm your ships, you will be no match for the Spanish men-of-war that patrol the coasts of Spain and Africa."

"Captain Conflans," Giovanni answered, "I have no intention of arming any of the four ships in this expedition. This is a voyage of discovery, exploration, and trading. We will carry only light weapons. And, yes, I certainly intend to follow a course a few degrees north of the course sailed by Columbus."

"Then, my good but naive mariner, you are either too inexperienced for this undertaking or you are simply foolhardy. You would do well to follow my advice, or turn the job to someone more capable. I wish you a good day."

With that parting shot, Conflans immediately strode away without waiting for a reply from Giovanni. Giovanni's face tensed as he watched Conflans walk away, and he vowed from this moment to change his soft approach to dealing with Conflans. "I swear that this Captain Conflans will soon see a different side of Giovanni Verrazzano," my brother said, throwing a dark look toward the retreating Conflans. "Tact is obviously wasted on a man of Conflans's arrogance."

April 20, 1523 Dieppe

Giovanni spent the past two days at Le Marin inn and tavern where we both have rooms. He said his thought was focussed on finding the best way to neutralize Captain Conflans, but it appeared to me when I joined him for dinner that he was more relaxed and doing much more than thinking about difficult captains. His dark-haired mistress, Marie, was entertaining him at the table in a private alcove and sharing small conversation over a cup of cider. Marie's quarters, for which Giovanni pays the rent, is adjacent to his. She is in no way one of the tarts sometimes found in these waterfront inns. Marie is a mature, sophisticated woman of considerable intelligence. Today she looked especially striking wearing a gold colored kirtle over a white smock. Over those items she wore an embroidered bodice and a light-brown gown with elbow-length sleeves so the beautiful golden kirtle showed. On her head she wore a French style hood. In short, Marie was elegantly dressed and also well protected against the chill of the room. Around her neck she had a delicate gold chain with a pearl pendant, which I recall was a gift from Giovanni after a voyage to Constantinople two years ago.

Marie is extremely loyal to Giovanni, and he values her as a passionate companion and a reliable confidant. Marie is one of the few people who can speak bluntly to Giovanni. She can tell him when he is wrong and he listens. He also listens to her advice, knowing that she hears much information around the city.

Giovanni had obviously enjoyed many tankards of cider, which probably accounts for his relaxation, and was beginning to complain to Marie rather loudly with tangled thoughts about dealing with the navy and their eternal procedures and pompous personalities. Surprisingly, he somehow managed to avoid mentioning Conflans by name. Many of the patrons in the tavern were naval officers themselves and word could soon get to the admiral if Giovanni became too loud and critical of the navy. Marie fortunately saw the problem and quickly maneuvered Giovanni to change the subject.

After we finished our dinner, we noticed a man watching us from another table. He wore the clothes of a gentleman and had an open, pleasant appearance. Giovanni, always a gregarious man, invited him over to our table and asked if he would join us for a round of cider. He told us his name was Jacques Beaudine. His clothing and his accented speech suggested he was not from Normandy, but he gave us no immediate clue to his origins. When asked directly, he told us he was a merchant from Marseilles. He said he is in Dieppe on behalf of a group of merchants to investigate trade with Normandy ports. He stayed at our table for some time, paying for all the drinks. It was a most jovial evening.

April 21, 1523 Dieppe

Today we again talked to Jacques Beaudine, the merchant from Marseilles. He told us that he is interested in finding out about trade with the new continents in the west. Giovanni, being very pleased to have someone seek him out on such matters, was eager to talk of the prospects for other trade connections. The voyage for this year has no room for additional investors, although some side agreement might still be made. In subsequent voyages, however, Giovanni and I will be in a strong position to make connections with new investors seeking trade with the new world.

This Monsieur Beaudine is a tall, lean man with a neatly trimmed black beard, and dark eyes showing forth an inner intelligence. Giovanni was eager to tell him about plans for our upcoming voyage to learn if Beaudine could offer insightful suggestions. We both think he would be a big asset in our future plans, and Giovanni is confident Beaudine is a man of honor. Beaudine will be in Dieppe for a few more days and we have made plans to meet him at the Le Marin for dinner while he is here. Giovanni is very enthusiastic about this new connection. Even though he has interested investors in Lyon for the foreseeable future, "More is always better," he said.

April 24, 1523 Dieppe

Marie is always present at our dinners, but says little throughout the evening. Tonight after we had finished our wine and bid our farewells to Beaudine, Marie finally spoke. "Giovanni, my sweet and foolish man, you must be careful of this man Beaudine. There is something unsavory about him. Please be cautious about giving information to him until we know who he truly represents."

"Do not be so negative, Marie," Giovanni admonished, "Beaudine is a man of integrity and I trust him. I think we may have business together in the future."

Marie shrugged her shoulders and said, "I think you may regret putting your trust in this man, Giovanni, you do not know who this man truly is. I truly doubt that he is from Marseilles. He has provided you no credentials. How can you be so foolish?"

September 6, 2010 Rouen

The late Renaissance was a time of stunning change. I would have loved to be there to see it. Of course, I'd want my laptop and a digital camera to make a record of it all. That period saw the spread of Italian culture and influence outward from northern Italy into nearby countries, especially France, England, and Spain. This cultural transfer involved not only artists, but craftsmen, businessmen, bankers, and navigators.

One particular migration I previously studied was that of the bankers and merchants from Florence who left to establish colonies of Florentines in major cities of Europe. In Lyon, for example, the Florentine merchants held trade fairs, operated banks, and made Lyon the premier financial center of France. Even King Francis the First traveled to Lyon to arrange for loans from the Florentine banks to finance his wars and expensive tastes. The migration of Florentines to Lyon and other cities in Europe created pockets of permanent citizens who became loyal subjects of the king while keeping their Italian culture and language intact. In addition, the king and other rich men invited artists, writers, and philosophers, mostly from Florence, to come work under their support. The host countries welcomed these highly skilled, innovative, and wealthy newcomers with the result that they advanced both economically and culturally. This migration did much to expand the effects of the Renaissance and change the culture of France. Despite this, the Florentines were not without problems in their adopted countries. Although they were welcomed for their contributions, they never were fully accepted as native Frenchmen, even after several generations. Very little was needed for them to be castigated as "a foreign element among us," or "they are not truly French."

In addition to merchants and bankers, the mariners from northern Italy were also in demand by the maritime nations. Columbus learned his skills in Genoa, then discovered the New World for Spain in 1492. John Cabot, born in Genoa, claimed Newfoundland and all the land beyond for Henry VII of England 1497. Then in 1524, Francis the First sent Giovanni Verrazzano, who had learned his skill while sailing the Mediterranean out of Venice, to find a passage westward to Asia.

One part of the Verrazzano family had come to Lyon as bankers in the 1450's. Typically the Florentine expatriates married within the Florentine community of Lyon. Thus, in 1480 Alessandro Verrazzano married Giovanna Gadagne, daughter of a wealthy Florentine merchant in Lyon. I have concluded that their sons Giovanni, born in 1485, and Gerolamo, 1487, left Lyon about 1500 to return to the family estate in the Val di Greve near Florence. There they studied at the University of Florence, acquainting themselves with Latin, Greek, mathematics, astronomy, and theology. By residing in Florence for those years the young Verrazzano brothers strengthened ties to Tuscany and their sense of Italian identity. So the probability remains that Giovanni and Gerolamo were from Lyon with strong family and cultural ties to Florence where they were educated.

Although Giovanni excelled in mathematics and astronomy, he had little patience for education and after a year went to Venice to learn navigation and become a merchant mariner. His intelligence and confidence were quickly noticed by Venetian businessmen and he soon found himself sailing the Mediterranean to ports in Egypt and Turkey. Not only did he learn navigation, but he learned to be a businessman, trading for Far Eastern goods brought to the Levant.

Gerolamo, on the other hand, found university studies more to his liking. He stayed in Florence a year longer and later joined his brother's Mediterranean voyages. He also learned navigation but his interests lay in mapping the routes and lands they visited. Although he taught himself to make maps he knew that to improve his skills he must study under the great cartographers. Fortunately a well-known cartographer of the day lived in Florence, and Gerolamo managed an introduction to Amerigo Vespucci, to work as an assistant. After some some months Vespucci saw great potential in Gerolamo and told him to go to the Netherlands to study under the cartographer, astronomer, and explorer, Johannes Ruysch. Gerolamo went to Ruysch with a letter of introduction from Vespucci, thus immediately finding his mentor and model for his life. Unfortunately after only a year Ruysch left Utrecht to continue his mapping as a monk in Cologne, Germany, leaving Gerolamo to return to Italy.

The elder brother, Giovanni, comes across to me as an aggressive and proud man accustomed to respect from peers, and respect with a pinch of fear from subordinates. He was an intelligent and clever man of many skills. His family gave him an assist in almost anything he undertook. Sometimes help came from their deep pockets, but their name alone opened many doors. He and Gerolamo appeared to be devoted brothers, though their personalities were quite different.

Gerolamo was satisfied with his studies and mapmaking. He was not a dominant sort like Giovanni, but enjoyed being part of the big things that Giovanni initiated. I think Gerolamo was more able to tend to tedious details, such as researching information prior to their voyage and making maps from the positional information in ships' logs.

In the Villon library collection I happened upon a book by Captain Antoine Conflans titled, Traité du Navigaige, *published by the French navy in 1518. This man clearly had the attention of admirals in the king's navy.*

Incidentally, most of this family history is my conjecture. There was a known Verrazzano family in Lyon, but no record of Giovanni's birth exists in Lyon nor in Tuscany. While it is all plausible and there are no facts to refute it, the actual evidence is very thin.

Chapter 4

April 25, 1523 Dieppe

Today was horrible! The king announced that all ships presently in Dieppe and Havre d'Grace are to be appropriated for sending French soldiers to Scotland. This is a black day for Giovanni and me, and for the expedition. Now this valuable adventure may be delayed for as much as a year and heaven only knows what new impediment may arise by then. Perhaps our voyage, our dream, may never happen.

Those damned English! They have been threatening to expand their small pale around Calais for several months now and finally they have made their move. How they managed to keep this tiny plot of land that belongs rightfully to France, I will never know. Now these English asses want to expand, perhaps to regain some of their former might on French soil. King Francis and his generals will now help the Scots open a military campaign against their rival Henry VIII in the northern border land of England. This might distract that audacious king's attention from Normandy. It seems only yesterday the two kings were trying to negotiate an alliance. That failed. And now this damnable disaster!

Giovanni was full of bitterness tonight when he came to dinner. Without greeting anyone, he sputtered, "I know in my heart that Conflans made sure that our assigned ships would be included in this damned appropriation. It would have been in his power to petition for an exemption for these four ships. He has shown himself to be the bastard son of a whore that I thought him to be. Now he can be the naval warrior captain instead of being bored to death by a voyage of discovery. He has made it very clear that he has no desire to sail to the new world, and if I have my way, I will see his desire granted. What a bastard!"

Again Marie was forced to calm her lover. "Giovanni, be still. You will only cause yourself more harm by letting these naval men hear your libelous talk. This could soon get back to Admiral Bonnivet and, although he likes you, he would not let your slander against one of his favorite captains go unpunished."

"Naturally, you are right, Marie, but I am sick of this arrogant pig interfering with my enterprise. I have dreamt of this voyage for years. It will be the attainment of my dream to explore beyond the western horizon and I will not let this imperious buffoon sabotage my expedition."

"If this voyage is successful in finding a passage and riches in the new lands, it will also be the turning point in my life. I will become governor of new territories and the beneficiary of their wealth. On the other hand, failure of the voyage in any of its aspects will relegate me to the life of a minor seafaring merchant of no consequence. Now this jackass Conflans has steered my promising venture toward a dunghill."

Marie responded, "Dear Giovanni, surely you can find a sympathetic ear for your Conflans problem. Why not speak again with Viscount Ango to find a solution to your plight? This man knows your abilities and wants to see this voyage be successful. So speak with him."

Le Marin was serving Giovanni's favorite sausages tonight, but in his state of agitation he could scarcely eat.

April 30, 1523 Dieppe

Tonight we heard another piece of startling news from Marie. The smooth-talking merchant from Marseilles, Jacques Beaudine, who now seems to have disappeared, was more than a merchant. His main reason for visiting Dieppe, was to learn as much as possible about Giovanni's voyage. It appears that a naval officer acting as an emissary from Francis the First has been in Dieppe and stayed a few days at the inn. Our landlord overheard him telling another officer about a Monsieur Beaudine who paid a call to the office of João da Silveira, the Portuguese ambassador in Paris. Insiders in the ambassador's office tell us the ambassador has since written a letter to the king of Portugal with details of the plans for Giovanni's voyage to the new world. Our informants found drafts of this letter and passed the information to the office of the king's principal secretary, a man who keeps his finger on all the intrigues among foreign diplomats. Thus, in this circuitous way, we now find that the "honorable Monsieur Beaudine" was much more than he appeared to be, and much different than he claimed to be. He is no Marseilles merchant at all but an agent for the Portuguese ambassador, and he had us all fooled, except for Marie, of course.

The Portuguese king is extremely concerned that France or England will encroach upon and lay claim to land rightfully belonging to him under the Papal Bull. Perhaps no harm has been done to the expedition by having the Portuguese king know details of our voyage. No one in France, especially the king, gives a damn what the king of Portugal worries about. Most of the information in the ambassador's letter was erroneous anyway. The ambassador wrote that the departure of the ships for Scotland indicated our voyage was cancelled. We have been assured this is not true, but uncertainty shrouds our optimism again.

May 3, 1523 Dieppe

The fleet is now loaded with provisions for six months to feed crew, soldiers and horses on the voyage to Scotland. God only knows if the ships will actually return. In four days the soldiers embark and the small armada will sail for Scotland. This is a sad day for us and at the moment there is no way to see anything but misfortune for our expedition.

We now have additional time to utilize Viscount Ango's extensive library of books and maps. I, for one, see this as the one good result from our delay. More preparation time is never a bad thing, and perhaps we will see something in a book or map that will inspire a new idea for the voyage.

Giovanni plans to spend a few weeks of this waiting period with his wife in Lyon. Because I have no such ties in Lyon, I will stay in Dieppe and Rouen visiting with friends, mariners, and the cartographers that are beginning to recognize Dieppe as a good center for their work.

I truly relish my unmarried state. It gives me unlimited latitude in my choice of locales and associates. The only problem is that well-meaning relatives and friends insist on finding me a wife. When I visit my parents in Lyon, they often have dinner guests who just happen to have a young beautiful daughter. If I wanted a wife I could find one on my own, but my family thinks I only lack the boldness or the initiative to look. How silly!

May 5, 1523 Dieppe

Giovanni sent a message to Viscount Ango asking if we could visit his library again and also have a few minutes of his time for a private conversation. Ango responded immediately by return courier that he would be delighted if we would come tomorrow around midday and, after our work in his library, join him for another of his always enjoyable meals. Naturally we will go. I am sure there will be other visitors present, but the good viscount will certainly allow some time for us to speak with him privately.

May 6, 1523 Dieppe

This has been one of those days I will long remember; all because of Viscount Ango and the remarkable man that he is!

As we walked to Ango's manor, *Pensée*, the breeze was blowing in from the sea giving the air such a delightful freshness mixed with the local smells of harbor and city. Giovanni, briefly shedding his dark gloom, appeared to be somewhat restored by the warmth of sun and air, commenting, "This is truly a good moment in our lives.

More than just this moment, I am convinced that we are living in the very best of times. The exploding expansion of knowledge and the stunning awareness of new worlds beyond the horizon makes this a unique time in history. How exciting it is! And how fortunate I am to be living at this time. I do not know of a similar time, nor can I imagine that such an exciting period would ever come again if this flow of energy were halted. I think, however, that this age of innovation and exploration could continue for a long time; probably well beyond my lifetime." In this belief Giovanni and I are in complete agreement.

We were met at the door by a servant and taken to Viscount Ango's study. He rose heavily from his chair to greet us, still not fully disconnected from his tasks at hand. The air in the room was surprisingly stale and desperately called for some open windows on this beautiful day. Viscount Ango seemed to be suddenly aware of this himself, and directed the footman to open shutters and sashes. The immediate rush of fresh air and light changed the entire mood of the room. Ango's mood seemed to brighten as well, as he turned his full attention to us.

Ango has obviously lived in comfort since his seafaring days of privateering and sailing trading ships for his father, and has begun to add girth to his waist. His warm camaraderie filled the room as he inquired after our health and well-being. He expressed genuine interest when Giovanni told him of his plans to visit his wife in Lyon, and asked Giovanni to convey personal greetings to our uncle. Given such an opportune opening, Giovanni wasted no time in raising his concern about Captain Conflans.

"My dear viscount and esteemed employer, I have only the greatest respect for you, as does everyone who knows you. And I know there is genuine feeling in your offer to help when you are able. I must ask for your advice or assistance in a very delicate matter, with your kind permission."

"Please proceed, Captain Verrazzano, I will help if I can, whether it is merely giving advice or taking some necessary action."

"My concern," began Giovanni, "is Captain Conflans…"

"Say no more," interrupted the viscount, "Captain Conflans is an outstanding naval commander, but he has no sense or skill when it comes to dealing with peers. He has no ability to think and solve problems other than naval strategies. He is often inept except in his command of a warship, and sometimes makes himself a fool. I am often surprised that the admiral regards him so highly."

Giovanni and I were both shocked at the sudden forcefulness of Ango's response. We were also surprised at the openness with which Ango spoke to us about a rather sensitive subject, and were not a little amused that he saw through Conflans so clearly, and to find that his opinion agreed with our own assessment.

"This is indeed a sensitive matter," Ango continued. "Captain Conflans is clearly a favorite of Admiral Bonnivet, and Bonnivet is a favorite of the king. But it also happens that I hold a strong hand and perhaps can play a card that will subdue our arrogant Captain Conflans. The fleet is away to Scotland for the time being and your expedition is delayed. This, in fact, provides an opportune period of time to oil the wheels of naval politics. Please, Captain Verrazzano, let the matter rest. I shall press some hands and drop some hints, and we shall see what happens."

A look of relief came over Giovanni's face. I have never seen such a sudden transformation in a man; in one moment his anxieties disappeared. He suddenly felt assured that the expedition would indeed occur, and that by some miracle Conflans would no longer annoy him. We were both pleased that the astute Ango had grasped the problem before Giovanni could even express it.

Viscount Ango preparing to return to his work said, "Go to the library and I will send a servant to call you to our dinner. There are a few guests visiting and I think you should meet them. This evening there will be a lively discussion between two visiting philosophers. You are both educated men and should find the evening very interesting."

After a few hours in the library, we were taken into the small paneled dining room. The tall leaded glass windows presented a beautiful view of the sea with the sun setting on its horizon. Giovanni stopped near one of the windows to admire the view and, I'm sure, to reflect on the thought of his expedition soon sailing toward that horizon.

I looked forward with some eagerness to meeting Viscount Ango's always interesting dinner guests. Only two other men joined us for dinner making a perfect group for intimate conversation.

One man was a professor from nearby Caen University, Doctor Professor Jehan Fortier. He is a man of some fifty years in age, who has a balding head and slightly stooped posture. His eyes seemed to penetrate mine as though looking for any sign of intelligent life. But his demeanor was congenial, which I'm beginning to believe is a requirement for guests at the Ango manor. At Ango's table we have yet to meet the overbearing guest who disdains anyone not measuring up to his level. I am sure the viscount screens guests for their conversational abilities. How fortunate we are to be included.

The other guest was a young student named Lucas Peeters, who comes from the Flemish university town of Leuven. There he was once a student of the great Desiderius Erasmus of Rotterdam whose humorous satire on society and the church, *In Praise of Folly*, was such a delight to read. I hope they did not expect me to equal their intellect and knowledge, but I am sure I was a good and responsive audience for this pair of philosophers. Viscount Ango himself is well read in philosophy, and skillfully guided the evening's conversation toward a productive direction.

The meal was brought in with steaming platters of roasted pork and fresh cod just off a ship from Newfoundland waters. No sooner were our glasses filled than the viscount asked Professor Fortier to explain to us Giovanni Pico della Mirandola's intent in his Oration of the Dignity of Man. "Why did this young man Pico think that man had the potential to be like the angels, or even above the angels? Did he truly think that man had the potential to be like God?"

I was shocked by this question. I had read Pico's work as a student, but gave it little thought as I was consumed by interest in mathematics and astronomy at the time. This new look at Pico now sounds blasphemous to me.

Professor Fortier or the viscount surely do not subscribe to such beliefs. Nevertheless, I know that philosophy is not a matter of belief, but of ideas. When ideas become belief, that is, faith, we have religion. Pico's ideas are certainly intriguing.

In the course of the evening Professor Fortier told us that Pico was himself a very pious man who received much criticism for his writings on the possible state of man in the celestial hierarchy. Fortier explained that Pico, born in Mirandola of wealthy parents, studied everything that several universities had to offer, wrote profusely, and died at the early age of thirty-one, perhaps due to poisoning by offended parties unknown.

"The crux of Pico's thesis," the professor said, "is that, as rational men we are set apart from the animals in creation and, through use of our intellectual and meditative abilities, can raise our being from that of the animals to that of the angels. Additionally, through contemplation, man could even reach the level of the Seraphim who are closest to God."

Professor Doctor Fortier continued by explaining to us that Pico came to these conclusions by looking at many philosophies, including Plato, Aristotle, Judaic discourses, and the early Christian fathers. "Pico, blessed with a great memory, could cite supporting evidence using Holy Scripture from Jesus, Saint Paul, or the Torah, as easily as Plato. He truly opened a new book on the concept of man's place in the hierarchy of men, angels, and God. Although the Church was not pleased with some of his writings, saying that he relied too much on pagan philosophers, Pico managed to escape punishment by agreeing to delete certain statements in his books. He never actually disowned his ideas, but as a practical matter he could change his words."

My brother could not hold back his contempt for such ideas that offended the Church and also his own sense of discipline. "This Pico should have been imprisoned for corrupting the faith in such a manner by questioning the authority of the Church. No seaman could ever escape unpunished if he questioned the authority of the captain so blatantly."

The viscount observed, for Giovanni's benefit, that seamen are perhaps a different case where life and death rest on the judgement of an experienced captain. "Sea captains are not dealing with ideas and concepts, Captain Verrazzano. They are concerned daily with the cold reality of survival when reliable decisions must be made instantly. In such a case there is, of course, no room for debate among the crew."

Giovanni quickly saw that he had spoken as a captain rather than a scholar, "Yes, Viscount, you are right. My mind enjoys a well-reasoned argument as much as anyone's. I read Pico's Oration when I was a student in Florence, and although I do not accept his conclusions, he certainly presents a thorough argument on man's potential for knowing God through his own efforts, independent of guidance by the Church." I thought, however, that Giovanni's analogy about sea captains was on the mark. The Church takes exactly the same position of authority as a sea captain when faced with men like Pico or Luther.

Footmen removed empty platters and replaced them with others filled with more pork and cod, then made the rounds to fill our wine glasses. Conversation about Pico continued throughout the meal without interruption and the table was eventually cleared. Immediately we were provided a plate of sweet honey-flavored bread and a sweet wine was poured into new glasses.

At this point Professor Fortier interjected, "We must remember that Pico never rejected the Church, nor did he intend for anyone to interpret his writing in such a way. The Church is a vital and strong organization ordained by God, but governed by men trying to understand God's intentions. The Church has withstood major schisms even within the Roman branch. Only a hundred years ago three men claimed the right to be pope, knowing well that God ordained only one leader for His Church. Yet this schism was resolved, and the strength of the Church was diminished only temporarily."

Viscount Ango followed the idea of possible schism in the Church by turning to the young scholar, Peeters. "Mr. Peeters, would you please enlighten us on your mentor, Erasmus, and his view of man and God compared with the views of the German monk Luther? Each seems to see man in a different light than does the Church, but Luther's view has landed him in conflict with the Pope, while Erasmus seems to be more acceptable to the authorities."

Peeters replied, "Kind Sir, your knowledge of the current thinking among scholars is excellent. To begin, my mentor Erasmus was in Leuven University only a short time before he felt constrained to move to Basel in order to be free of any institutional affiliation which might inhibit his freedom of expression. In Leuven there were authorities who objected to the influence of his liberal ideas on students. He had heard that Basel is more open to new ideas. Therefore, I was graced by his wisdom for only one year."

"Despite his concern for freedom of expression, Erasmus has exerted *de facto* constraint on himself when speaking of Church matters. He has the greatest respect and tolerance for diverse ideas regarding man's relationship to God, and especially respects Martin Luther. But Erasmus cannot totally accept Luther's ideas that justification comes only through faith in God.

Luther believes that God grants salvation through His grace to any man who has shown unwavering faith. In Luther's view, God's salvation does not depend on good works but rather that good works may come forth from a man who has received salvation through faith. Luther particularly objects to the Church collecting indulgences with the pretense that the gift of money constitutes good works and, therefore, salvation."

"But where does Erasmus stand in this issue?" I asked.

"Erasmus feels strongly that many of Luther's points are valid," Peeters continued, "and that the Church is in great need of change to correct its error. Many voices said that Erasmus was weak, or worse, cowardly for not raising his voice in protest against the wrongful practices of the Church. Erasmus, however, felt that his influence for change could best be exerted within the structure of the Church, and if he were to break away he would be ineffective. Erasmus believes that too much bitter haranguing prevents truth from emerging. Only with an orderly and harmonious discussion can opposing parties find the truth. Whether this signifies weakness or strength is, I think, beside the point. The crux is that Erasmus has not crossed the line leading to excommunication as happened to Luther two years ago. Luther is now in no position to help the Church improve, while Erasmus's great reputation still carries some level of influence among Church authorities."

"As I reflect on Erasmus's writings," Peeters continued, "I see that he parts with Luther on the point of salvation by faith alone. He agrees with Luther that scripture should be the only basis for any sacrament or practice of the Church, but takes exception to Luther's belief that faith alone leads to salvation. Luther's belief gives great independence to the layman who could potentially read scripture and achieve God's salvation without guidance or dispensations from the Church. This would leave the Church in the role of dispensing Holy Eucharist and little else. Some might begin to think that even the Eucharist is unnecessary."

This stimulating and enlightening conversation extended for another hour or more before the diners began to grow weary. Our gracious host, Ango, excused himself and begged Giovanni and me to make ourselves comfortable as his guests for the night. The other guests were there for indefinite visits. We were free to spend more time in his library in the morning before leaving.

As we left the room, Ango told Giovanni, "Captain Verrazzano, you may rest assured that your problem with a certain other captain will be resolved by the time the ships return from Scotland."

Pondering on our discussion this evening, I believe there is certainly an undercurrent of change taking place in our society. Pico wrote on the importance of an individual's intellect in finding God. Luther is preaching to all that will listen that man can achieve salvation by faith without the requirement of good works in the form of indulgences, which are nothing more than a fund-raising effort by the Church. We did not discuss Zwingli of Zurich, but he has become a disciple of Erasmus, and is also deviating from traditional church practices. To me, it is all evidence that we are living in an exciting time of transition, but to what end I cannot imagine. However, of this I am certain, whatever transpires will be far different from today.

Chapter 5

May 15, 1523 Dieppe

Giovanni and I are leaving Dieppe and will be away until we receive word from Admiral Bonnivet that the four ships are back in port and ready to be refitted for our expedition. We leave with confidence that the issue with Conflans will be resolved in a reasonable way that satisfies Giovanni's concerns without offense to Admiral Bonnivet.

Giovanni will go to Lyon to be with his wife, Beatriz and family. She has no desire to travel to Rouen or Dieppe with Giovanni, nor has she been invited. Giovanni has very tender feelings for Beatriz, and it sometimes bothers him that he has chosen the traveling life of a seaman. It is easy to see how Giovanni was attracted to such a beautiful young girl. At the time of their marriage she was eighteen and well into the blossoming, both mental and physical, that turns a young girl into a mature woman. Her dark eyes and midnight-black hair against her lightly tanned complexion come from her mixture of Spanish and Moorish ancestry going back several generations.

Giovanni repeatedly spurned his parents' attempts to make a match with daughters of various merchants in Lyon, choosing to do his own search. In March of 1519 Giovanni was in Spain, trying to persuade Ferdinand

Magellan to hire him as captain of one of his ships on his voyage in search of the Spice Islands. Giovanni was disappointed that there was no need for his services, as all command positions had been given to Spanish captains. Although many other crew members were Magellan's Portuguese countrymen, as well as from other European maritime countries, the Spanish insisted on Spanish commanders.

In the end Giovanni was glad not to have been on that voyage. They were gone a full three years. Furthermore, Magellan was killed in a skirmish with savages halfway through the voyage. If he had gone, Giovanni could not have seized this opportune moment to make plans, preparations, and a proposal for his own voyage.

While in Seville for several months Giovanni became well acquainted with Spanish sea captains, whom he found to be a very hard, but likable lot. One of them took Giovanni to his parents' home for a visit, and there he met his future wife. He was immediately smitten with Beatriz and extended his stay in Seville for weeks so he could convince her family that he was indeed a worthy husband for Beatriz. This young woman could read and speak Spanish, Italian, and French, as well as play the lute and dulcimer. When her family was finally convinced, Giovanni persuaded them to bring her to Lyon for a wedding. The Verrazzano family first thought Giovanni was making a big mistake and made life difficult for him. But as they began to know Beatriz, they also fell for her sweet charm. From that point all went well and the couple were soon wed. As Giovanni often goes to sea it was agreed that Beatriz would live with the Verrazzano family. So far their marriage has brought no children.

For my part I plan to stay in Rouen until our ships return to Dieppe. A boyhood friend, Felice Conti, is a curate at the Rouen cathedral and shares my interest in discussing ideas, and is always entertaining in conversation. His living quarters provide rooms for guests, and there is a good library in the cathedral where I can spend days reading. My evenings will be in the tavern eating and talking. For me it is an ideal time to study, have long stimulating discussions, and perhaps satisfy some other urges.

Felice and I were neighbors in Lyon and shared the same tutor as boys. We also shared the same mischief and punishments. Secretly we shared our discovery of our emerging manhood. Those moments were of great importance to my life. At age sixteen, Felice began preparation for the priesthood, while I moved to Florence for university studies. The separation caused us to lose contact for a number of years, and I had no expectation that I would see Felice again…that is, until I made a visit to my parent's home in Lyon. I heard from them that Felice had become a priest and was assigned to the cathedral in Rouen. Although I had lived in Rouen some of that time, I had not known he was there.

May 19, 1523 Rouen

On arriving in Rouen today, I went to the cathedral to find Felice. I have yet to see this cathedral without scaffolding on some part of it, as it is constantly in repair. At present there is a bustle of workers as the central and west portals undergo reconstruction. This poor old building has suffered fire damage, war damage, and lightning strikes. I wonder if it will even survive long enough to be finished in some future time. The appearance is changing from the early thirteenth century style that the Florentine architect, Vasari, referred to as “gothic” because of its crude appearance to his modern eye. The present style reflects the newer architecture of northern Italy. Who knows what style may emerge from this forever-under-construction building with its ever-changing chief architects? Inside it is cool and dim but for me it is not an inviting place.

Felice was busy in a meeting with other canons for a time, so I went to the library which is usually unoccupied. This library is an irresistible place with tables and interesting volumes to be perused. After a short time Felice arrived and we sat for a long period of uninterrupted conversation. I was elated to see his boyish smile again and see that he still has the familiar habit of occasionally running his fingers through his blond hair. Felice is tall and thin with a handsome face and blue eyes. It seemed strange to see my old friend wearing a cassock. It made him look much more important than the young boy I knew. We reminisced about past pleasures and disappointments, the many friends we shared in common, and eventually our mutual interest in learning. Felice recalled our youthful escapade when we let cows in the school. We wondered if the hated teacher ever recovered his dignity. We both suffered dearly for our scornful prank but we agreed that seeing the teacher so flustered was worth the cost.

I told Felice about my interesting visit with the philosophers at the manor of Viscount Ango. He then added some interesting comments from the viewpoint of the Church bishops.

Felice gave me some details on Luther's movement that is now attracting great attention in the Vatican and bishoprics all across Europe. "The Church is now considering ways to stem the growing urges for change. This change has become a force like the tide and, just as with the tide, efforts to stop it may be futile but they must try. When they squelch those heretical ideas in one place they suddenly pop up in another. It is more than a little disturbing to think that the culture we have known and loved for our entire lives may be undergoing a cataclysmic change. I would love to say that the effect will be minor but I fear that in a few years we will not recognize our beloved Church."

Someone passed nearby and we both fell silent for a few moments until he left, not wishing to be overheard. Felice is careful not to seem too interested in these seditious men.

I asked Felice what he knew about the Swiss preacher, Zwingli. He noted that, "Huldrych Zwingli is a devotee of Erasmus but has been far more vocal than Erasmus and has made a complete break with our Roman Church. While Luther may have intended to reform from within, after he was excommunicated he had no choice but to respond to the large following of people who liked what they heard from him. Zwingli, on the other hand, never felt a need to try to reform from within. The problems he perceived were far too great and the Church hierarchy far too conservative to hope for the radical change he wanted."

"Zwingli makes a practice," Felice continued, "of reading the Gospels and Epistles from Erasmus's translation and interpreting them as he goes. He wants to put the people more directly in touch with the entire Word of God without a priest choosing what the people should hear. This has brought Zwingli many followers, who apparently relish the idea of a relationship with God without an intermediary priest. Zwingli objects also to the excessive use of trappings designed to set priests apart from the people. He attacks those he sees living corrupt lives, especially monks who indulge themselves in earthly pleasures. He rejects the idea of hell and damnation for unbaptized children. His most strident message is that tithing is not ordained by God, as some priests have insisted. Poor Zwingli nearly died when he contracted the plague while ministering to hundreds of dying people of Zurich. His recovery is regarded as miraculous, and has greatly expanded his following." Felice finished with, "To tell the truth, I think Zwingli, Luther and their followers should all be in jail, and they will be lucky to escape retribution from the Church."

This additional information about Zwingli is most interesting to me for the connections I see with the writings that Pico produced nearly forty years ago. I do not know who among these reformers actually read Pico's Oration, but it is clear that change is underway in Europe. Perhaps they all read Pico, but it could also be that the reform idea came to many men at the same time. That would be even more fascinating and somewhat mysterious too. Such a simultaneous awakening could be construed as the action of God Himself. It is very exciting to think that perhaps God has helped us return to the importance of each person feeling a closeness with Him.

May 20, 1523 Rouen

What a pleasure to see Felice again and feel the warmth of his companionship. Since that first meeting we have continued renewing our friendship and I will now visit him as often as time allows. I think each of us feels a growing fondness for one another. Gradually we are realizing that our adolescent sexual experimentations have reappeared as mature, but forbidden, love. This creates a dilemma for us. Such activities between men are prohibited by law, though seldom prosecuted. Nevertheless, we must be careful in public and our words or behavior must not give suspicion to any of Felice's superiors in the Church.

The bishop is sending Felice to Lyon on an important errand of church business and Felice obtained permission for me to travel with him. This is a great opportunity for us to have some time alone for further conversation and for continuing the rediscovery of our great attachment for one another. Each of us will also have time with our families, even though that is not always a good thing for either of us. It has become easier for Felice since he is a priest—he is no longer pestered about marriage. We leave at dawn tomorrow. Felice will be in Lyon only a few days, but I will probably stay longer as it may be some time before I see my family again. I will stay until we hear from Admiral Bonnivet that our ships have returned from Scotland.

Translator's note: Gerolamo offers no explanation for the large gap in his diary during his visit to Lyon. Perhaps he felt that the diary was intended only as a chronicle of everything related to the voyage of exploration. Perhaps he felt that the mundane life with the parents was not worthy of writing. This is unfortunate. It would have been valuable to learn more about the Verrazzano family.

Chapter 6

September 12, 2010 Rouen

Coincident with the break in Gerolamo's journal, I persuaded Nicole to join me for a Sunday afternoon in a museum or park. I must take some time away from the tedium of translation in the library basement. My back is beginning to ache and my legs need some real exercise. My daily path from my comfortable room in the Hotel des Carmes to the Bibliothèque Villon takes only five minutes, and offers little of particular interest along the way. A day of diversion and exercise is needed.

I met Nicole as planned on the steps of the Rouen Museum of Fine Arts, which is just around the corner from the Villon library. She arrived in sleeveless blouse, with hair pulled up in back, and oversized sun glasses, which she shoved to the top of her head as she walked up the steps. In the mellow September sunlight, I could see her blond hair reflect a momentary trace of redness. Very attractive sight.

She gave me a peck on the cheek, and I instinctively took her hand as we walked inside. Nicole said, "Ross, I have been to this museum many times, but I look forward to this visit so I can see what interests you."

I told her, "I am curious about the collection of paintings by artists whose work is contemporary with Viscount Ango. I'm hoping to find paintings that could have hung in his manor in the sixteenth century. It's fascinating to think that perhaps some of Ango's art collection found a permanent home here almost 500 years later."

Within thirty minutes I encountered exactly what I had hoped to find: a 1509 painting by an artist of Viscount Ango's time, and a work which could have hung in his home.

"Look, Nicole. This one is titled The Virgin among the Virgins *by the Flemish artist Gerard David. I've read about this painting. It depicts the Virgin and Child surrounded by a dozen presumed virgins dressed in clothing worn by nobility of the Renaissance. In addition to two angels near the Virgin, David painted his self-portrait in the upper left corner of the group of ladies. A woman in the right corner is thought to be David's wife. On that basis, I would suppose that all the women in the picture are from important sixteenth century families in Rouen. This painting is probably a 'who's who' of the time."*

I found no Jean Clouet paintings, which Gerolamo mentioned hanging in Ango's house, but the museum collection included a painting by Clouet's son François, Le bain de Diane (The bath of Diane). *François Clouet's work would not have been in Ango's home in 1523, but I presume that his style was similar to his father's. The expression and brilliance of these paintings must have created quite a stir in the sixteenth century.*

Nicole and I stayed in this museum until my legs ached up to my shoulders. Another day I hope to visit the nearby Notre Dame cathedral of Rouen where Gerolamo visited his priest friend Felice. Late in the afternoon Nicole and I had a light snack at a nearby cafe, and enjoyed a long, rambling, easygoing conversation. For the evening she had a dinner arrangement with her family, and I went for a long thoughtful walk. I imagined that Nicole felt some affection for me, as I did for her. Maybe it was just the balmy September afternoon that led me into such a fantasy for a few moments.

This evening I was stunned by an email from Lorena announcing her plans to visit me in Rouen. There was no mention of how long she will stay. Although I enjoy her company a lot, this news in troublesome. My work is progressing so well mainly because I have no distracting demands on my time. Lorena's presence will require time away from my work. She will expect me to take some time to see the area and will be offended if I don't comply. The letter left no room for approval from me—only, "I'm coming." The note lacked her usual upbeat tone, and gives me the uneasy feeling that something is bothering her. I've been so wrapped up in my work that I have not written or called her for…I don't know how long, and she made it clear she feels neglected. That alone was probably enough to cause her to book a flight for September 20th. Damn! That's only two weeks from now. I'll never finish my translation before she gets here. I might phone and ask her to wait, but that could make matters worse since she's already booked. In spite of all the confusion, I will be glad to see her and I'm sure that once she gets here, we'll have a good time. Her note sounds like some smoothing of ruffled feathers will be needed.

October 15, 1523 Lyon

Today Giovanni finally received a message by courier from Admiral Bonnivet. The four ships are now at our disposal, and we leave Lyon tomorrow morning for the return to Dieppe. The message added one bit of encouraging information. It said, "Giovanni da Verrazzano will assume full command of the fleet by the 30th day of October." What has happened to Captain Conflans? Is it too much to hope that the thorn has been removed completely? Now we are nearly beside ourselves with anticipation for our return to Dieppe. One thing is clear: our great benefactor, Viscount Ango, played his hand and played it well. He said that he would look after the situation with Conflans and apparently he succeeded. His reputation and royal connections once again opened the right doors. What a relief for Giovanni to hear that he is no longer sharing command.

It has been a long, almost unbearable, wait through the summer in Lyon. In the first place, there is simply not enough of interest here to make the time pass quickly for us. And on the other hand, we, especially Giovanni, have spent the whole time in a stew over the situation with Captain Conflans. Now, assuming that something has been resolved, we can make progress. We are both eager to hear the details. The roads are dry this time of year and we will make good time on the journey to Dieppe.

October 22, 1523 Dieppe

Soon after arriving, we requested a short meeting with Admiral Bonnivet. He greeted us warmly as usual and after exchanging polite conversation briefly, he told us of the new command arrangement. Captain Conflans will be in command of the *Normande*, and Giovanni will have full authority in the organization and command of the whole expedition. We were further told that Captain Conflans took the news of changes in command of the expedition rather well but had left muttering about "that damnable Italian fisherman."

We also heard some detail about the outcome of the Scottish venture. We might have guessed that the voyage to Scotland was for nothing. King Henry VIII of England judiciously backed away from his ambitions to reclaim additional French lands around Calais. Perhaps knowing he was about to be attacked again on his northern borders by the Scots, with the help of French troops, caused him to rethink his plans. Never mind, that fiasco is in the past. The ships have returned in time to prepare for a departure, perhaps as early as January. We then went quayside to inspect the ships

What a mess these poor ships are in! After having troops and animals quartered on the ships for a voyage to and from Scotland, the ships are now in great need of cleaning, mending, caulking, tarring, and resupply. How fortunate that we have been so amply funded by bankers and merchants of Lyon. Otherwise I fear we would quickly consume our money just preparing the ships. The *Dauphine* received serious damage in a storm during her return, and now she needs a new main mast, along with sails, spars, and braces. The *Normande* needs sails and spars along with all brace lines. Much needs to be done.

Giovanni immediately went to see Lieutenant Fournier and Ensign First Class Bonnet. Surprisingly, they had already received instructions from Admiral Bonnivet. In fact, there is no question of clearing orders with Captain Conflans.

Despite this happy circumstance we are still faced with an important remnant problem regarding Conflans. Although Giovanni will command the expedition and also command the *Dauphine*, Captain Conflans is still involved as commander of the *Normande*. Giovanni hoped that Conflans would be dismissed from the expedition altogether but he is reconciled to accepting Conflans as a subordinate. I still have a question about how well Captain Conflans will accept the role of subordinate to the "Italian fisherman." Giovanni and I both also wonder what concessions were promised to Conflans to assuage his injured pride. There had to be some honey to soothe such an ego. No one has mentioned any conditions but perhaps it will eventually come out.

This fisherman epithet irritates Giovanni enormously. He made a voyage to the fisheries of Newfoundland fifteen years ago aboard the *Pensée* with Captain Aubert, one of Ango's seasoned mariners. Giovanni has since repeatedly proven his worth as a trading merchant mariner but the disparaging title "fisherman" is still used by those who resent an Italian commanding ships sailing with French crews. No one but Conflans has dared speak the word openly, but Giovanni knows from hearsay that among French naval sailors he is always "the Italian fisherman." He is certain that Conflans encourages such disrespect. "Such unforgivable behavior for a senior officer!" Giovanni muttered.

It makes little difference that Giovanni and I were both born and raised in Lyon, France, we are still part of the Lyonnaise Florentine community. Within that group one would certainly think they were still in Florence by the language, styles, customs, and the names given to children: all is Italian. Most families have Florentine tutors for their children and we all grew up speaking and writing Italian first. Only when we mix with people outside our community do we speak French. I suppose our accent sounds a bit foreign to Frenchmen, but we are totally fluent. Some in our community feel their true loyalty lies with the Italian homeland but they never let that feeling be known. In truth the majority of us feel loyalty to France and the king. Despite our loyalty and our competence as mariners, merchants, and bankers, and our attractiveness to foreign kings and ship owners, the common French seaman feels resentment, even superiority, toward us as foreigners.

Most of the time these feelings stay hidden, but if anything should favor us to a Frenchman's disadvantage, the resentment breaks the surface. Giovanni, to his great credit, has learned to deal with French crews under his command so that these subsurface resentments cause no problems. When something unpleasant arises he deals with it quickly and sternly and it seldom recurs thereafter. I am not sure that Captain Conflans will not foment such trouble, but I know that Giovanni is now in a position to deal with him. With luck we will not see Conflans again until near the time for departure.

Translator's note: Only the French historian, Jacques Habert, posits that the Verrazzano brothers were part of the Florentine community in Lyon. Lawrence Wroth wrote that they came from Florence, but concedes that the argument for Lyon is equally plausible. Others say with apparent certainty that they are from the Verrazzano estate near Florence, Italy. A Verrazzano castle still exists there today to show that the family had roots there. In fact, there are no birth records for Giovanni or Gerolamo in either place, but records of the family name exist in both places. Gerolamo's journal clearly shows that the brothers lived in Lyon, had family ties in Florence, and received most of their education and vocational training in Italy.

September 20, 2010 Rouen

I met Lorena at Charles DeGaulle today and we took an early train to Rouen, where I moved her into my room at the Hotel des Carmes. I think we are in for an exuberant and passionate reunion. It suddenly occurred to me when we met that her beauty is probably a lot like Giovanni's Spanish wife Beatrix, with her black hair and beautiful complexion. As she flashed her electric smile, my heart melted under her charm. The moment we embraced all my misgivings about her presence immediately evaporated. My translating can wait for a while. I'll use this time for a visit to Dieppe with Lorena. I need to acquaint myself with the layout of that city anyway. She quickly admonished me for my poor communication but not enough to change our happy mood.

I promised to shorten my days at the library so we could be together each afternoon. Also I provided her with a Michelin Green Guide to Rouen so she could see some sights while I'm working at the library. I thought Lorena might balk at the prospect of being on her own each morning, but surprisingly, she accepted the plan without complaint.

The next morning at the library I mentioned to Nicole that I would be spending time with Lorena. She said, "That will be a good chance for you to see the area. I would be glad to spend a day with you and Lorena to show you the sights of Rouen." When Nicole saw the "bad idea" look on my face she immediately withdrew the suggestion. I cannot even imagine living through such a day.

October 25, 1523 Dieppe

Ensign First Class Bonnet informed us today that we will have to wait for a new mast for the *Dauphine*. The masts in the naval warehouse are suitable only for the smaller ships. New masts from Sweden are expected soon but this means another delay until the mast arrives. In the meantime work will continue on the caulking, tarring, and general cleaning that can be done without the new mast. Giovanni has explained his plans to the naval carpenters about expanding the officer's quarters in the *Dauphine*.

October 26, 1523 Dieppe

I met with Giovanni and Marie at the Le Marin for dinner tonight. As we gathered in a private dining room at Le Marin Giovanni was in fine form, feeling expansive and generous. "Now I have that Captain Conflans under my thumb," Giovanni crowed. "That arrogant captain will learn to show some respect in the future." Giovanni seldom relaxes so fully, and I think his mind is more at ease because he is now also in command of Conflans. The wine may have helped. Giovanni no longer expresses the wish that Conflans be dismissed but I know he is hoping that Conflans will find a reason to excuse himself from the expedition.

I expressed that thought myself as I raised my glass with a toast, "Let us drink to smooth sailing and a humbled Conflans remaining behind in France."

"That would be indescribably sweet," Giovanni said as he raised his glass." We both know better than to expect such a miracle.

Marie told us of happenings in the port over the summer. While we were in Lyon, the Portuguese agent, Beaudine, appeared in Dieppe for a few weeks to determine the status of the now-well-known Verrazzano expedition to the New World. Beaudine was a bit shocked when he discovered all the expedition ships missing from the pier in

Dieppe. His inquiries into the reasons led him to hear about the disgruntled Captain Conflans and the discovery that Conflans had been reduced to second in command, along with an overblown account suggesting great friction among the sailors in the port over the matter. Beaudine concluded that this friction was the cause of the delay of the Verrazzano voyage, and that perhaps the voyage had been cancelled. The fact that the king had requisitioned the ships for moving troops for an indefinite period of time gave further support to his belief that our voyage was unlikely to occur.

Armed with this information the misguided Beaudine wrote a letter to the Portuguese ambassador relating his findings and his conclusions. The ambassador in turn relayed this distorted and partly erroneous misinformation to the King of Portugal. In our happy mood of the evening this news gave us great amusement, and we continued to jest throughout the evening about the hapless Portuguese and how foolish they are. What fun it is to have someone to ridicule!

November 1, 1523 Dieppe

We hoped for a mast raising on All Saints Day but unfortunately the new masts are still on the Swedish ship waiting to be unloaded. Raising a mast is an important moment in building or refurbishing a ship. Such things require the proper ritual and ceremony, especially for such a momentous voyage. At a mast raising there must be blessings from a clergyman, a bishop if possible, and appropriate prayers. Without these formalities the ship may as well be condemned. Sailors would hear of this irregularity and rightly refuse to go aboard such a doomed ship.

Sailors are a strange lot. On land most of them show little sign or interest in religion. A few of them may go to church occasionally but their style of living belies any profession of belief in the Christian faith. But once they set forth on the sea they suddenly become devout believers. Most of them, that is. Others would be inclined to behave in the whoring, gambling lifestyle they lead on land if ship rules were not so strict against all vices. The captain sets the tone of behavior on the ship and, almost without exception, the captain of any ship will enforce a pure lifestyle on these immoral men. Orders of the captain usually forbid gambling, swearing, fighting, and slothfulness. Disregard for these orders is considered a serious offense, the same as disobedience of any order. Prayers must be attended by all sailors daily. Terce is scheduled at the time of change of the mid-morning watch. At that time there are a few minutes when most of the men are available for morning prayers. They recite the 107th psalm, called the sailor's psalm, the Salve Regina, and the Paternoster, plus a prayer for good passage that day. At vespers much of the routine is repeated.

Everyone on a ship feels the heavy presence of hazards and dangers that can destroy a voyage. Men may fall from the rigging into the sea. This is nearly always certain death unless they are lucky enough to catch the trailing line. A ship under sail simply cannot turn around in a short distance. Even if they were to turn around, there is little chance they could find the exact spot where the sailor fell and see the small dot of a man bobbing in the waves. Many sailors have never learned to swim and they simply flounder and sink out of sight. If the water is cold survival is brief, and they are unlikely to find him alive even if they find the right location. So the ship will usually sail on without attempting a rescue. Their best hope is trusting God to protect them from such accidents, hence the temporary turn to faith and prayer.

Of the dangers at sea, storms are a greatly feared event because high winds and waves, especially when hitting abeam, can swamp a ship and drown all hands in a matter of minutes. An equally dreaded hazard is running aground. If a ship becomes stuck on a shoal, the waves and wind will soon batter her to bits. Often a hole is gouged in the hull of a grounded ship, causing it to sink on the spot. Given the many dangers seamen face during a simple voyage on the sea it is clear why they are careful not to offend God, their patron saints, or any incidental saint that may offer them safety at sea.

November 20, 1523 Dieppe

At last the new main mast is ready to be raised on the *Dauphine*. Tomorrow is a feast day commemorating the Presentation of Mary, a very important day in the church year and a most suitable time for raising a mast.

November 21, 1523 Dieppe

Today the mast was raised, or stepped, as we call it, and what an impressive affair it was. Not all mast-stepping gets this much attention when it is only a replacement mast, but this is for a ship about to depart on an important mission of exploration expected to bring glory and riches to

France. Her access to the spices and silks of Cathay will radically shift the balance of the political duel between France and her adversaries, Spain and the Holy Roman Emperor. Truly this is a voyage that holds the aspirations of kings and merchants, not to mention the elation for those of us who will conduct the momentous journey. All our preparation has given rise to hope…hope that this will be the voyage that enters France into the scramble for pieces of the New World.

The weather turned cold and overcast by mid-morning with a bone-chilling wind blowing from the sea. Unpleasant weather lent a sense of haste to finish the mast-stepping ceremony. The ritual began with the bishop from Rouen offering prayers for the safety of the ship and all the men who sail her. He went on at some length, asking for protection from God and invoking protection from St. Christopher, St. Elmo, and Our Lady, Star of the Sea: all patron saints of sailors and travelers. The bishop paced about the deck swinging a censer and trying despite the wind to direct its fragrant smoke into all corners of the ship. Then he retraced his steps while sprinkling holy water over all parts of the deck from fore to aft. While dispensing his blessings, the bishop gave special attention to the new mast suspended from a hoist built alongside the ship. We felt certain by this time that no demons could have remained in any part of the *Dauphine*, and I, for one, felt grateful that I would be traveling with this blessed ship.

Giovanni held up a gold *écu au soleil*, a coin of the realm, for the bishop to bless. Then Giovanni gave the coin to a sailor who went below deck into the bilges, where he placed the coin in a slot-shaped mortise that forms the spot on the keel, the step, where the raised mast will rest. This practice has little religious meaning, but it is a sea-faring tradition to put a coin under the main mast. I have heard it originated in pagan Rome or Greece when they believed sailors lost at sea would need a coin to buy passage into the afterlife. The tradition continues today with the addition of Christian invocations and prayers.

Carpenters created the new mast from a tall spruce tree by chipping away with an adze until the surface was smooth and perfectly round. Our ship's carpenter cut a tenon in its base and shaped it to fit the mortise cut into the keel. I admire these shipwright carpenters in Dieppe. I think they are the most skilled in France. We certainly should have one of them on our crew to make repairs as needed during our voyage. The sailor returned from the bilges and announced that the coin was in place. The bishop recited another prayer and again invoked the guardianship of Our Lady, Star of the Sea. Then the mast was lowered through the hole in the main deck with sailors below to guide it through the opening in the lowest deck. Carpenters waited in the bilges to guide it into the mortise slot on the keel and peg it securely. The bishop intoned a benediction and processed with his retinue onto the dock.

No one lingered after the stepping ceremony on the deck of the *Dauphine* today. A cold, fine mist had begun to blow, making the whole affair a rather miserable test of will. Viscount Ango apparently decided it was too much and left shortly after he had greeted the bishop and invited him to come to his nearby home after the ceremony.

A mast-stepping ceremony was a minor thing in my mind before today, but it had a surprising effect on my thinking. I now feel a great excitement that this voyage is imminent. Until now it seemed far in the future or perhaps I was uncertain that it would actually occur. Now I am almost dancing with anticipation. I am sure this will be the biggest event of my life, and it is truly about to happen.

December 3, 1523 Dieppe

The sailors have rigged the new sails on the *Dauphine*. All the ship's supplies and provisions are assembled on the dock and sailors are starting to load them into the hold. Lieutenant Fournier and Ensign First Class Bonnet have worked efficiently to bring all our needs together for a timely departure. The *Normande*, the *Intrépide*, and the *Égyptien* are also docked nearby and are likewise nearly loaded and ready for the voyage. Most crew members of all our ships have been retained for this voyage, but Lieutenant Fournier added a new cook to the crew of the *Dauphine* and, at Giovanni's request, a ship's surgeon. I am eager to meet this surgeon. He has served on naval vessels, has an education, and will be quartered with the officers. Perhaps I can learn from him.

December 10, 1523 Dieppe

Lieutenant Fournier informed us today that all ships will be ready to depart anytime after the 27th of this month. Giovanni would be happy to leave at the next high tide, but the 28th is a Friday. No seaman wants to begin a voyage on Friday as that is the day of the week that our Lord was crucified, and it would bring the worst of luck to flout such a rule. Of course there is no rule, it is simply another seaman's superstition. Even though most of them agree it is only an old sailor's belief, none of them are willing to take a chance. What if there were truly something to it? Therefore Giovanni has decided to wait through the sabbath and begin the voyage on Tuesday, January 1st.

December 15, 1523 Dieppe

Lieutenant Fournier presented us with a bill of lading for provisions and supplies that are ready for moving onto the ships. The list is impressive both for its variety and its quantity. The lieutenant has conveniently broken the consumable provisions into amounts per man so we could appreciate how well our crew is provided.

Food and drink are loaded in sufficient quantity for each sailor to have the following amounts per day: one *livre* of hard bread, one *galon* of cider, one *livre* of salted pork. One dried cod is to be shared among four men on fast days, with oats and dried peas available for porridge in case the fish supply runs low, a quarter *livre* of butter, a half *livre* of cheese. Wine is provided for officers. For the cook, the load included a barrel of oil and two barrels of vinegar, fishing hooks to be used when fish were available, and guns, powder, and balls for hunting on land. I am glad to see that the ship's surgeon ordered a barrel of *aqua vitae*. This distillate does wonders for one's health. Why else would it be called water of life?

The men eat well, but their hard work requires a large intake of food. More importantly, the spirit of the men is always much higher when the food supply is ample. There is nothing worse for morale than an empty stomach.

Translator's note: The Old French term livre is nearly the same weight as the English pound. Galon is a French Norman term roughly equivalent to the English gallon.

December 17, 1523 Dieppe

Giovanni arranged for a posted notice on the quay announcing that the expedition will depart at high tide on the morning of January 1st.

NOTICE TO ALL SEAMEN

All crewmen assigned to the *Dauphine*, the *Normande*, the *Intrépide*, and the *Égyptien* will report to their ships by noon on Thursday the 27th of December and complete stowing all gear and provisions in the lower deck in preparation for departure January 1st. Master and boatswain of each ship will be present to supervise stowing operations. The cook will begin preparing meals on the evening of the 27th. Officers must appear for duty by noon Monday, December 31st.

By Order of
Captain Giovanni da Verrazzano

At last, the long wait has ended!

Translator's note: Posting such a notice was only a formality, as none of the ordinary seamen could read. Nevertheless word of mouth assured that everyone heard the news.

Chapter 7

December 31, 1523   Dieppe

At noon today Giovanni and I formally boarded the now fully-rigged *Dauphine.* We were met at the rail by the ship's master, who introduced himself as Matthieu Ango, a nephew of Viscount Ango. As Matthieu spoke we were called on board by the boatswain with his pipe. This infernal pipe with its irritating shriek is a necessary annoyance. It is the only efficient way to relay the master's commands to the crew even in a raging storm. Matthieu immediately gave Giovanni, as the new commander, a thorough tour of the entire ship to demonstrate its readiness for the voyage. This included brief identification of some of the principal crewmen.

"Captain Verrazzano, this is Boatswain Christophe. He is my assistant, and will serve as master on certain watches." The boatswain gave Giovanni a sharp salute. Christophe is a young seaman with bright, alert eyes that bespeak confidence. He was smartly dressed like Matthieu in a leather jerkin over a loose-fitting linen shirt. His hose and shoes indicate good grooming and personal pride. I expect this young man has a good future with Ango's fleet of ships.

As we moved along the deck, we stopped before a burly, square-faced man with dark eyes and beard. "This well-seasoned seaman is Leclerc" Matthieu said. "In the navy he serves as a gunner's mate, but on this voyage will be the master rigger with responsibility for condition of sails, ropes, spars, and masts while under way." Leclerc gave a salute to Giovanni and introduced the seaman next to him.

"Captain, this is able seaman Paul. He will be my rigger's mate." Paul gave a brief salute to Giovanni, but said nothing. Leclerc and his mate were dressed similarly to Christophe, but with sailcloth jerkins.

Next we stood before a small and slightly twisted, weatherbeaten man of greater years than others. "Captain, this is our cook Carlito. He is known to work wonders with meals." Carlito likewise touched his forehead to show his respect for the captain. We passed before the rest of the seamen, most of whose names were not provided to us, but we observed that we have a crew of fifty, counting officers, mates, able seamen, and boys.

Below main deck we saw the provisions loaded neatly in every available space. Barrels, crates, and many coils of rope were all packed efficiently and tightly to prevent shifting in a stormy sea. Each container was identified by a number and recorded in the master's inventory book. By reference to his book, he easily told us exactly the contents of any container.

Then the master escorted us into the bilge where we could see more containers and ballast stones. In the center near the mainmast, Matthieu briefly demonstrated that the pumps are operational and in good repair. As no ship is without some leakage, these pumps will be in use at least once daily.

Topside again, Matthieu showed us to the newly remodeled officers quarters below the quarterdeck. We each have a tiny space big enough for a bunk with a shelf for stowing gear. Our little spaces open onto a larger room with a table for dining and charting. Astrolabes, quadrants, and cross-staffs were securely stowed in a cabinet along with parchment and ink for writing and charting. We stowed our personal bags and settled into our quarters for the first night aboard, ready to cast off at the early morning high tide when the ebb flow will help us out of the harbor.

January 1, 1524 Dieppe

Before departure every man on board was required attend Mass to confess his sins, receive absolution, and the Eucharist. Giovanni wrote in his log, "We received the holy sacrament of the Eucharist on the very day we began our voyage." A cheering crowd came to the quay to see us off as the sun rose above the horizon and immediately passed behind a cover of clouds. Of course Marie was there, dressed in her finest hood and woolen cloak, waving to Giovanni as he complained to me that he would miss her company terribly while we are gone. "She is by far the best and most captivating woman I have ever known, and I will be eager for the day when I return to her," he said. I have never heard Giovanni express any such sentiment for Beatriz, or any person for that matter. The priest from St. Jacques parish church came to sprinkle the *Dauphine* with one last blessing. Probably the *Dauphine* is today the most blessed ship in France.

Captain Conflans boarded the *Dauphine* briefly to greet us in a very civil and courtly manner. He seemed to be in a jovial mood; completely different from any previous encounter. He made an offhand comment about finally agreeing with Giovanni that the southern course would be better than the northern route he first proposed so vehemently. With a friendly smile and a slight nudge of Giovanni's shoulder he said, "Who knows, perhaps on this route we will find some Spanish vessels loaded with riches for us to plunder." Giovanni entered the happy spirit of the moment with a brief smile, but solemnly responded, "My good Captain Conflans, I love wealth as much any man, and I am certain our king would be happy to see his treasury grow with Spanish gold, but I pray that you speak in jest and will not deviate from our true objective. We simply cannot take any risks that may weaken or endanger our expedition." Conflans laughed at Giovanni's serious turn, and assured him there was nothing to worry about. Conflans offered his wishes of good luck for our venture and left our ship to board the *Normande*. Giovanni watched Conflans for a few moments as he walked down the quay and said, "That man's sudden brightness of mood does not cheer me at all. I still have little trust of him." But immediately Giovanni turned his attention toward getting our ships underway.

In the cold dawn with overcast skies we slipped our moorings and moved slowly into the estuary of the Arques River that forms the busy port of Dieppe. The spring tide had just peaked and its ebbing flow helped the *Dauphine* move toward the sea. Giovanni stood on the quarterdeck instructing the oarsmen as their long wooden sweeps moved us out into the river and toward the sea. In such limited space as this harbor we must depend on the deck oarsmen, as well as oarsmen in the ship's boat, to move and steer us until we pass the jetty where we can unfurl the sails. Just as we began to feel the tide carry our ship toward the sea, we both looked back at the pier and saw Viscount Ango standing at his upper window. He returned our wave and watched us move toward the main channel. His days of sailing are over but he has often told us that he never sees a ship leave without wishing to be on it.

This moment of departure is filled with emotion. On one hand, I feel the excitement of beginning a new voyage. I have sailed with Giovanni many times and always the first emotion is excitement. But with the anticipation is an undercurrent of apprehension. When at sea one never knows what will happen in the next hour. We know we are competent and can handle the ship, but the unknown looms at all times. The storms, the shoals, hostile ships in Spanish waters, illness, injury, as well as unknown hazards in uncharted waters are only a few of the potential hazards. Are the tales of monsters true? Are there cannibals in the part of the New World where we are headed? Will we find a passage to Asia? If so, will we see the Chinese? The list is interminable. Going to sea and facing the fears of the unknown is truly an act of courage.

In a short time we reached the lighthouse at the end of the jetty, and the master gave the order to unfurl the sails and set our course. The men in the tow boat quickly came aboard, hoisted the boat out of the water, and stowed it on the main deck. We set a course for west by south, just one point off west, to get us out of *La Manche*. We expect to hold this course for about 100 leagues before turning toward the island of Madeira.

Translator's note: La Manche, *the French term for English Channel, was shown on some early maps as the English Sea. The length of a "league" varied from country to country and through time, but an average conversion is 1 league = 3.18 nautical miles. French historian Jacques Habert writes that the French league in the period of Verrazzano's voyage was equal to one-twentieth of a degree of latitude, or 3 nautical miles (3.45 statute miles).*

The schedule of watches was established at noon and changed according to formula. Solar and stellar observations are made at fixed hours. Speed estimates are done a certain way for consistency. Any deviation from routine practices would be resented by the mariners. They know that their safety and success depends upon each man doing his job correctly. Malingering seldom occurs as anyone attempting to shirk his work is often harshly dealt with by the other crew members, or certainly by the boatswain under orders of the master. All officers, seamen, and boys are divided into three watches of four hours. Each watch is headed by an officer and a third of the men. Life at sea is driven by the watch periods. A boy is assigned to maintain the thirty-minute sand glass and turn it at the proper moment. If he becomes inattentive or dozes the helmsman raps him soundly. Missing a turn of the glass is a serious offense because of the errors it makes in our reckoning of distance traveled. The boy also must strike a bell at every second turn of the glass. The sound of this bell is the only time that matters on a ship. I must remind the helmsman to make a time correction every few days as we move westward. This is easily done by a gnomon at the center of our compass. At noon the shadow of the gnomon should touch the north symbol of the compass. As we sail west the bell marking the end of the second morning watch, following Prime prayers, will ring slightly earlier each day. If we do not make an occasional correction on the compass, the changes of the watches would begin to come at wrong times.

By the end of the third watch we had progressed about sixteen leagues. Vespers, the Salve Regina, and the Ave Maria were said at the main mast and the first hot meal of a mutton stew was ready. These first two days out may be the only days with fresh meat until we can hunt on land again. With so many experienced crewmen, little time is needed to settle into an orderly routine. We have a fair northeasterly wind off the aft starboard quarter and are making good progress. A large gathering of clouds on the distant northwest horizon concern me at the moment. We shall see how they look by morning.

Sailors stop by the cook's station under the shelter at the forecastle. Each man brings his own wooden bowl and utensil and goes to the cook's fire for a portion of stew and biscuit. Then he sits wherever he can find an unoccupied spot. When a watch goes off duty, those men then take their turn eating. The officers, including Giovanni, me, the surgeon, and the ship's master, are brought plates by a steward, a young boy brought along as an apprentice seaman. The men each receive an allotment of cider and the officers are served wine. For other meals the men are given dried herring or salted pork, and biscuits with a ration of cider. Today the evening meal after vespers is the only cooked meal of the day. Beginning tomorrow the cooked meal will be at midday.

January 2, 1524   At sea

Since leaving port we have maintained a west by south course. Giovanni reckoned our distance to be thirty leagues, a very good day. I also made an estimate and arrived at the same result. We always follow a practice that each of us makes calculations of course and distance. Also we both do the celestial observations. We carry a cross-staff, an astrolabe, and a quadrant. The cross-staff is preferred by both Giovanni and me, but it is difficult to make a reliable observation on a moving ship with any of these instruments. Nevertheless they are better than nothing, and we must know when we are nearing the latitude of our destination. We also estimate our latitude by dead reckoning, but it helps to have the instruments as a check. On the other hand, longitude depends entirely on dead reckoning, unless reliable measurements of lunar angles can be made. But these lunar measurements cannot be made with sufficient accuracy on a moving ship and the necessary computations are beyond the skill of most mariners.

January 3, 1524   At sea

Weather remains unsettled with dark clouds in the northwest. Fair wind on the aft quarter. Still making good time at one point south of west. I calculate we made another thirty leagues today.

A pleasant surprise awaited me when I met our tall, blond surgeon, Berthram Peeters. He dresses well and has a courtly, gentle manner. He appears to be an educated man with many abilities. His education differs from mine in many ways. He has read little of the philosophers but has good curiosity about everything, having spent much time as an apprentice under French physicians. In addition to caring for the sick and injured on our voyage, Peeters is expected to record observations of nature and the ethnic character of people we encounter. This is a new innovation for exploration voyages as usually such observations are made only by the captain or pilot. Giovanni and I will be making similar observations but with fewer details than those Peeters intends to make.

I was surprised to hear that Peeters began preparation for priesthood before changing to his medical apprenticeship. He told us he keeps in close touch with the writings of the church leaders, and explained that he is especially concerned about the widely popular and heretical writings of Luther. I hope he can inform me more on the subject as I know only hearsay and rumors about this German priest that everyone is concerned about. Also I am curious to see the array of medicines and medical tools he carried on board. Medicine is another area about which I am terribly ignorant.

January 4, 1524   At sea

Today, after consultation with me, Giovanni ordered a change of course to south-southwest. Now by my reckoning if we keep this course at two points west of south for 400 leagues, we will reach the Portuguese islands of Madeira. Although the Portuguese do not approve of our voyage, they have so far made no effort to prevent it.

We plan to avoid them as we approach their Madeira Islands.

Until then we hope for a continuation of this fair wind that is now on our aft quarter. We continue to make about thirty leagues each day. The clouds in the northwest are much closer and I expect the wind will veer as they approach.

January 6, 1524 At sea

Before departure Giovanni ordered the captain of each ship to make every effort to maintain visual contact. Each ship is capable of the same speed, so visual contact is not difficult in fair weather. Today the wind changed to the west and became much stronger. The seas are beginning to become rough and it is clear that the storm so long on the horizon has finally found us. We have already lost sight of the *Normande* in the gathering rain and I fear for our other two ships as well. They know our first destination is the most westerly islet of the Madeiras. Giovanni gave instructions to meet there if we became separated.

January 8, 1524 At sea

Yesterday the north-northwest wind became a raging gale. We saw almost constant lightning flashes in the northwest and waves began to wash the deck abeam. We had to change course quickly to keep waves from swamping or capsizing the *Dauphine*. Our course could not be to the east or southeast, away from the wind, because land lies in that direction, and we could risk being driven into the coast in the dark of night. To avoid such a disaster we set a course to the west-southwest. At Giovanni's direction, Matthieu gave the order for a course change and a reduction of sail. Christophe, the boatswain, whistled the command into a howling wind and the seamen quickly responded. They struggled against the wind as they moved across the deck and grabbed for handholds to keep their balance. With unbelievable courage they climbed up the shrouds, stood on the foot lines in the driving rain, furled the foresail up to the yard, then reduced the mainsail to the minimum needed to maintain some necessary bite for the rudder. What but God's protection kept them from being tossed into the sea? The spritsail was furled by the previous watch before the winds hit and the mizzen sail has been furled for several days.

When last we had a momentary glimpse of the other ships we could see they also had changed course. Then we lost sight of them as the rain began and visibility barely extended past the prow of the ship. The wind had now increased in strength by threefold, and items on deck began to slip from their lashings and slide around the deck with each roll of the ship. Crewmen worked desperately in the gale to secure everything that had come loose. The intensity and force of such a storm tests the strength of everything—men and ships. If I had to be up on the main mast or standing on the foot lines furling a sail, my courage would fail lest I be thrown into the sea by the sweeping side-to-side gyration. At times it seemed uncertain that the Dauphine could return to its upright position. Thankfully our ship is well-ballasted and always rights herself. As darkness settled in the storm winds worsened and I felt the dreadful sense of struggling for survival, as if our ship were merely a tossing bit of flotsam.

Even the most seasoned sailors began to fear for their lives, and they hurriedly drew lots to see who among them would do a pilgrimage of penance for all our sins if God would save us from this tempest. The boatswain, Christophe, was thus selected and upon our return he has made a solemn promise to travel as a pilgrim to Vézelay Abbey where the relics of Saint Mary Magdalene, who so loved our Lord, are held. Every sailor prayed for God to save us from the perilous storm and stop its engulfing waves.

Despite the boatswain's pledge, the storm continued unabated for a seemingly endless time. The enormous waves appeared to come from two directions and where they intersected, a giant pyramid of water appeared. Any one of these pyramids could have capsized our ship if hit at the right moment. A lesser ship would have been unmanageable and sunk without the *Dauphine's* excellent balance.

Waves coming from behind made steering difficult, as our rate of movement was almost the same as the advancing waves thus causing the rudder to lose its bite. Without rudder control our ship could be turned by a wave hitting us hard from starboard. In one instance the helmsman could not bring her back around and called for help with the tiller. Everyone was drenched from the rain and waves.

A report came to Matthieu that the strain on the ship from twisting and turning with the impact of waves had loosened caulking in the bilge, and he ordered two men down to man the pumps continuously until fresh oakum could fill the leaking strakes in the hull. Amid the frantic activity on deck I heard a shrill whistle of the boatswain's pipe relaying the master's commands for adjusting the sails. No human voice could have been heard above the roar of our northwesterly gale. I was fearful that one of the men would be washed overboard before this storm ended. No one could move without grabbing something to keep from being swept away as waist-deep water repeatedly washed over the deck. Fortunately at the first sign of a severe storm approaching Matthieu had ordered grab lines strung between the masts and along the gunwales. This precaution saves many men from drowning when a wave floods the deck with a torrent of water.

After many harrowing hours the wind began lessened slightly and the extreme danger eased. Our relief at seeing the wind abate gave hope that we would survive this storm. All the crew now are certain that the boatswain's vow to a pilgrimage saved us.

January 9, 1524 At sea

The storm subsided in the night. This morning waves are still large but no longer dangerous. Rain continues but visibility is better, but the low-riding clouds allow us to see distances of only one-half league. God help us, we see nothing but water. There is no sign of our other ships. We can only hope for a successful rendezvous with our missing fleet in Madeira.

The overcast sky and the heaving waves following a storm leave me with the sense of smallness on this vast and powerful sea. My memory of the fear that grips a sailor during a storm moved me to compose a few lines.

Roiling seas, heaving and ominous, pewter gray and cold.
Waves driven by Aeolus' breath burst upon our deck.
My meager shell trembles, frail before such fearsome force.
Prophets say God's power swells the waters of the sea.
Would that He show mercy in our peril.

Translator's note: Gerolamo's poems have a meter and rhyme that I am unable to recreate in translation.

Giovanni and I made an effort to determine our location. The storm disrupted our routine procedures that help us keep a record of time, speed, and course. My brother relies on his great experience with dead reckoning in a time like this. He instinctively estimates speed of the ship even when it is impossible to time the passing flotsam. The helmsman tried to recall how much he was able to maintain course despite the waves turning the ship from time to time. To determine our latitude we took a sighting on the sun that was weakly visible through thinning clouds. The conclusion of this terrifying storm is that the winds moved us along very quickly toward our destination in Madeira. Now, instead of fifteen days from Dieppe to our rendezvous point in Madeira, we expect to be there in thirteen. Because we moved westward during the storm, we must now change our course to south by west in order to reach our rendezvous with other ships of our fleet.

January 10, 1524 At sea

The sun is shining brightly for the first time since we left Dieppe. The air has that sweet balmy feel that one senses as the weather grows warmer, and we can enjoy the lift of spirit that comes with the southern climes. How sweet! The horrifying tempest would soon be forgotten were it not for the fact that we still see no sign of the other three ships.

At the end of the third watch today at noon Giovanni ordered an extra session of prayer and thanksgiving. We particularly gave thanks to the Virgin Mary for her intercessions on our behalf. Prayers were said also to Mary Magdalene, for whom the boatswain will make a pilgrimage to Vézelay. The words of the Ave Maria, familiar to us all from childhood, gave comfort. Ave Maria, gratia plena, Dominus tecum. We especially felt the meaning of the words of the 107th Psalm:

> Then they cried out to the Lord in their trouble, and he brought them out of their distress. He stilled the storm to a whisper; the waves of the sea were hushed.

The Lord certainly responded to our cries in the night and to the boatswain's pledge. Everyone is in a state of extreme gratitude for our deliverance.

January 13, 1524 At sea, nearing Madeira

For the past three days lighter winds have slowed our progress to a regular twenty-three leagues for the day and night. We have maintained a south by west course. Under such good sailing conditions the days seem long and routine. But after living through the intensity of the storm, routine days are truly a blessing.

Giovanni's rutter describes the profile of the mountain on Madeira, and it corresponds perfectly with the view ahead of us. By the end of the fourth watch we anchored near a deserted islet at the far west end of the Madeira Islands. The Portuguese are very negative toward anyone who might be traveling their waters along the west coast of Africa, so we avoided going near their island ports. Now there is nothing to do but wait a few days and hope the other three ships arrive as planned.

In the meantime there is much that can be done aboard the *Dauphine* to repair damages from the storm. The caulkers are busy filling leaks that worsened from the twisting and turning the ship endured when waves pressed her from all sides. The pumps, which had to be manned constantly during the storm, now need repair. Several casks of water stored below broke loose during the storm and spilled water as they bounced about on the lower deck. The carpenter, who also serves as cooper on this voyage, is making new barrels. We will need them when we are again able to go ashore to replenish our supply of water and wood. Luckily the sails were furled before the wind became too severe and they suffered little damage.

Translator's note: Every captain owned a rutter, a written guide to ports, courses, and coastal appearances with prominent landmarks indicated by sketches.

January 16, 1524 Near Madeira

Today the *Normande* arrived with obvious damage to sails. The foremast was broken and the rudder badly damaged. Captain Conflans reported to Giovanni as soon as they dropped anchor and gave us a greatly distressing report. He had seen one of the other ships capsize soon after the wind and waves became most perilous. He was almost certain it was the *Égyptien* that capsized and sank. He said the *Intrépide* appeared to have severe damage, but was lost from view in the rain. Conflans did not know if *Intrépide* survived the storm.

The most serious part of the report was Conflans's account of an encounter with a Spanish ship. This new development served to renew Giovanni's mistrust and disgust with Conflans. With great self-satisfaction at his escape, Conflans said, "After the storm we could see no sign of our fleet, but we chanced to sight a Spanish ship returning from a voyage to the New World. The Spaniard was limping along with severe storm damage to sails and rudder. Being a one time privateer, I could not resist the temptation to take this prize as a bonus for King Francis. Usually a minimum of fire power is needed to capture one of these prizes, as the Spanish ships are often not armed."

"I soon discovered to my horror that this Spaniard was very well armed with cannon and could still deliver a lethal bite, though crippled by the storm. As soon as we fired a warning shot from one of our cannons the Spanish ship realized our intention and her gunners began firing. I was confounded by this sudden turn. I was stunned that the *Normande* was greatly out-gunned, could not return meaningful fire, hence we sustained heavy damage. I was fortunate that we could manage to turn and escape without sinking. The Spaniard's damage prevented their giving chase."

Giovanni jumped in at this time, his voice rising in anger. "Captain Conflans, tell me by what authority you carried cannon on the *Normande*. I explicitly instructed there were to be no heavy weapons."

Conflans answered, "They were added to the *Normande* by my own orders with the Admiral's knowledge, and there is every reason for cannon to be aboard such a voyage. You are in error to think you could survive without them."

At the end of this report, Giovanni, visibly reddened, burst forth, "Captain Conflans, your arrogance has finally destroyed you. You have broken the first rule of the seaman to obey orders. Your over-grown self-esteem caused you to throw caution to the winds, thinking the reward would mollify me. You, sir, are terribly mistaken, and I will do my best to publicize your transgression. It would be no less a misdeed if you had been successful. You have put the entire expedition at risk, and I wager that may have been your intention. For you, Captain Conflans, this voyage is ended immediately."

Conflans blustered with great indignation, "How can you dare to speak to me about arrogance and obedience? You are arrogant in the extreme to imagine that you have the ability to make this voyage alone. And as for obedience, with a Spanish prize I could have made you a hero in the eyes of Admiral Bonnivet, Viscount Ango, and the king. Now your incompetence and inexperience will cause you to be lost at sea. You cannot possibly succeed without my experience and my knowledge of French seamen. When you fail to return from your voyage, I will gladly expose you as a novice who should never have been given command."

Conflans tried to continue with his thundering rant, but Giovanni interrupted him and told him in a firm voice to be silent. "There is nothing more to say, Captain. You are dismissed. Go see to your ship and make her ready for a return to Dieppe. You will give Admiral Bonnivet a complete account of your failure, as I will also upon my return."

Giovanni took the only action possible in the situation. He ordered Conflans to make rudder repairs sufficient to sail and make all haste to return to Dieppe. Giovanni promised that when the expedition is completed, Conflans will be paid a retainer fee of 100 *livres au tournaise* to compensate for his brief participation in the voyage. I thought this a surprisingly generous gesture from Giovanni, considering how much he dislikes this tiresome man. Before the *Normande* began its return voyage, Giovanni gave Conflans a sealed letter addressed to Admiral Bonnivet with instructions for Conflans to deliver it personally.

Giovanni told me later that his anger was lessened somewhat by the clear opportunity for ridding himself of Conflans permanently. But the most horrible side of the debacle is that Conflans, through his foolishness, has put the entire expedition in dire jeopardy. His irresponsible act, plus the probable loss of two ships in the storm, could very easily bring an end to our venture. Fortunately Giovanni is not that easily diverted from a goal. He will, of course, continue with the *Dauphine* alone. A man so focussed on a noble goal is not easily thwarted.

The loss of the *Normande* to our expedition is very great indeed. We will now be without help in the event of disaster, forcing us to take extra precautions against accident. Nevertheless, if the lost ship *Intrépide* fails to arrive today we will begin our westward sail alone. Our crew spent the day transferring essential provisions and equipment to the *Dauphine*, leaving a supply sufficient for the *Normande* to return to Dieppe.

This evening Giovanni and I went ashore to get the best possible sightings of the northern stars. How different the heavens look from Madeira. Here Polaris is only thirty-two degrees above the horizon compared with nearly fifty degrees at Dieppe. At this latitude some of our familiar stars dip below the horizon during their rotation around the North Star. One advantage in stopping at Madeira for our rendezvous is its precisely known location. The correct latitude and longitude of this spot results from frequent measurements made by astronomers, using angular distance between the moon and certain stars to compute the longitude. Much of this is due to the great efforts of Prince Henry of Portugal and his many assistants some seventy-five years ago. From this known point we can now gain a fresh start on our dead reckoning navigation. Tomorrow we leave with the early tide.

Chapter 8

January 17, 1524 At sea, westward

We are away. The *Dauphine* weighed anchor shortly before dawn. In the days since leaving Dieppe we had barely settled into a routine before the storm changed everything about the expedition. Now we are alone on the sea with many days of routine sailing ahead. The steady northeasterly winds that served Columbus so well are now pushing us steadily on our course due westward along the thirty-second parallel. Everything is perfect for sailing. The weather is fair and the wind is right for following the course without tacking. The foresail and mainsail are each set to catch the northeasterly wind and give us good speed, and the mizzensail is furled. I am sure we will make good time until we reach the New World.

Until now I have had little opportunity to write about the men on board the *Dauphine*. With quieter days at sea, I have begun to talk with officers and sailors in an effort to know them. We officers are quartered reasonably comfortably around a common space below the quarter deck. We use this space for sleeping, eating, charting, and writing. This area will also be an ideal place for meeting and conversation for officers not on watch.

First there is the ship's master, who is second to Giovanni in the command chain. As is often the case, the master is the ship's owner or his appointee. Because the *Dauphine* is owned by Viscount Ango but on long term lease to the navy, the master, as I wrote earlier, is his nephew, Matthieu Ango. Matthieu is a quiet man not yet twenty-five years of age. He is pleasant enough, but seldom enters into conversation among the officers. He is a tall, well-formed man with light hair and a clean-shaven face, giving him a very youthful appearance. Matthieu is second to none in seamanship however. He is firm with the crew, and has the experienced seaman's sense of wind, weather, and sail. He sees immediately if the sail should be taken in a bit to reduce strain on the ship. He has considerable skill estimating a ship's speed, and we often rely on his opinion when making our estimates of distance traveled.

As second in command he is charged with managing the ship, including loading, getting under sail, and maintaining an orderly ship. He is well-respected by the seamen because he is competent and fair, but the crew like him particularly because he is French. Without Matthieu, Giovanni would be much more subject to the crew's resentment that he is not sufficiently French. Matthieu can discuss with Giovanni the mood of the sailors. Already he has mentioned hearing of a murmur of discontent among crewmen over Giovanni's dismissal of Captain Conflans. This is certainly no great surprise, but bears close watch lest it erupt into open resistance. Giovanni may never shake Conflans's "Italian fisherman" epithet, and apparently some in the crew share the sentiment. Knowing Matthieu's acceptance by the crew, Giovanni instructed him to keep an ear open to discover the source of fomentation.

January 18, 1524 At sea

In the past day we have sailed twenty-eight leagues, still going west on the thirty-second parallel. This is much better time than we made on the first leg of the voyage from Dieppe to Madeira. If this fair wind continues we will make the destination in good time.

Our ship's cook, Carlito, is an unusual man, although I find his speech difficult to understand. It is a mixture of Spanish and French, spoken with a raspy voice. He is of such small stature that I have trouble imagining him as the able seaman he claims to have been in his youth. He told me he has always been an orphan and has no family name. Matthieu knows a little more about Carlito, and told us that he was abandoned at birth, then rescued by Cistercian monks at the Monfero Abbey in northwestern Spain. There the monks called him Carlito, Little Carlos, and made him a kitchen helper. He left the monastery at the age of twelve and went to sea. The abbot arranged for a small payment to a ship's master with the promise to train Carlito as an able seaman. Thus began a new life for the young orphan. Always small in size, he made up for this deficiency through his high energy and hard work.

After years as a seaman, Carlito had a serious accident. He fell from the rigging onto the deck and became a cripple, thus preventing him from carrying out the duties of an ordinary seaman. This incident would turn most young men into beggars on the street, but Carlito's familiarity with cooking provided him with a new opening for employment at sea and since then he has been a ship's cook. His food is not wonderful, but in the monastery he learned the secret of using herbs to improve the unpalatable flavors of boiled or salted meat and fish.

Best of all, Carlito learned the secret of making a tasty bread. If the Cistercians taught him nothing else, this skill with bread was a fine education. It is said that Carlito insisted that a keg of beer be included among the provisions loaded on the *Dauphine* at Dieppe. Apparently Carlito saw the Cistercians add a bit of beer to wheat dough and then allow the dough to stand for a time. The happy result was that the bread became much lighter and very flavorful. He told me he used ordinary ingredients; rendered fat, honey, flour, and beer, making certain to include just a bit of the sediment from the bottom of the barrel and a bit of the foam from the top. The benefit for Carlito was steady employment aboard ships as his reputation for bread making became known. Carlito makes bread aboard the *Dauphine* on Saturdays and Wednesdays which provides a welcome change from the hard biscuit we eat on other days.

Carlito produces food for the men and officers from a simple open fire built on a bed of sand and rock on the deck under the shelter of the forecastle. Most of his cooking is done in a pot hung over the fire, but he cooks his bread in a simple oven made of a small ceramic dome that covers a shallow flat-bottom ceramic bowl placed directly on the coals. When both ceramic pieces are hot, Carlito puts the puffy bread dough in the bowl and covers it with the dome. On baking days he produces ten delicious round loaves that are quickly devoured by everyone. This practical oven, which Carlito calls La Campana for its bell-shaped dome, is his prized possession and is his assurance of continued employment at sea.

In addition to his cooking skills, Carlito is full of stories and legends. Many of his tales are pure nonsense about sea monsters, cannibals, and other fantasies intended to feed the sailor's superstitions. I cannot determine if Carlito himself believes these stories, but they are intriguing and always attract a circle of believers.

Carlito also is a repository of other stories meant solely for entertainment. When I notice a group of sailors gathered around Carlito, I make it a point to join them to hear his latest story, many of them quite humorous. Today I heard such a tale, which I will summarize.

A blacksmith in a certain village had killed a man and was to be condemned for his act. The villagers came before the judge and beseeched him to spare the smith, affirming that they had no other blacksmith, nor was there another for a great distance. They further argued that the poor smith had many important skills. He was a good farrier, he made locks and keys, and he could make all manner of ironworks for carts or plows. The judge answered, "My good men, I have heard your allegations, but I must consider that a man is slain. If I spare your smith, how shall justice be done?" The spokesman for the villagers replied, "We beg your grace to consider this alternative. We have in our village two weavers, and the better one of them will serve our needs well enough. We pray you, therefore, hang the second weaver, and save the smith."

As always Carlito swears the story is true, but he refuses requests to finish the story and leaves the fate of the poor weaver for the men to ponder.

January 19, 1524   At sea

This is the most favorable location imaginable for sailing westward. We have constant winds requiring little adjustment to our sails, and fair weather daily. Our course continues directly west along the thirty-second parallel. We appear to have made another twenty-nine leagues from Madeira. All is well.

I have watched our boatswain at work for the past few days. He is a bright young lad, with more years at sea than you might guess from looking at him. This young man, called Christophe, is the son of a friend of Viscount Ango, and Matthieu agreed to train the boy at sea. He is now nearly nineteen and in his eighth year of training. In another year or two he will become pilot of one of Ango's ships, and later become a ship's master. Matthieu said he expects Christophe to be an excellent master one day.

As boatswain Christophe does the work of communicating Matthieu's orders to the crew. He is responsible for keeping the pumps manned, for stowing and caring for provisions in the hold, and arranging for repairs to sails and spars when necessary. He is first among the seamen and not yet an officer. He is an effective liaison between officers and seamen and trusted by both. I find him an agreeable, pleasant man.

I discovered it was Christophe who told Matthieu of the grumbling among some seamen about Giovanni's dealing with Conflans. Christophe passes this information without divulging names of crewmen in order to protect their confidence in him. The crewmen know that Christophe talks frequently with the master and they use him as a means of telling the officers if something is amiss. It is a delicate line for Christophe to walk without offending or betraying confidences of either side. Of course, if serious matters arise that might lead to open confrontation between seamen and officers, Christophe would certainly tell the master the names of agitators so they could be dealt with quickly. Apparently Christophe passed word to Matthieu today that the man Leclerc is quietly stirring discontent over the dismissal of Captain Conflans. Leclerc, a former crewman under Conflans on the *Dauphine*, is a strong and dominating man feared by many of the crew. This is a bad mixture and I need to learn more about this Leclerc.

January 20, 1524 At sea

Our course is the same: west along the thirty-second parallel. We continue to make about thirty leagues each day. Nothing new to report. High thin clouds are now overhead, trailing off to the west, suggesting that a change may come. Not another storm, we hope.

Today I chanced to speak at length with our surgeon Berthram Peeters. He has so much of interest to talk about that I hardly knew where to begin our conversation. As we became more acquainted, I asked him, "How did you choose to make medicine rather than the Church your life's work?" I knew from his brother, Lucas, that Berthram had also considered the priesthood.

"This was a simple choice for me," Berthram began. "My brother and I were both planning a life in the priesthood, and I think Lucas may yet enter that profession. But I felt another calling. I wanted to see the world and satisfy my sense of adventure. There is, however, a more important reason. Two years ago I met a beautiful woman and in due time asked for her hand in marriage. Her father agreed and the lovely Alaina willingly agreed to marry me. Marriage is simply not an option for a priest. So I made the choice."

"Our marriage is unusual because Alaina and I found each other without prior arrangements by their parents." I told Berthram that my brother, Giovanni, followed the same path in finding a bride.

"Many people have told me," Berthram continued, "that the marriage is sure to be an unhappy one because we did not rely on the better judgement of our parents. Alaina and I are already certain we have an excellent union."

They live in Rouen where Berthram expects to practice his trade after this voyage. The voyage to the New World fulfills his need to see other places and to gain some medical experience. When he returns he will begin his medical trade in earnest.

Berthram told me, "Surgery today is gradually becoming a separate trade. Most surgery today is still done by barbers, but I became enthused when I learned that some men in the field had discovered new methods that are far beyond the abilities of most barbers. Such simple things as tying off an arm above the point of amputation has saved many men from bleeding to death. Also cauterization with hot metal prevents death from amputation. Some physicians," he continued, "have found that tying off blood vessels after amputation works better than cauterization. As new methods are discovered, few barbers ever hear about them. Only someone who devotes his life to knowledge of surgery and communicates with others working in the field can hope to learn new techniques as they are discovered. I expect to travel to Paris regularly to listen to men who are studying the human body."

Berthram told me that dissection of a Christian human body is illegal and considered a desecration by the Church. Despite this stigma a few men with medical curiosity have managed to dissect non-Christian bodies if they can be found and dispel some of the mystery about the insides of humans. Furthermore some have begun to think that disease is caused from particles outside the body, rather than from a disorder of the four cardinal humors of blood, phlegm, yellow bile, and black bile.

Berthram said, "I traveled to Padua a few years ago to work as an apprentice to the prominent physician Gerolamo Fracastoro. This Italian has new insights on the causes of diseases, and is currently thinking that diseases are transmitted by tiny disease seeds or spores that travel in the air. He even observed that some diseases are transmitted from person to person."

I admire that Berthram wants to devote his life to this pursuit and that he has gone to such lengths to obtain the best training possible. I think he is at the threshold of great changes in his field.

Later in the day Berthram showed me the tools of his trade. God forbid that I should ever be subject to such devices! At first sight his tools seem to be similar to those a carpenter might use: a drill, a saw, pliers, and tongs that he called forceps. The most bothersome was a metal tube for use as a catheter, the thought of which sent a small chill down my spine. He told me that most wounds to the arms or legs resulted in amputation, so little more was needed than the small package of tools in his possession. He showed me the sharp cutting tool he uses for bleeding a patient. He explained that this procedure is used to return proper balance to one of the humors that has caused illness. Despite his practice of new medical methods Berthram often falls back on the long-tested knowledge of the humors.

In addition to his tools Berthram has a box of bags containing herbs from which he can concoct medicines to suit the ailment. I could see bags of garlic, willow bark, wormwood, bishopwort, cropleek, celandine, and red nettle, each having its value for illness. Also he has herbs carried in from Asia including tamarind and nux vomica, a poisonous nut from Asia whose name reveals its use. Other poisons were monkshood and wolfbane. I have yet to learn how Berthram uses these seemingly dangerous herbs. He explained to me that his training under Fracastoro taught him proper dosages adequate for the ailment, but insufficient to kill the patient. He told me the objective of most of these medicines was to induce vomiting or purging. Those procedures along with bleeding appear to comprise the practice of any medicine other than amputations.

January 23, 1524 At sea

Course still due west. Northeast wind holding steady.

I had an unsettling exchange with Giovanni today. As I told him about some of the interesting crewmen on board, he listened with interest for a while, then blurted out, "Are you trying to undermine my authority with the crew?" I had no idea how to respond to his question, and asked him to explain his meaning. "I have enough problem keeping their respect," he continued, "without your diverting their attention to yourself."

I could only guess that he referred to my fraternization with crewmen. "Giovanni," I replied, "I have never said or done anything that would make a crewman think any less of you. I have no idea what you are talking about."

"I will tell you one thing," Giovanni said intently, "You have spent your life trying to match my accomplishments and now I see you gaining favor with the crew, while they continue to distrust me."

Giovanni then changed the subject as though he wished to say no more about this brief rift, and he began talking about the good distance we were making with the hope that our good fortune continues. Later in the day he spoke in a friendlier manner and told me to ignore his earlier outburst. For the rest of the day I have tried to understand his words, which he now wants me to forget. As young boys can I remember a sense of rivalry between us. Perhaps the feeling remains without my being aware of it. Maybe Giovanni sees a rivalry and I do not. Something I have done or said irked him, of that I am sure, but what and why I do not know.

As boys he would tease me because I spent more time with studies under our tutor. His teasing would upset me and sometimes I would ignore my studies to stop his taunts. But soon I would return to my interests. When we went to the university in Florence, Giovanni did very well in his studies, but he was eager to begin making his way in the world as a seaman and trader. He went to Venice and began his life at sea while I stayed longer in Florence to pursue further reading in astronomy, languages, mathematics, and philosophy. My only hope of understanding Giovanni's outburst today, is to suppose that he feels bothered that he stopped his education while I continued. Perhaps this has been bothering him all these years.

January 24, 1524 At sea

Course west. Wind is steady and little adjustment of sails is necessary. Often in the afternoon we see tall clouds building up on the horizon, but by morning they are gone with no rain or storminess.

Today we adjusted the change of watches to match solar noon. We have gained time by a little more than one glass. The third watch of the day had to stay on duty thirty minutes longer, one turn of the glass, but everyone is willing to adapt for the sake of keeping the routine steady. Also we have begun to see a change in our compass. Our evening sighting of the North Star began to differ from north on our compass. This is easily corrected by rotating the compass an appropriate amount, but it is curious that no one understands why this change occurs. The needle is obviously attracted to the northern constellations, and those constellations change position steadily through the day. But why must a ship sailing west across the Atlantic Ocean experience this change of compass direction? The reverse happens on the eastward return. Giovanni experienced this on his voyage to the Newfoundland fisheries, and Columbus and others commented on it too. Now it has become routine to adjust the compass, rather than fret about a loss of dependance on the compass. If we failed to make this correction, our course would soon veer south of our intended destination.

The young boatswain, Christophe, has been talking with Carlito again and relayed some of the conversation to me. Carlito made several voyages along the coast of Africa in his early days as a seaman. He swore to Christophe and other listeners that he saw many strange creatures in those unknown lands. Men with only one leg and one eye, animals with two heads, but most worrisome are the cannibals that live on human flesh. The old cook foretells that this crew had better expect similar inhabitants in the lands of our destination. As no one has visited these shores where we go, no one can dispute his prophecy, but some sailors expect the worst.

January 26, 1524 At sea

Wind conditions remain the same as yesterday, but we continue to make good about twenty-five leagues due west each day.

January 27, 1524 At sea

Today is Sunday and Giovanni ordered a special prayer service in thanksgiving for the good fortune we have had on these eleven days since our departure from Madeira.

The fair winds have returned and no mishaps have occurred. We owe great thanks to God, who has brought us such good sailing.

Giovanni began the prayers with the Salve Regina, always a part of sailors' prayer services, and the oft repeated words come easily from Giovanni's lips. "Hail, holy Queen, mother of mercy," he begins, and the crew repeats his words. Sailors regard the Holy Virgin as one of their patron saints, as do many travelers. "The life and sweetness, and our hope, hail." Giovanni shouts the words for all to hear and echo. "To thee do we cry, poor banished children of Eve," he pauses again for their response. Then finishes with, "to thee we sigh, mourning and weeping in this valley of tears."

Then Giovanni reads selections from the 107th Psalm, emphasizing the words of thanksgiving we should all take to heart. "He stilled the storm to a whisper, the waves of the sea were hushed."

The sailors respond, "Thanks be to God!"

"They were glad when it grew calm, and He guided them to their desired haven."

"Thanks be to God!" comes the response.

"Let us give thanks to the Lord for his unfailing love and his wonderful deeds for mankind," Giovanni says.

The crew answers, "Thanks be to God."

Giovanni is very sincere about his devotion to God and has additional prayer times alone in his bedchamber. Most of us feel we have given sufficient notice to our Maker and Protector through the regular daily prayers for everyone, but in the midst of our recent terrible storm I heard prayers on many lips.

Chapter 9

January 28, 1524 At sea

Once again the winds have weakened and shifted northwesterly. This required much additional labor to manipulate the sails as we tacked back and forth across our due west course. Distance made good today was down to twenty leagues. The extra work involved in tacking seemed to enliven the spirits of the men, who had little to do but routine maintenance during our time of sailing constantly on west course. With extra time on their hands they applied themselves to other tasks such as caulking leaks, swabbing the deck (a daily task under any circumstances), and making repairs to sails and lines. The master allows no time for idleness on any ship under his direction. Mathieu's repeated maxim, "Idleness leads to discontent; discontent leads to mutiny." The men have a renewed energy. They weathered the storm and we have had many days of steady sailing. They all knew the voyage is going well, and I can sense their pleasure at having more tasks involving actual sailing.

Today I had a pleasant conversation with Giovanni. He, too, seems more at ease since the change of winds has caused new activity on board. He talked of Marie and this long separation, and that he missed her wise counsel on many and various matters. But he is still greatly enjoying this voyage and feels that he is at last fulfilling a dream.

"Giovanni," I asked, " tell me more about this dream. You have often mentioned a dream without adding much detail." He thought a few moments, as though considering whether to divulge his innermost thoughts.

"The simplest way to describe it," he began, "is that I want to conquer the horizon."

He paused again and I interjected a question. "But how can one conquer the horizon? It moves continuously ahead of us, and stays constantly at the same distance."

Giovanni had clearly given this some thought but had not expressed it before now except perhaps to Marie.

He said, "The horizon is my temptress and she has me under a spell that cannot be shaken. I could no more ignore her call than I could live without nourishment. The poets have their Erato as their inspirational muse, astronomers have their Urania. I, as an explorer, have Orizontas, I am certain of her existence and she drives my ambition to explore. She is a seductress muse that draws an explorer toward the unknown that lies beyond the horizon. A true explorer is defenseless against her lure. Any mariner has the skill to sail, but few have the ambition and imagination that drives them to explore the unknown and find what lies beyond."

I responded with my own source of motivation, "You are different from me, Giovanni. I love to sail and make voyages to new and interesting places, and I love the art of navigation. But I have no compassion or drive to explore the ever receding horizon. I would be just as happy to make my mark as a cartographer, which I hope to do when we return.

My motivation is the map that I will make as a result of this voyage, and the satisfying knowledge that this will be the most thorough map of the land that the cartographer Waldseemüller called America. I want to make a map based entirely on direct observation by a cartographer, without conjecture and fanciful fabrication. This map will have my name on it for all time to come."

Giovanni continued, "Your goal is a good and proper one for you. You are a good navigator and a good companion on the many long voyages we have made together. Your dream is attainable only because you have cartographic skills; my dream is also attainable because of my skills. A merchant may wish to travel foreign lands as a means of expanding his wealth, but he lacks the skill to get there so the merchant's dream is not attainable. That is why merchants and bankers from Lyon have financed this voyage…to realize their dream. Likewise without them I could not realize my dream."

"You will indeed attain your dream Giovanni," I said, "not only because you have the skills for navigation, but also because you have the skills for bringing together all the necessary parts: the money, the support of the king, the assembly of a crew, the acquisition of ships, and much more. This is a great event with many parts that only you could have executed so well. This voyage will itself have your name upon it for all time."

Of course an unmentioned motive for us both is the prospect of wealth resulting from the discoveries, and future development of resources we hope to find in the New World, but at the moment we are discussing ideals.

January 29, 1524

We are still having to deal with the changed wind, now coming from the northwest. Giovanni heard some details of the voyage made by Columbus, and most Spaniards over the thirty-two years since then; that the winds blew steadily from the northeast for the entire voyage to the New World. The only difference is that the Spaniards sailed twenty-eight degrees latitude and less, which is four degrees farther south than our course. Most mariners have known for many years that winds blow from the northeast when they sail south of thirty degrees. Also it is known that north of thirty degrees latitude, winds are from westerly directions. We happen to be sailing within a latitude between the two wind directions, where the winds shift direction seasonally. So now we have good sailing with northeast winds, even though we must work harder to make headway sailing with the wind on our forequarter.

January 31, 1524

Northwesterly winds, fair weather with many clouds. Course continues on thirty-two degrees.

Today I had another chance for conversation with Berthram Peeters, the surgeon and probed him about his views on Martin Luther and the church's reactions. This man, Luther, has caught everyone's attention. Some hate him for questioning the Church, some like what he says. I am eager to know more about his thinking.

Berthram told me that Luther has been excommunicated by the church authorities for the past four years, but excommunication did nothing to silence the renegade former priest. If anything he has become more vocal and has gained a larger audience. Berthram said many of the common people were waiting for such a voice as Luther's. It is said that Luther did not create his audience among the common people, rather he found an eager audience waiting to hear his message. The fact that so many were ready to listen is exactly what startled the church authorities into action against Luther. His popularity is the only thing that saved his life from the flames. Berthram said he had heard much support of Luther among his friends in Flanders.

Giovanni, who was sitting nearby, said, "It would have been better for all if Luther had burned. His movement is now getting out of control and the church is suffering seriously. The church is the only true guardian of the faith. Their 1,500 years of maintaining a pure faith has given us a bulwark we can rely on in times of trouble. Where else can we turn for sustenance and salvation but the true doctrines of the Church? There is nothing else! Luther does not offer us absolution for our sins, nor does he want us to have most of the sacramental rites that we need in our lives."

With that outpouring of his thoughts Giovanni left us and went up on the quarterdeck. He has never enjoyed a discussion of ideas and much prefers to avoid it when possible. He feels very comfortable with the security provided by the church and wants to hear nothing to shake his foundation. There are many who feel the same about the changes happening over much of Europe. Later in the day as we were changing watches, Giovanni cautioned me against contamination of my mind with false doctrines. Always the elder brother, his subordination of me grates terribly. My faith is not shaken in the least nor have

Luther's ideas swayed me. I simply love discussing new thoughts and attempting to trace from whence they come.

The young surgeon was somewhat subdued after Giovanni's words. He certainly does not want to offend the captain, but I reassured him that Giovanni was much more tolerant of such talk than he sounds, he merely wants to keep it contained. He cannot tolerate those who actually leave the faith of the church. What would bother Giovanni is for us to begin criticizing the church as Luther did, rather than just to discuss Luther's ideas. He would be very concerned, and probably forbid our conversations if we began to believe Luther's talk.

February 1, 1524

Made good twenty-five leagues today after several major tacks to the southwest then back to north by west. We never can sail the *Dauphine* closer than four points into the northwesterly wind. This requires some big swings in direction but never strays too far from our planned course.

Berthram said he had more to tell me about Luther and wanted to continue our discussion about his ideas. It is clear to me that Berthram is somewhat swayed by Luther as are many of his countrymen. So far the changes seem to be restricted to Germany, Flanders, and Switzerland. France, unfortunately, has begun to feel a noticeable infusion of Luther's ideas, but, not so much as Germany.

Berthram has memorized many sections of Luther's book, *On The Liberty of a Christian Man*, and related some quotations: "The Church of Rome, formerly the most holy of all Churches, has become the most lawless den of thieves, the most shameless of all brothels, the very kingdom of sin, death, and hell; so that not even antichrist, if he were to come, could devise any addition to its wickedness."

This startling statement was written just five years ago, about a year before Luther was excommunicated. Such a statement surely earned him a place at the stake.

Berthram continued with other quotes from Luther's writing on what he sees as errors of the Church, namely that the pope has the sole authority to interpret the scriptures. "The large problem being that there is no proof announcing that this authority is the Pope's alone, thus they have assumed this authority for themselves."

Berthram added his own thought, "Hence there are many who can interpret scripture, and it was for this reason that Luther undertook to write a new translation of the Bible in German, his native tongue, and make it available for anyone who is able to read. This great work was finished and published only two years ago. Unfortunately the very act of translating the Bible into vernacular is punishable by death in the eyes of the Church, so Luther remains apostate."

"One great asset for Luther," Berthram told me, "has been his skill in logic and his memory for scripture. When speaking he quickly convinces others with his adroit intellect and command of debate. When Johan Eck desired to defend the church he challenged Luther to a debate of ideas to be judged by a panel of academics. Luther easily showed the errors of Eck's arguments and seemed to be a clear winner in the debate. Nevertheless, the judges appointed by the church claimed that Eck won the argument. Few in the audience were convinced. Nearly everyone except the judges thought Luther had made his case much more clearly than Eck."

February 2, 1524

We are continuing our tacks against brisk northwesterly winds, and made good twenty leagues. Skies are overcast much of the time now, I wonder about a change of weather coming our way.

Christophe told us today that he continues to hear grumbling among men when not on watch. Their concern is that the Italian captain may be incompetent. It is a different reason every day. Some have said that the foreign captain will not be able to bring us through another storm. Survival of the first storm was due to good fortune and the pledge to a pilgrimage, and had little to do with seamanship of the captain. Each day there are variations on this theme. Sailors are expected to complain, but no one pays much attention unless work fails to be done, or plots are hatched. Matthieu, knowing that one man is often the agitator, presses Christophe to learn who is fomenting this kind of talk. Christophe told him Leclerc's name has not been mentioned again as the one responsible for keeping this talk alive. Rather the men are silent about what or who started the murmuring against the captain. Matthieu pressed further, "Christophe, you must not keep this man's name to yourself. If you hear his name, I must know it." The young boatswain promised he would tell if he heard a source of this mutinous talk.

Christophe also told us more stories that Carlito continues to provide to the crew. The cook foretold that this ship has offended the spirits of the sea, suggesting that dismissing Conflans was the offending act. "When a person of rank is dismissed without good cause," Carlito told Christophe, "some misfortune is sure to befall the voyage as punishment for an unjust deed." He went on to say that "Aeolus, master of the winds, would soon open his bag of winds and end this idyllic sailing we have so far experienced." The sailors, who regard Carlito as something of an oracle, have no knowledge of Greek mythology and the story of Aeolus, but nevertheless nod in agreement according to Christophe. We have had seven days of fair weather and good winds, but every sailor knows that good weather eventually ends. The mere mention of Aeolus's bag of winds sends a shudder through some long experienced sailors. No doubt we will experience another serious storm on this voyage; it is almost inevitable, and a few sailors will swear that Carlito foretold the storm and its cause. I must alert Giovanni to this undercurrent of anxiety among the crew, despite his recent outburst over my association with the crew. We must demand that Carlito cease connecting all misfortune to the dismissal of Conflans. Carlito himself may be the primary cause of unrest among the crew.

February 4, 1524

Wind changed toward north. This veering of the wind is enough to make fewer tacks necessary. Sailed better distance, thirty leagues made good.

Today I stood on the quarterdeck watching sailors in their work routine. Their experience shows clearly how a group must work together when adjusting sails for a change in direction during a tack maneuver. Each one understands the importance of working together to hoist a yard for example, and they sing a song to help them coordinate or to develop a rhythm to their effort. The songs usually have many verses depending on the duration of the task. When raising the yard of the mainmast or weighing anchor, there is always a chorus of nonsense words that helps them heave in unison:

"Ah la ira lahoula chalez" sings out the leader,

"Ah my boys faladoue," respond the men as they heave on the rope lifting the heavy spar and sails.

"Into the port of Dieppe we shall come again," sings the leader,

"Ah my boys faladoue," the men respond with another heave on the ropes.

Another working song I enjoy hearing has to do with a drunken sailor and has many verses, some of them quite ribald in tone. Each verse suggests what to do with a drunk sailor.

"Put him in the longboat 'til he's sober," and a chorus, "Weigh hey, and up she rises, weigh hey, and up she rises," is sung on the heave of the ropes as the yard rises up the mast.

"Throw him in bed with naughty Margo," followed by, "Weigh hey, and up she rises, weigh hey, and up she rises," while heaving the yard upward.

All this is beautiful to watch and the men enjoy their work when everyone is pulling together and singing. Giovanni says it helps their morale to sing together and I am sure that is true. The female name Marguerite appears in their song frequently, and Margo is a familiar form of Marguerite. This may have been a particular woman referred to at one time but she is long forgotten except among sailors.

February 5, 1524

Now nineteen days out of Madeira and sailing remains good. Spirits are high. Matthieu Ango made another correction to our compass based on sightings we took on the North Star. Again our compass was indicating one point to the northwest and had to be turned by that amount.

I talked with Giovanni about the frightful tales Carlito has been telling the crew about impending storms and the reasons why our ship may be in disfavor. This upset Giovanni considerably, and he had words with Matthieu giving orders to root out this kind of talk before it causes problems. Matthieu talked with his protégé, Christophe. The talk against Giovanni may stop, but we wonder if damage has already been done. The message sent to Carlito included a serious threat of severe punishment to him if any future stories dealt with the dismissal of Captain Conflans. Carlito is wise to the ways of the sea and knows that the master makes no hollow threats. But Carlito is also very clever, and will no doubt find a way to continue his delight in frightening the sailors. He is smart enough to avoid any mention of Conflans again, but the men now have it on their minds.

Christophe reported further that several crewmen have a complaint of malingering against a young able seaman named Miguel. That surprised me because I have watched the men at work on deck, and this Miguel works as hard as any seaman. Christophe added that the rigging master, Leclerc, complains that Miguel is slow because he is Spanish and cannot keep up with French sailors. I wonder if Leclerc is also the one who stirs discontent about

Giovanni supposedly being Italian. Leclerc served under Captain Conflans and may retain a strong loyalty to him. Could he also bear resentment of anyone perceived to be foreign?

February 6, 1524

Continuing along thirty-two degrees latitude, made good twenty-eight leagues again today. Wind is still northerly. Once during each watch, Giovanni or the officer on duty, has a sailor throw a piece of wood into the water from the forward starboard rail. The movement of the ship past the floating wood is timed by reciting the verses of the 107th Psalm in a regular meter. When the stern of the ship passes the wood, the speaker notes how far into the Psalm he has progressed. Giovanni's experience has taught him to accurately estimate the rate of the ship's movement from the final word he speaks as the ship sails past the wood.

Each time we change course during a tack, we must know our speed and direction during that leg of the maneuver. The helmsman keeps a record on his traverse board by moving pegs showing the number of watch periods he maintained each course. This provides time and direction to our speed estimates, and thus we are able to find our distance traveled along each segment of our course. Another computation tells us the actual distance made good along our intended course, or "distance made good." To the ordinary seaman, the art of navigation seems to be almost magical. They are often in awe and a little suspicious of men who can take a ship to sea and return safely to port again.

February 7, 1524

We have entered an area of seaweed near the water's surface. This is very disturbing for everyone as we fear running aground more than anything. Matthieu orders soundings taken almost continuously whenever these mysterious weeds appear but our thirty fathom line has never yet found a bottom. The weed appears to be unattached and floating in this area.

The boatswain reported to us that Carlito knows of shipmates sailing with Columbus who saw the same weed. They also feared running aground but even more they feared becoming entangled in the thick cover of the weed in their path. Despite their fears neither problem occurred. The weed seems to be floating freely without forming a heavy mat and we are so far able to sail freely through it. This weed must be unique to these waters for I have never heard a mariner tell of seeing it in another place. We even see little fish and other tiny sea creatures living amid its long fronds.

Partly as a precaution against the weed Giovanni ordered our first major change of course since leaving Madeira. We set a new course for northwest by west, just one point off northwest. He wants to continue this route until we reach thirty-four degrees latitude, then resume our due west course.

The strange water plant was the reason Giovanni gave to the crew for the change of course but he confided to the master and me that he had other reasons. Giovanni knew that the Spanish captain Lucas Vázquez de Ayllon had sailed up the coast of the land they called Florida to some point above thirty-one degrees. He learned of this from his

Florentine connections, but he has not heard if the Spanish established a settlement or an armed naval presence there, so he has decided on the side of caution to avoid any possibility of contact. We will approach the land that lies ahead at thirty-four degrees, then turn south and move carefully down the coast. If we should see a Spanish ship ahead, we would then have time to turn and head north again before they could intercept us. This would be much wiser than sailing directly into their den.

Translator's note: As it turned out, Ayllon never exercised his grant to colonize, so Verrazzano need not have worried. Nevertheless, given the information he had at the time, Verrazzano was right to use utmost caution...especially because he was sailing alone and without cannon.

Chapter 10

September 25, 2010 Dieppe

I needed this extended break from the tedium of translating tedious Italian manuscripts in a windowless room of the library. I must have some time in the open air. Lorena and I came to Dieppe, partly for a holiday, but also for me to become more familiar with the harbor area that Gerolamo writes about in his journal.

We checked into the Aguado hotel with a room facing the sea and a beautiful boulevard with a broad esplanade along the beach. After dumping our bags, we walked about a hundred yards to the waterfront of the harbor at the center of Dieppe. Certainly this was the city center in the sixteenth century. One of the most noticeable features is that this neighborhood of Dieppe has far fewer graffiti on buildings compared to my neighborhood in Rouen. It gives the place a cleaner look.

Today the small harbor is lined with recreational boats of all sizes, but no major seagoing vessels. In 1524 I would have seen a maze of masts and spars with caravels and nefs unloading their wares from exotic places. The present array of small boats and the many modifications to the harbor make it like a man-made lake, not a place that sent forth sea-going ships to trade and explore the world. I hoped to imagine what Verrazzano would have seen in 1524. It's pretty difficult after nearly 500 years.

This view of Dieppe harbor in the 1850's is probably very similar to the view in Verrazzano's time. From *Dieppe et ses environs* by Eugène Chapus, 1853.

A tourist information center directed us to the site of Viscount Ango's town home, Pensée, *but nothing remains after ages of deterioration and wartime destruction, especially the naval bombardment by an Anglo-Dutch fleet in 1694. The site now has a college built around a courtyard. I was told the basement of one of the buildings has some floor tiles that are the only remnants of Ango's house.*

A few structures from Verrazzano's time still exist. The first one we visited was the thirteenth-century church, Saint Jacques. Inside is Ango's tomb and a frieze depicting New World natives encountered by explorers and traders from Dieppe. The name Ango appears in a street and the name of a bridge across the Arques River at one end of the harbor.

The other visible remnant from Verrazzano's time is the Castle of Dieppe perched prominently atop the sea cliff just southwest of town. The castle has been occupied by noblemen, used as military barracks, and now is an interesting historical museum. The present structure was built in 1435 on a cliff overlooking the sea and the town of Dieppe in order to protect the fortified town from attack by the English. An earlier castle on the same site was built by Henry II of England and Richard the Lionhearted about 1195. The present castle was spared from the 1694 naval bombardment that destroyed much of the town. Such bombardments clearly demonstrated the futility of walls as a protection for a city.

I can only imagine where the Le Marin inn might have been, but my best guess is that it was facing the harbor, which is the obvious location of an inn for seafarers. I saw an attractive brewery and bar named La Marine *facing the harbor not far from the site of Ango's former home. Perhaps that bar might be on the site of the old inn, Le Marin. Gerolamo wrote that Le Marin was only a short walk from Viscount Ango's house.*

Today the streets around the harbor are lined with inviting little bistros and restaurants beckoning to tourists arriving on the cross-channel ferry from Newhaven, England. British tourists love it as a short holiday. They can be over and back home in one day of shopping and eating if they're unfortunate enough to be in a hurry. Our first stop on the waterfront was a place touting their Fruits de Mer. *This had to be a good choice in a town that has been a fishing center since the eleventh century. For a historian I spent a surprising amount of time today exploring the food of Dieppe, rather than its history. I think my soul needed this refreshing break from history after so many days in the library archives.*

September 26, 2010 Dieppe

After a morning of sightseeing, we found a nice spot with tables outside for a quiet cup of coffee with a snack. The pleasantness took a sudden turn however when Lorena said she might stay for several weeks. She wanted us to see more of France and spend some time in Paris. I tried to gently put a quietus on that idea. "Lorena," I said, "I can't do that. I have a deadline for finishing this work before my grant expires at the end of the year. I'm not sure just how much longer I'll need for the work, but I do know that translations cannot be hurried."

Lorena became silent for a while, then said, "I dropped everything I'm working on to come over here, and I think you should be willing to do the same. Now your coolness makes me realize I sacrificed my own work for nothing."

"Coolness? That's rich! You may recall, even though I didn't ask you to come, I was actually glad to see you, and my passions certainly were not cool. Why are you making so little of my work? If you appreciated how important this project is to me, you would not suggest anything that might jeopardize it. You surely know how important it is to me. I still cannot understand what possessed you to make such a sudden trip, and to tell the truth, I think it would be a burden if you stayed as long as you planned. In fact it would completely screw up my work schedule."

"Oh! So now I'm a burden and it's all about you and your work!" her voice showing a too familiar icy edge. "Well, I can certainly relieve you of your burden. I'm out of here tomorrow! I'll not inconvenience you any more. Furthermore, I'll tell you exactly why I decided to come so suddenly. When I didn't hear from you for so long I supposed your new friend, Nicole, was taking too much of your time. I wrote emails asking you to write, but you never answered. What else

was I to think? But now that I'm here you have not even mentioned Nicole and that makes me wonder why you're avoiding the subject."

"Nicole? That's why you came? My God, Lorena, that's just stupid." My voice rose and hardened to expose more annoyance than I intended, but I couldn't help wondering if she sensed that I had become involved with Nicole.

"Oh, I see. Now I'm a stupid burden. Ross, I think you've stepped in it big time now."

Fortunately we both stopped short of the shouting match that was about to happen. An ensuing tense silence lasted through the afternoon with both of us angry and confused. By dinner time we had calmed a bit, and we both agreed it would be hard for her to remain knowing my feelings. Even if she stayed, the air would be charged with electricity and the slightest spark could release a blast of lightning. I cannot not stop my work and she cannot, or will not, be a tourist without me. Needless to say the visit to Dieppe was cut short. Tomorrow Lorena leaves for Paris. I'll travel as far as Rouen and she is heading home. I've always loved Lorena's spontaneity and I thought it would work out for her to come. But this time her sudden appearance was too much for me. I'll feel a lot better just getting back to my work and trying to forget this episode, if that's even possible.

February 8, 1524

Now sailing northwest by west to reach thirty-four degrees longitude. Made twenty-eight leagues with little need for making tacks. The wind is still from the north and we chose a course as close to the wind as possible, which is between four and five points.

Translator's note. Sailing ships cannot, of course, sail directly into the wind. The square riggers of the day could sail no closer than 45° to 50° (four points) from the wind direction. This required sailing a distance with the wind 45° to the port, then turning (tacking) to sail with the wind 45° on the starboard, resulting in a zigzag pattern along the intended course. Part of the navigator's job was to determine the actual distance traveled (distance made good) along their intended course. This was done using a traverse board with a compass rose diagram printed on it. The traverse board had holes radiating in a line for each direction of the compass. With each turn of the sand glass (thirty minutes) a peg was placed in an appropriate hole on the traverse board to indicate course for that period. At the end of each four hour watch the course recorded on the traverse board was plotted on a chart.

We still see this mysterious weed that appears to be floating on the water, but I believe it is less dense, and we now find large areas where it is missing altogether. I think we are nearing the its edge. But Giovanni and Matthieu continue to order frequent soundings. So far, no bottom has been reached with our line.

During our evening meal, I asked Berthram Peeters a few more questions about the fate of Martin Luther. This subject is one he heard discussed frequently when he was in training for the priesthood. His bishop apparently ranted often about the depravity of this renegade priest.

He told me about the Diet of Worms, an assembly of clerics, which met in the city of Worms, Germany three years ago to make a decision about Luther. They gave Luther a chance to come to recant his writings, but he refused and was declared a heretic. From that time all men were prohibited from defending him and his life was in danger. An edict resulting from the Diet of Worms declared Luther an outlaw and ordered him to be arrested and punished. Furthermore it was to be considered a crime for anyone to give Luther any form of aid, including food and shelter, and he could even be killed on sight by anyone without legal consequences. Clearly this man was doomed.

During Luther's return from Worms to Wittenburg, he was kidnapped in a forest by masked horsemen and taken to Wartburg castle near Eisenach. As it happened the kidnapping was arranged by Frederick III of Saxony as a means of protecting and saving Luther's life. Luther could not have had a better protector. Frederick of Saxony is a powerful man and an Elector of the Empire. Luther continued to be safe as long as he remained in Frederick's castle. While there he continued to write against the pope and expand his translation of the Bible into German. After about one year Luther secretly returned to his home near Wittenburg and preached among his followers. He claimed that they needed him there to prevent their slipping back under the pope's rule. A year later Luther helped a group of nuns escape from a convent by hiding them in barrels. He also married one of those nuns.

This was all Berthram knew about Luther, except that he continues to live and irritate the Church with his preachings and writings. I am not sure how I feel about Luther and his daring deeds. He may have done irreparable harm to the Church if his beliefs continue to spread. It makes me very uneasy to see changes happening when it is impossible to guess what the outcome may be.

As I think about it I see other changes taking place that could alter our world as much as Luther's protests against the Church. The sudden surge of discovery since 1492 has opened up endless possibilities for new realms with new resources and expanded commerce. I see countries facing the great ocean are already reaching higher prominence than ever before. Soon the king of France and the king of England will be as powerful as Spain and Portugal. Increasingly they will assert their place in the expanded world and will win some of the spoils from the contest. I myself feel the excitement at being a part of this change during this voyage. I believe much of this change attends an increasing urge among men to realize their own desires. From whence this urge arises I do not know.

In my limited understanding, I see the writing of Pico della Mirandola as a good starting point for thinking about the importance of free will for mankind in his driven quest for knowledge. I think it possible that an extension of Pico's thoughts could lead to the kinds of changes that Martin Luther has begun, as well as the adventures of Columbus, Cabot, and our own voyage. It supports my feeling that we are living in a most exciting time of new events and ideas.

I am pleased that Berthram was chosen as surgeon for this voyage. He is very well informed on certain subjects.

February 9, 1524

Continuing on course northwest by west and made good a distance of thirty-two leagues. Weather is good, but clouds are increasing and wind is stiffening. Perhaps some change is awaiting us ahead. We have seen almost no floating weed in the past day. It appears that we have passed through this strange mass of vegetation.

Today for the first time I had a chance to speak with the chief rigger, Leclerc. We happened to be near Carlito's fire pad at the same time so I seized the opportunity to learn more about this man who some say may be the source of foment among the crew. His physical size and apparent strength could indeed make him a formidable foe and crewmen are probably careful not to cross him. I can see it would be easy for him to exert his will among the men.

"Greetings, Leclerc," I said, "how goes the voyage for you?"

"Well enough, Sir," he answered. Then silence. It is not unusual for seamen, even as experienced as Leclerc, to avoid speaking to officers.

"Tell me," I persisted, "do you believe the *Dauphine* was unduly weakened by our previous storm and will she continue to withstand future storms?"

This question opened his mouth and he informed me of the many storms our ship had weathered. "I have served as chief gunner on the *Dauphine* for many years under the good Captain Conflans, and we have been through many a storm together. Never once has this faithful ship given me cause to doubt her strength. If she is well commanded and properly ballasted she will carry us through any weather God provides."

"Then apparently she is well commanded and ballasted for this voyage, or we would have found the bottom of this ocean," I said.

Leclerc said no more, but turned to ladle some of Carlito's fish stew into his bowl, and found a place to sit in the sun.

February 10, 1524

Today at the noon change of watch I informed Giovanni that we had reached thirty-four degrees north longitude. He made an effort to verify this using his cross staff to measure the height of the sun above the horizon. Although such measurements at sea are not very dependable, Giovanni concluded that we had indeed reached our desired parallel and ordered a change of course to due west again. For the day and night we made good twenty-six leagues. Wind has become strong and causes breaking waves. Wind direction has veered again to the northwest, forcing us to tack back and forth to make progress on course.

Judging from the dark clouds with flashes of lightning on the horizon, I feel certain we face a bad time tonight and tomorrow. The crew began making early preparations for a storm by securing everything on deck. The increasing winds required a reduction of sail on both foremast and mainmast. The spritsail and mizzensail were likewise furled. Carlito doused his fire early and we now face a cold dinner of dried pork and hard bread with our cider or wine. After a cold breakfast and noon meal, we anticipated a good hot meal tonight but that is not to be. And this is a Sunday as well when the meal is often better. His decision to douse the fire was well founded…a light rain has already begun. Soon the deck will be awash with breaking waves again. I am writing my journal early today knowing the sea will soon be too rough for pen and ink.

February 11, 1524

A gale began in the night with the screech of demons and banshees while it also issued a horrifying whistle as it vibrated the taut halyards. All hands were summoned to again risk life to haul in the sail for high wind. In the darkness and the chilling wind they furled the foresail and reduced the mainsail by more than half…just enough. We must keep some sail power to maintain control. We had to give up all pretense of maintaining our west course as the wind had veered to northwest by west.

We changed to a south course in an attempt to keep the wind at our aft quarter, rather than abeam, lest we take water and be swamped. Now the ship was swaying broadly side to side. Each time the *Dauphine* dipped to the port until water was washing over the gunwales our lives hung in the balance. She would linger in that precarious situation for what seemed eternity, then slowly begin uprighting and swaying to the starboard but slightly less than the swing to port. This back and forth continued through the night and each of those swings felt like the end. Fierce waves broke over the deck making life perilous for seamen. Lines were strung between masts and along the gunwales for men to grip as they moved on the deck. We all realize at such moments that our lives depend solely on the seaworthiness of the *Dauphine*. The men on deck risk their lives just moving about not to mention climbing out on the yards to furl sails. Each swing held us in suspense wondering if she could right herself one more time. We know that the best of seamen using all the correct procedures can go down if the ship is incapable of withstanding a storm. Fortunately she maintained essential rudder control and rigidity. We felt very thankful, and a bit surprised, each time she managed to recover from a blast of wind and right herself.

The *Dauphine* wallowed in the sea like a dying whale. The wind blew unabated: it blew without mercy, without rest. Our world became nothing but immense foaming waves rushing at us under a sky low enough to touch. Hour after hour and day after day there was nothing around the ship but howling of the wind, raging of the sea, and a crashing wall of water pouring over the deck. There was no rest for the *Dauphine* and no rest for us. She tossed and pitched, she rolled side to side, she groaned from the relentless wrenching of her beams and planks. It was a constant, life-threatening effort for sailors and ship.

The gale tore at the rigging and sails throughout the night and into the morning without abatement. Later in the night our mainsail began flapping and fluttering uselessly in the wind. The wind broke a main sheet line and the sail lost its wind. I am certain this storm was worse than the one we experienced on the way to Madeira and our lives were sorely endangered. The men knew the peril was very great and in the night they again drew lots to determine which of them would go on a pilgrimage in an attempt to draw God's favor and salvation on our desperate situation. Not surprisingly our boatswain, Christophe, won the task again. Pure chance came his way during the first storm, but the most experienced seamen learn to manipulate the short stick. Christophe, being one of the youngest aboard and having already drawn the short stick in the first storm, was bound to get the honor of making the trip to Vézelay in thanksgiving to God for his grace and salvation if we survive our storms. Now Christophe can combine the two trips as one. The Lord is still honored, the pledges made in our moments of greatest fear will be kept, and there is no harm in having one man do penance for both storms. If we have more storms I am certain that Christophe will win again. He will merely have to remember to recite prayers of thanksgiving for each storm. Carlito tells us that the same happened on Columbus's first voyage but the Admiral himself won the short stick twice.

February 12, 1524

The gale has waned somewhat and the peril is lessened, thanks be to God, but we cannot yet return to our due west course. Giovanni predicts that by tomorrow morning we can resume our voyage on course. He has miraculously managed to maintain a sense of distance traveled during the storm and the helmsmen have done well at keeping close to our southerly course. By taking in as much sail as possible we were able to slow our speed despite the fierce winds. In brief Giovanni estimates that we have gone only fifteen leagues off course and, with due care, we can hold it to no more than another five leagues before the storm ends. This means that we will be only one degree off our thirty-fourth parallel when we turn back to the northwest. This amount can be recovered in a little more than one day of sailing, putting us back on our intended course again. God has truly been generous with His blessings. Most of the crew attributes our good fortune to the involuntary pledge made by our young boatswain,

Christophe. I am inclined to give ample credit to Giovanni and our able ship's master, Matthieu, as well.

As it turned out the storm abated enough by the time of vespers to begin our turn-around and return to our course. This is another stroke of good fortune as we will gain almost a day over our estimate for getting back on course.

An unfortunate event came to light this morning. Christophe reported that one of our able seamen went missing in the night during the storm. Strangely no one saw anything happen to the man, the Spaniard known as Miguel. Master Matthieu and I together are questioning each man on the crew and so far no one knows what happened. Also no one but Carlito knows anything about Miguel's life. Most of the crew just calls him "Spaniard."

Only a few days ago I had a chance to talk to Miguel for the first time. It was a baking day for Carlito and on such days he enlists Miguel as cook's helper. Carlito told me he hopes to teach Miguel enough that he will one day become a ship's cook. Carlito also told me that he had known Miguel for years and helped him find a place on this crew.

Then Miguel briefly told me his story. "I first met Carlito in the monastery," Miguel began, "and was brought to the kitchen to wash cooking pots and tend the fire. Carlito was much older and took care of me because because we were both outcasts and orphans before coming to the monastery."

Miguel continued, I heard that my father was an important man in northern Spain, but I never knew his name. My mother was a servant girl in the rich man's household. But when she became pregnant she was immediately turned out of the house and forced to fend for herself."

"After I was born, my mother, whose name I never learned, took me to the father's house and tried to get the servants to tell the father I was his son. Her efforts were rebuffed so she left me at the door of a convent, where I was taken in."

"I never knew what happened to my mother, but the nuns told me that she lived only a few months existing on scraps until she died of starvation, but I am not certain that is true. I stayed in the convent until I was about six years old, when the nuns took me to nearby Monfero Abbey. Those Spanish Cistercian monks accepted me just as they had Carlito years earlier."

"Eventually I left the monastery, but the monks made no effort to arrange an apprenticeship as they had for Carlito. I had no ship's master to take me in and train me. After some time I happened to be in the port town of Havre d'Grâce where I chanced to meet Carlito again. Carlito helped me find a place on a ship as a grommet, a ship's boy. I worked hard at learning all I could, knowing that in a few years I would be given a job as an able seaman with pay. I was extremely grateful to Carlito for helping me find me work and for the chance to learn a skill. That was the beginning of my seafaring days."

At the end of his story Miguel said he could not understand why some of the seamen said he shirked his duties. "I have worked hard and have not once claimed illness to avoid work. It never bothers me that some call me

'Spaniard.' I am sure I carry my share of the load during my watch."

All this story sheds no light whatever on the whereabouts of Miguel today. The only interesting bit of information is that several men thought Miguel was a shirker. Yet Miguel seems sincere when he denies malingering. Shirking duties is a serious charge and one that should have come to the boatswain's and the master's attention, however seamen often avoid bringing problems to the attention of officers and try to handle things themselves. This distressing trait, combined with the fact that Miguel was a Spaniard in a crew of Frenchmen, leads to some dark suspicions regarding Miguel's disappearance. The questioning of crewmen continues to no avail. I am puzzled that no one could explain Miguel's disappearance, even though all hands were on deck to tend the ship during the storm. Even Carlito, who would seem to be Miguel's friend, offers no information. Our investigation continues.

February 13, 1524

Today we sailed a course northwest by west and again reached our latitude of thirty-four degrees by noon. The wind has veered to the north again and with a minimum of tacking we made good twenty-five leagues. The sea has very large swells but sailing is not difficult. The sky remains cloudy with light rain falling, but clear blue sky far in the west bodes well for tonight and tomorrow. We are not entirely out of the weed, for large clumps of it continue to appear at times. Today is Friday and we are observing it as a fast day by eating dried fish and bread. Throughout the voyage Giovanni has kept a careful schedule of both fast days and feast days, with prayers of thanks for the protection given by our Lord.

Further questioning of the crew about Miguel's disappearance finally led to one man who saw Miguel swept overboard when a large wave hit us amidships. This was a time when we all feared being capsized and sunk; a time of greatest danger of being washed into the sea. This information will probably settle the matter as we have little else, nevertheless uncertainty remains. Why did only one man see this happen? Why did only the man accused of malingering fall into the sea? Matthieu and I both feel that Carlito knows more than he is telling, but we cannot induce him to talk about it. If we find that a crewman pushed Miguel overboard, the consequences would be dire indeed. We have instructed Christophe to be alert for additional information.

Today is Wednesday, the first day of Lent. During this time we will add Wednesday as a day of fasting. Fish and cheese will be acceptable, but we will avoid the dried pork and mutton. We will also add a short prayer service every morning. Now all the men know the Salve Regina very well and much of the 107th Psalm. Giovanni always adds an impromptu prayer for our safety and protection. Today he offered a special prayer of thanksgiving for our safe passage through the recent storm. He also reminded God, and all of us, that our boatswain, Christophe, will complete his pilgrimage to the shrine of Saint Madeleine at Vézelay when we return.

February 14, 1524

Skies are again sunny and the north northwest wind is most favorable. Frequent tacking is required to maintain our west course, and again all appears to be a normal routine aboard the *Dauphine*. Our sturdy *Dauphine* sails on in the serene weather. The sky is a miracle of purity, a miracle of azure as though it had never known a storm. The sea is polished, it is blue; it is clear; it is sparkling in the sunlight like a gem. An aura extends on all sides to the very horizon—as if the whole sea had become a single sapphire cut by a celestial gemcutter. And on the glistening, calm waters the *Dauphine* glides effortlessly.

February 15, 1524

Made good twenty-five leagues over the past day and night. Wind is north northwest. Good sailing.

Able seaman Louis came to Berthram with an injury. First he asked permission from Christophe to see Matthieu, who gave him permission to see the surgeon. Berthram examined the man in the officers' room where I was updating my charts. I was pleased for a chance to watch a trained surgeon work. The sailor had cut his arm while splicing ropes. The wound had swollen, was full of pus, and obviously inflamed. My understanding is that most festering wounds eventually lead to amputation. I was interested to see what this trained surgeon might try.

Berthram first admonished the poor seaman for not coming for treatment immediately, rather than waiting until the wound had festered. "Louis, you will be damned lucky if this arm is not amputated," Berthram told the sailor. He felt the sailor's skin and saw that he had a fever, which is what made him feel ill enough to finally see the surgeon. "This infection is a serious situation and could lead to the man's death," he told me. The surgeon talked as he worked, explaining his actions. He told me that his Italian mentor, Fracastoro, had taught him to cut away the blackened flesh around the wound using scalpel and scissors and to clean it with salted water. The unfortunate sailor writhed and groaned in agony with each of these operations. Next Berthram used a syringe filled with wine to flush the wound again as he had earlier with salt water. He could not say why the wine was important, but that it sometimes seemed to prevent festering.

"I am following Fracastoro's belief that infections and other ailments come from outside the body rather than from humors within," the surgeon explained. "Few other doctors accept this new idea but I saw near miracles of recovery resulting from my mentor's treatment of wounds." Berthram said he hopes to return to Italy to learn what new methods his medical mentor has devised.

Our surgeon next prepared a poultice made from a mixture of egg, rose-infused water, and pine oil; spread it on the wound and wrapped it with strips of cloth. The sailor suffered considerably during the cutting, the application of salted water, and once more with the wine on the fresh opening in the flesh. Berthram explained very calmly as poor Louis grimaced in pain, "This is all considered a radical approach to treatment, and many physicians are not ready to accept it. My mentor thinks that anything can carry the seeds of infection, even the very clothing we wear. He believes the salt water and wine may wash these infectious seeds away."

Next Berthram undertook to reduce the fever in the sailor. He began by giving the man a mixture of ground willow bark and water to drink. This was followed by drinking water infused with chamomile, which Berthram explained would reduce excessive yellow bile that was causing the man's fever. Then the surgeon applied leeches to the man's leg. Berthram explained that bleeding would further help bring the humors back into harmony to aid in healing. Puzzled at Berthram's treatment using both old and new methods of treatment, I asked for an explanation.

"Medicine today is changing with the help of men like Fracastoro, but we also continue to rely on certain healing practices of Hippocrates that have been rediscovered in our time," Berthram said. "I am straddling the transition from Hippocrates' belief in the four humors to new ideas based on observation. I find myself practicing parts of both philosophies just to be sure I have covered all possibilities." Berthram told Louis to go back to his duties and return tomorrow for another look at the wound. After Louis left, Berthram said, "If the fever has not gone by tomorrow, I will bleed him again. Leeches are effective for small quantities of blood, but more aggressive bleeding may be required,"

February 16, 1524

I estimate that we should see indications of land in the next fortnight. This is, of course, uncertain because we really have no idea how Cabot's Newfoundland connects to Ponce de León's Florida. Our latitude, thirty-four degrees, has never been visited by anyone with navigation instruments. There is simply no reliable map based on actual measurements of location, and I will be the first to make one!

February 17, 1524

The storm we experienced seven days ago set us back and now we will try to regain as much as feasible. Giovanni has directed the master to spread as much sail as possible in the hope of hastening our arrival to the New World. Today, as a result, we made good twenty-nine leagues. I pray we are not putting undue strain on our sturdy *Dauphine.* She constantly makes groaning noises, and the pumps must be manned…often three times in a day.

February 22, 1524

For the past four days I have been ill and felt near death, hence the gap in my daily journal. In the night of the 17th I became ill with a fever and repeated vomiting. I cannot image the reason for this agony but Berthram cared for me through out my ordeal. Most of the time I was so feverish I was not rational, so I am told. Berthram and Giovanni feared that I would not recover, but Berthram's care no doubt saved my life. Berthram is perplexed because his herbal remedies did nothing to control my fever, which rendered me unconscious much of the time and incoherent at other times. He credits frequent bleedings for breaking my fever. Fortunately I was unconscious most of the time and have no memory of any treatment. My only recollection is repeated terrifying dreams. I truly felt the devil had sent his demons to torment me. Apparently I shouted out in terror while in my severe state. Berthram said such hallucinations often come with high fevers, and discounts the idea that the devil was after me. Our ship's master, Matthieu, and several of the sailors became ill with the same ailment. Matthieu fared much better than I and returned to health after only a day.

Berthram is at a loss to explain this sudden illness. When his herbs failed, he had filled a basin with my blood three different times in an effort to bring my humors back into balance…something about my yellow bile that I have never even tried to understand. He attributes my recovery to the old Hippocratic method, and expressed his disappointment that his newer methods let him down. My own feeling, which I expressed to him, was that two other factors have helped in my recovery. One was, of course, my brother's prayers, both during vespers and in his own private prayers that he said every night at his bed. The other factor I believe may have been either good luck or perhaps my own robustness. Berthram conceded that some patients recover from serious illness without the help of a physician.

Berthram feels that his mentor, Fracastoro, is vindicated in one respect at least. When several of us took the illness at the same time, the cause had to be something from outside our bodies; from the air, water, clothing, food, or I know not what. Fracostoro would explain that a simultaneous illness such as Matthieu and I acquired can only be caused by external conditions, which he calls "seeds of infection." This is an interesting idea, but I doubt it will catch on among physicians for a long time. Even Berthram ultimately relied on the treatment of our humors because it seemed to be working. Other physicians will be less likely to try these new treatments.

I discovered that Berthram had spent much time beside my bed trying to reduce my fever. He told Carlito to prepare some meat broth in an effort to give me some nourishment. Most of the time I immediately vomited and lost the broth. I am touched that he gave me so much attention. Giovanni came in abruptly and said, "It is a damn good thing you are well again, we will soon see land and I want you ready to start mapping."

When Giovanni left, Berthram said, "Unfeeling though your brother may sound, he spent almost as much time caring for you as did I."

Chapter 11

February 23, 1524

Our fine sailing weather continues, praise be to God. The illness set me back considerably. My record keeping, map plotting, and journaling have a gap that can only be partially retrieved. The map is simple enough to bring current; I merely get the essential distances and bearings from Giovanni. My record of winds and other observations are secondary to the main log that Giovanni keeps, so a gap in my record is not a serious loss. However, my journal is more than a record of the voyage; it gives the views of some men on the crew, and their work. Perhaps over time the gap of a few days will make no difference, but I wonder what transpired while I was in my agony.

February 24, 1524

Our trustworthy *Dauphine* is performing beautifully. In the past day and night we made good thirty leagues under full sail. We continue backing and forthing to maintain our desired course. The ship is responding well to the extra stress of full sail in a fair wind. Leakage in the bilge has increased only slightly during the time of this extra strain. Boatswain Christophe must still muster a pumping crew at least twice daily, morning and evening. Caulkers are at work on each watch keeping their eyes open for seepage in the hull and fixing problems with oakum and pitch immediately. The ship is in fine shape. We are very fortunate to have such a seaworthy ship as the *Dauphine*.

February 25, 1524

Distance made good since yesterday is twenty-eight leagues on our thirty-four degree latitude course. Giovanni is constantly looking for signs of land…birds or bits of floating vegetation. He is beginning to anticipate our contact with the unknown shore, Giovanni's horizon.

I talked at length with Giovanni today about our experiences on this voyage, and he expressed some remarkable ideas on the meaning of a ship to him. He told me, "I see our ship as a real place, like a small village in the midst of a wilderness. It is a very unusual place because it moves, and it is so isolated in this wilderness that no one can come to it. Only three or four men in the world know where it is located, and they are all on board. It is a moving place, fully self-sufficient with food, shelter, and fuel to maintain life for quite a long time. We are a complete community, living and working as a well-ordered community."

This was an unusual observation for Giovanni. "What an interesting thought," I replied, "you are right. A ship is a very special sort of place. Yes, we are an operating community, and we appear to be a single unit. But just as the ship is a completely isolated place, so each one of the men is also isolated. Each person is alone in this world even though we have a community, friends, and workers around us. We are always alone with our thoughts, even when engaged in dialogue. No one knows our thoughts completely, even when we attempt to express them."

Berthram, our surgeon, was listening to our conversation and added another aspect to our idea of the ship. He added, "The ship is a place, but it is also a space…a space that is bounded by its hull. Without the critical size and shape of this ship's empty space within the hull, it would be nothing more than a pile of timbers nailed together and would sink under the weight of its cargo and ballast. The size and shape of the *Dauphine* are decisive in determining how much cargo, provisions, and crew it can carry. This feature makes the ship a unique type of place that is far different from a city's place or a country's place. A city may build a wall, and it will soon begin to grow outside its wall. Likewise, a country may expand or contract its borders. But a ship has a fixed size and shape; to change it would destroy it. Its inner space is essential to its existence. The same may be said of any vessel, even a cooking pot."

Giovanni spoke up again, "If that is the case, then the importance of any container is the inner space it creates, whether it is a pot, a building, or a ship."

"That is exactly my thought," replied Berthram. "Think, for example, of a church. It may be a beautiful building, but its importance is the space within. The nave of the church derives from the Latin word for ship, navis, which brings us back to the thought that the ship was important for its space within. Furthermore, the main function of the church is the Mass, and one focus of the Mass is the chalice. What is the chalice, but a space…a vessel for holding wine. With this view of objects, we begin to notice spaces created by objects more than the objects themselves: cooking pots, sea chests, or chalices, all these objects are important for their inner spaces."

After this brief exchange, the topic of our conversation drifted to more immediate concerns of running the *Dauphine*.

February 26, 1524

Thirty leagues made good over the past day and night. A brisk wind continues from northwest by north, and is frightfully colder than I expected for this latitude. I remind myself that it is still February, and winter has not yet lost its sting. Crewmen have reported bits of vegetation floating in the water. Excitement grows as the men sense that land may be near.

The elation of the men at the thought of land brought on a bit of merry-making. I enjoy watching them sing their merry sea songs and stomp their feet in a sort of dance. A few of them could actually make a good show of dancing. Two crewmen brought out their tambours and pipes and played traditional songs of the seamen.

> For the months we've been a-sailing; Marguerite expects us home:
> Well, well, here we come. Hey, hey here we are.
> We won't go away: We will come back my dear;
> We will not leave again, 'Til the winds blow Nor West.

They switched to another favorite, but the music sounded just the same. I think the piper knew only one tune. The words fit anyway, and the men are busy with dancing and singing. Like the other song, the words are partly nonsense, but express the long time at sea and the expectation of returning home…until the next ship leaves.

> Ah la tra laloo chalez; Ah my boys faladoo.
> Into the Port of Dieppe we shall come again.
> Ah my boys faladoo.

This dancing and singing went on throughout the afternoon. Several men apparently know only one song apiece, so they take turns leading the singing. Giovanni enjoyed watching too, but he was careful to see they kept their cider drinking to a minimum. After all, it is still Lent and he wants no drunkenness that would offend God. But occasionally the men need a little pleasure and release from their hard work. Giovanni joined the joyful spirit by ordering the steward to bring a cup of wine to each of us on the quarterdeck. I saw Giovanni laughing and enjoying himself more than he has for many weeks. He must sense that he is about to visit his seductress, Orizontas. He called a halt to the dancing at the two-hour watch. It was time for vespers and the evening meal of fish with Carlito's bread, and of course, more cider for the men.

The sailors' dancing and songs of returning home to Dieppe roused a latent loneliness that sleeps while men are intent on their work. But these days of easy sailing have brought a longing for home in many of us. Even Giovanni, who rarely shows his softer side, made a simple passing remark that he would like to see his Marie. He awakened to how much he enjoyed her company. Bertram felt it as well. He said the sailor's songs reminded him that Alaina loved to dance to such lively tunes, and that this voyage suddenly seemed very long.

At such times I must admit to myself that life at sea is not quite natural for me. I would not evade this unique opportunity for my map of the New World, but I miss the quiet excitement of a scholar finding a new book on an unexplored shelf of a library. Nostalgia for a long conversation with Felice on religion and philosophy fills my heart. These are feelings of land creatures imprisoned on a ship and exiled to a vast isolated ocean. Fortunately we are not truly prisoners and the yearnings will again be subdued. The watch changes, we take our posts and the voyage continues.

February 27, 1524

Wind is still northwest by north, and weather continues fair. The men have reported more tree branches floating in the water. We know that land lies not far ahead.

February 28, 1524

During the night the wind veered to southwest by west. This requires some tacking to maintain our course, but we continue to make good time. The good thing is that the change of wind has brought warmer temperatures and clearing. That northerly wind chilled my bones; the overcast sky covered me with gloom .

February 29, 1524

Wind has veered one point farther to southwest, and we can again make headway with a minimum of tacking.

Today is the Leap Day that traditionally a woman may propose marriage to a man, and if he refuses he must pay the penalty of a special gift of gloves. Who knows where such a silly idea started? It might be helpful for a woman interested in a very shy young man.

March 1, 1524

A warm wind continues blowing from the southwest, and we make excellent time under full sail.

The young sailor, Louis, who came to Berthram with a badly infected cut in his arm, returned for the third time today. His fever is long gone and the arm is no longer festered and is healing well. I am truly amazed. I have seen many lesser injuries result in amputation as soon as signs of infection began. This man's infection was well advanced and Berthram managed to save the arm. This sailor is indeed lucky. Berthram's study with Fracastoro has served him well. Because Berthram also bled the sailor several times, I suppose one could claim that Fracastoro's teaching had nothing to do with the healing. I am perfectly willing to give credit to Berthram no matter which method cured the man. Berthram was, in fact, the healer.

March 2, 1524

Wind is steady and skies are fair. The warm air continues to cheer us and gives a good mood to all. I think the fair weather greatly reduces grumbling among the crew. Giovanni seemed quite cheerful today. He senses that landfall is not far distant, and he can then begin his quest in earnest. The recent sighting of tree branches excited him greatly.

March 3, 1524

Warm wind continues steady from the southwest.

Giovanni has taken the precaution of ordering the foresail furled and reducing the mainsail by half during the night. In daylight we return to full sail and full speed again. Giovanni wisely guards against plowing the *Dauphine* headlong into land in the middle of night when visibility is low. He has ordered more frequent depth soundings with the lead and line. His greatest concern is to avoid grounding us on an unknown, and possibly hostile, shore.

March 4, 1524

We made good twenty-three leagues in the past day and night. This is remarkable time, I think, considering our reduced sail at night.

We are fortunate that the wind is holding steady from the southwest. We are sailing as close to the wind as is possible for the *Dauphine* and maintain our due west course at thirty-four degrees of latitude with a minimum of backing and forthing.

Two seamen came to Berthram recently complaining of extreme fatigue and sore muscles. Today the two reported that old scars had begun to fester like a fresh wound. They continued working with great difficulty, but soon found that their teeth were coming loose. This development frightened them, as all seamen recognize these early signs of the seaman's dreaded disease, scurvy.

Berthram had feared this disease would eventually show its face on our voyage, and confessed that his medical knowledge meets its limit when scurvy haunts a ship. Therefore he resorts to herbs and bleeding as they are the only devices available to him. About six or seven weeks from land is often the time for it to first appear, but strangely, some voyages never have a problem with this terrifying sickness. The victims can only lie helpless on the deck and wait for certain death as black splotches appear over their bodies. How long before other seamen contract this fatal curse? Are these two guilty of some horrible sin? If so, then perhaps the curse will be confined to them and not bring down our entire crew.

Berthram feels certain the scurvy came to these two men because of the foul air in the bilge where they had worked manning the pumps for an extended time. Other sailors think eating spoiled food may cause scurvy to appear, but none of our food is yet spoiled. They also tell of Portuguese sailors who sailed to China learning that sailors there ate some special food to prevent the disease. Poor Giovanni now has an additional fear for the ruin of his expedition, which would occur if there were too few able-bodied men to sail the ship.

March 5, 1524

We continue with reduced sail at night. It is odd to feel the ship in slow motion after so many days of traveling full sail day and night.

Yesterday we suspected it, but today it is obvious. We are in a current drifting northward. Furthermore it is a very warm current flowing directly from tropical waters. We have to compensate for its effect by additional tacking to the southwest, or be swept along with this strong northward flow. In this current we see many fish, which Giovanni ordered the crew to begin catching. Throughout the course of the day the men caught more than 100 fish which, cleaned and sliced, will provide delicious meals for the next day or two.

Also this warm current carries many signs of land...mostly tree branches, with a few entire trees. The eager anticipation of land has led Giovanni to offer a reward of ten *livres au tournaise* to the first man who makes positive sighting of land.

When I returned to our quarters, I found Berthram with his mid-day meal, and we reopened the subject of spaces. He seemed to have further ideas on the subject, but our earlier conversation was cut short by other urgencies. I took a glass of wine and sat down with him.

"Berthram," I said, "you spoke about spaces of ships and churches, with a brief mention of our own personal inner space where our personal thoughts and feelings reside. I would like to know if you think it possible that God is also in the inner space of each person."

"But of course," he replied, pushing his plate away, "that idea goes back to the ancient Greeks, such as Pythagoras, and certain sects of the earliest Christians. The fact that the pagan Greeks had believed such an idea was enough reason for the early fathers of the Church to reject it. That much I learned in the time I was preparing for the priesthood. Those early philosophers called it the 'seed of God.' Remember Jesus's statement in the gospel of Luke, 'the kingdom of God is within you,' is really an expression of that old idea."

I could see how that applied to my own thinking, and said, "Then that helps me better understand Giovanni Pico's *Oration on the Dignity of Man*. He said that man could raise himself through his own intellect to levels of the highest angels closest to God, the Seraphim. I now see that the intellect Pico refers to may be the same as the God seed."

"I have not read Pico," Berthram replied, "but I know men like Luther and Zwingli are preaching that each of us has a connection to God without depending on the intervention of the church. This is the crux of the church's effort to suppress those men and others. However, the reason it cannot suppress them successfully is that very many people like and accept the idea of having a direct pathway to God. It is an idea whose time has come." He reached for the wine and poured some into our glasses.

"I am devoted to the church," I said, "and sincerely hope she can learn to accommodate the changes taking place in her midst. Changes that I personally think have great value, even though I love the church."

"This is another example of the many kinds of changes taking place in our time," I continued, "Think of it, Berthram. We are seeing immense changes in philosophy, religion, exploration, science, and our knowledge of the world…all in our lifetime."

March 6, 1524

We are still slowed somewhat by having to compensate for the warm, north-flowing current. The warm water, the sudden abundance of fresh fish, and the sightings of tree branches have all the crewmen keeping an eye toward the horizon in the hope of winning Giovanni's prize. A new sense of anticipation has enveloped these seasoned sailors. Giovanni, more than anyone, wants to see that first glimmer of something different on the horizon. He has come to feel it is his own private horizon.

The recent abundance of fish oddly brought a remedy for the scurvy. Carlito, with his head full of sea lore, recalled a remedy learned in his youth. A few days ago he told sailors gutting the fish to bring him all the roe they found inside. Carlito stirred the roe into a paste and fed it to the stricken sailors three times a day. Today we can already see improvement in the two sailors; their gums are returning to normal color and teeth are becoming firmer. Giovanni declared this a miracle and said special prayers of thanksgiving for the recovery of our men. Carlito has proved again to be a great asset to this voyage.

Translator's Note: Fish roe has 4.6 mg of vitamin C per ounce. The sailors would have to eat about fourteen ounces per day to reach the minimum requirement of sixty-five mg needed to keep scurvy at bay.

March 7, 1524

During the first of watch of the morning, perhaps about two hours past midnight, a sailor high on the main mast supposed that he saw a fire glimmering in the far distance. It disappeared after a few minutes, and was not seen again. The commotion he made caused everyone to strain to see the fire, but no more light was seen. We all began to think the poor man's eyes had played a trick on him, and he suffered a lot of mocking and teasing about needing a new pair of eyes. Nothing more was seen through the night.

Soon after Carlito set out biscuit and fish for the midday meal the lookout sent up the shout for all to hear, "Land Ahead!" Land could not yet be seen from deck level, but after another two sandglasses were turned, everyone could see the thin, dark line of land on the horizon. The mainmast lookout who first saw the land was Denis, a young seaman from Dieppe. How apt that on this fourth Friday of Lent, a namesake of one of France's most revered saints should win the prize for sighting land! Our Saint Denis's grave is one of many pilgrimage sites for Christians. I suspect this young sailor will want to make his own pilgrimage to Saint Denis to give thanks for this sudden windfall of Giovanni's prize money.

The rest of the day was consumed by watching the ever-growing line in the distance. Giovanni ordered additional soundings and quickly discovered that we could now touch bottom at twenty-eight fathoms with our lead line, with each new cast of the line showing a shallower depth. Our crossing to this new shore, never before seen by Europeans, has taken fifty days and 1,200 leagues of sailing from Madeira. There were many long routine days with a few days of terrifying peril.

When the sun sank low in the west, we anchored well offshore in twelve fathoms of water. Lookouts reported signs of shoals ahead, and Giovanni would go no closer to shore. Nor did he send men in the ship's boat to examine more closely for possible land sites. He had no desire to encounter unknown men just as the sun was setting. At vespers we gave special thanks to God and to Our Lady, Star of the Sea, our patron saint of sailors, for bringing us safely to this shore.

Chapter 12

March 8, 1524 Offshore new land

We anchored about one-quarter league offshore through the past night and part of today with no intention of landing. Giovanni wanted to take advantage of the smaller swells and the cessation of forward movement of the ship to take some reliable celestial readings during both night and day. He determined that we are located at latitude 33° 45' north. He is elated to arrive so close to his intended latitude, after the problems we had with the north-flowing current for the past three days. Giovanni anticipated he might have made insufficient compensation for the current and arrived too far north, or made an over-compensation and arrived too far south. His expert navigation brought us within five leagues of our target.

March 9, 1524 Offshore new land

This morning he turned our course to west by south, one point off west, and began to sail along the coast, following its large arc in a southerly direction. We sailed slowly along the coast for twelve leagues and anchored again for the night. During the night we saw large fires on shore, indicating that the area was inhabited, but we saw no humans.

As the night breeze drifted from the shore, it brought wonderful aromas of the trees growing there. The shore is a sandy beach with large hills of sand. Beyond the beach we can see a low profile forming the horizon with no prominent hills or other features, and the land is densely forested with tall trees. This appears to be a most appealing land that would surely be suitable for settlement with agriculture. We agreed that the pleasantly sweet smell is that of laurel. There are beautiful fields and forests with varied colors and as much beauty and delectable appearance as it is possible to express. These are like the Hyrcanian forests, or the wild solitudes of Sythia, and northern European countries, full of rugged trees. The forests appear to consist of laurels along with other trees unknown to Europe. For a long distance the forest exhales the sweetest odors drifting to the ship on the land breezes. Giovanni named the area, Forest of Laurels. Unfortunately there is no deep bay or cove that invites us to make a landing and examine the land.

Translator's note: Hyrcania and Sythia are ancient names for areas in central Asia, including today's Afghanistan, parts of Iran, and the area surrounding the Caspian Sea. The Dauphine was sailing near present day Myrtle Beach on the north coast of South Carolina. The aroma of leaves and flowers of the myrtle provided the pleasant scents on the breezes blowing out to sea from the land.

March 10, 1524 Offshore new land

Giovanni ordered us to sail cautiously on a southwest by south course, staying well away from possible offshore shoals. We managed to maintain that course despite the countervailing push of the warm current. We made ten leagues.

Bertham reported to Giovanni that the scurvy had been stopped, and the two men are back on full duties. Carlito vows the healing was the result of feeding men fish roe, and Berthram is inclined to agree, but cannot explain why that should be so. Giovanni chooses to believe the miracle explanation based on his special appeals to Our Lady, Star of the Sea. Whatever the answer may be, everyone feels a great relief to have avoided this potential disaster.

March 11, 1524 Offshore new land

As we sailed southwest by west, making good eight leagues against the strong current, we saw the shore broken by inlets and rivers flowing into the ocean. Giovanni is eager to find an inlet suitable for anchoring so he may go ashore and make accurate celestial readings. The trees beyond the beach are cedars and some palm trees. We see shining lakes and pools of living water among the trees. This would be a good place to replenish our water and wood supplies if we can find a quiet anchor site. The smoke and aroma of burning cedar logs reach the ship. Numerous birds are along the shore and fly out to sea as far as our ship. Occasionally we have seen humans emerge from the brush and trees. Upon seeing us, they immediately retreated into the trees.

March 12, 1524 Offshore new land

We sailed another eight leagues, moving slowly down the coast against the current. Giovanni spoke with me about his feelings as we move past this strange unknown coast. He said, "Gerolamo, this coast as it slips by the ship is an enigma. It beckons us to come, yet warns us to stay away, it is both benign and savage, it is always mute, but is telling me, 'come and see.' Little did I imagine that my muse, Orizontas, would remain so mysterious and unattainable even after I came to her side. I have won the prize, but I cannot yet have it."

"Dear brother," I responded, "sometimes I think you are the enigma. In you I see many of the same traits that you ascribe to this beautiful land we are discovering. You are both inviting and repelling to associates. They fear you as much as they love you. There is often a wall around you that warns others to stay away. Your quest for the shores of the new world is so far a great success, yet you express dissatisfaction. Perhaps you will never be satisfied that you have conquered your Orizontas, because this fascinating land will always keep most of her secrets from you."

My bluntness left Giovanni silent for a few moments. He wiped his hand across his face, as he does when thinking, then said, "I suppose what you say is true, and I will take it to heart. Perhaps the lesson is that we can never completely finish any effort. Just when we think we have achieved the goal of a lifetime, the very next day we see our task is incomplete. Reaching this shore is a great accomplishment, but I already have thoughts about what comes next. The best part of this voyage of discovery has only begun, and I have already begun to move on to the next idea, which is simply a continuation and extension of this venture. Surely we will see enough on this voyage to entice our good king that this jewel could be his for the taking. If we find a passage through this land, it could mean another voyage that explores the way to the Orient! If not, this land will still offer many opportunities for exploitation, for which we will be needed as developers and administrators." With this he went back up to the quarterdeck to resume his estimations of our speed and distance traveled. Giovanni is justly proud that his navigational skills have brought us directly to our intended destination on this voyage.

Today I talked with seaman Denis and asked him what he would do with his sudden bonus of ten *livres*. He quickly responded that this money is equal to many weeks of pay for him, and he intended to save it for a pilgrimage. He wants to go with Christophe to Vézelay Abbey, where he hopes to stay for some time as a postulant, and eventually become a monk. I was surprised to hear this plan, as young men who go to sea at his young age seldom leave to seek another profession. Usually they become attached to the seafaring life or simply never have the means nor the ambition to change.

"Monks live an austere life," Denis said, "but in many ways a sailor is similarly austere. I think the transition to the cloister will not be difficult for me."

This was the first I had ever heard a sailor compared to a monk. A sailor faces many challenges at sea. It is a hard life with many deprivations. In port, however, he often lives a shamelessly immoral life.

Denis continued, "I simply cannot live in the company of these men, but once begun I could see no way out until now. I have long dreamt of finding my profession at Vézelay more than any other place. Now it is possible."

March 13, 1524 Offshore new land

Made good another seven leagues in the past night and day.

Giovanni has named this area the Field of Cedars, again for the new aromas coming to us from the shore. I have applied that name to the rudimentary map I am making of this coast. When we return to Dieppe, I hope to have all the information ready for a completed map.

March 14, 1524 Offshore new land

Another nine leagues on a southwest course. Giovanni has decided not to proceed farther in this southerly direction. He knows that Lucas Vázquez de Ayllon, probably came at least this far north as he explored the Florida coast. This assures us that no possible passage to the Orient lies south of this point. We have no knowledge of any Spanish presence in this area, but we have no desire to run into them in our small unarmed ship. Traveling alone as we are, thanks to Captain Conflans, our first business is survival.

Giovanni spent considerable time in the night obtaining an accurate reading of our position. He determined that we have reached 32° 30' north latitude and have traveled fifty leagues southward from the place where we first sighted land. Tomorrow we will begin our northward survey of the coast of this continent, if it truly is a continent. Giovanni named this turning-around place Dieppe in honor of our home port, and it is also to be the starting point for our survey of this mysterious coast.

March 15, 1524 Offshore new land

We are moving northward with the warm current and making good progress on a northwesterly course. The wind is steady from the west-southwest, requiring little tacking to maintain course. Nevertheless, we have reduced sail to avoid moving too quickly along the unfamiliar coast, and we continue to anchor each night. In the past night and day we made good twelve leagues, reversing the route we sailed a few days ago.

March 16, 1524

Made good another twelve leagues on a northwesterly course with a wind that has veered to west.

We see fires on shore at night, and see people on the beach occasionally. We wave and make friendly gestures toward them, but they always run into the forest when they notice that we have seen them. Giovanni is eager to find a suitable landing site so we can make direct contact with these indigenes.

True to his nature, Carlito has renewed his stories of strange men and cannibals dancing around the fires we see burning on the shore. He enjoys feeding the natural fears that lie within us when faced with the unknown. His stories have enough ring of truth to make even the skeptics listen. But we all hope that Carlito is wrong.

One story he told, just for our amusement, was about the lives of sailors. A townsman complained to a ship's captain that certain of his sailors had robbed him of all that he had. The old captain answered the distraught man, "Tell me, my friend, wore you that fancy doublet when they robbed you?"

The townsman answered, "Yes, indeed, this doublet is all they left me."

"Then bother me no more," the captain stormed, "for I know well, had they been my sailors they would have left you without a rag to your back."

Carlito was obviously elated by the raucous laughter of his audience.

March 17, 1524

Made good twelve leagues. Wind continues from the west. Our course has altered to east by north, as the coastline curves from northwest to east.

March 18, 1524

Made good fifteen leagues on an east by north course. We ended the day very near the location where we first sighted land after our long crossing. Giovanni identified a small inlet with calm waters and ordered us to anchor. We need a replenishment of water and wood. If game is available, we will hunt for fresh meat tomorrow. Also we must get a celestial reading on solid ground to verify our latitude.

March 19, 1524 Ashore at last

Early this morning, immediately after morning prayers, nine of us went ashore; Giovanni, myself, Berthram Peeters, and six oarsmen. We took tools for cutting wood and kegs for water, along with a musket. How good it felt to have my feet on steady ground! Unfortunately no game was found.

As we came ashore some indigenes fled quickly into the nearby forest despite our friendly gestures. We stood still and beckoned for them to return. They began to return slowly and Berthram stood ahead of us, becoming our representative, trying to communicate our friendly intentions. He gave the first man some swatches of bright cloth and a small knife. This gesture broke their reticence and they all returned; about fifteen men and boys.

The men were completely naked except for an animal pelt around the loins and a narrow belt made of grass about the waist. From this belt they attached items of adornment, such as animal tails or bird feathers, that hung to their knees. They are a well-proportioned race of medium height, a little taller than we, black hair tied back like a tail behind the neck. Their skin is dark, almost like Ethiopians, with no beards. They have large black eyes with an attentive and intelligent appearance. To us they resemble the Orientals, and we feel certain this is an indication that we are not far from China.

As they came near us, they marveled at our clothes, our lighter skin, and our beards. They were fully as curious about us as we about them. They welcomed us by offering some of their food, which appeared to be some kind of root vegetable and a legume like our beans. It was ground into a paste with water and mixed with an oil or animal fat. Not very palatable to us, but no doubt nourishing.

We indicated to these men that we wanted water for our kegs. They obliged by leading us to a nearby stream that ran with the clearest and most delicious water imaginable. We readily filled our vessels and chopped wood from fallen trees that was already well dried. This land is most delightful and captivating! I can easily conceive the eagerness with which our king will want to develop this beautiful place for his realm. The only weakness we notice is the lack of precious metals among these people. The king will be hoping to hear of gold and silver, and possibly gemstones. I feel certain that exploration of the hills to the west will surely yield evidence of treasure fit for a king, but for now, it is missing.

We are fortunate that Berthram made the effort to learn about communicating with people who speak an unknown language. He corresponded with Italian, Spanish, and Portuguese mariners who had traveled the coasts of Africa, and received a few general suggestions. The main thing he learned was that many hand gestures and facial expressions are widely used in common among many peoples. Gestures, however, must be used with the awareness that they may mean something different outside your own world. For example, they told Berthram that all people smile at times, but some groups reserve smiles only for friends and relatives. Strangers may be suspect if they smile too much. Beckoning for a person to come closer should be done with an open palm, not just a finger, which may be offensive or insulting. Likewise, many indigenes find direct eye contact offensive or a sign of aggressive intentions. Whatever Berthram uses seems to work well. These people respond to everything with enthusiasm. They readily understood our need for water and wood. Their offer of food was clearly a gesture of acceptance and trust. I am greatly impressed by how easily Berthram communicated after a few minutes of wariness by the indigenes.

Translator's note: This first landing occurred near Cape Fear, North Carolina. A map of Verrazzano's voyage up the east coast is on the last page.

March 20, 1524

We continued sailing slowly northeasterly, following the coast from half a league or more offshore. The coastal area shows signs of shoals and places where water is too shallow for the safety of our ship, and the coast appears to make a large northeast trending arc. We have seen no other locations that would be suitable for anchorage. Berthram would prefer to sail closer to the shore so he could see more details of natural features on the land, but Giovanni's well-reasoned caution prevails.

Giovanni again expressed his growing concern that this voyage will not be successful. He spoke to Berthram and me, "Since our landing and our contact with the indigenes, I feel there will be no satisfaction from this venture. We saw no sign of gold adornment among the inhabitants. Although they perhaps resemble Orientals, they are essentially different from the men described by voyagers to China. I confess that I have never seen a man from China, so my fears are based on hearsay. But I see no indication that these people have ever had contact with the Orient, and that makes me anxious about finding a passage through this continent."

Berthram tried to soothe Giovanni's anxieties, "My dear Captain, you face the enigma of seeking something without knowing its characteristics nor even a certainty of its existence. You have found the object of your quest, but you are troubled because what you found is incomprehensible. It simply does not resemble what you expected and hoped for. Jesus spoke of this dilemma when he said, 'Seek and you shall find,' but he does not make it clear exactly how we will know when we have found it."

After a short pause, Berthram continued, "You have reached your destination, but feel disoriented or confused about what you see here. It simply fails to meet your expectations, and therefore you fear there is little value to it. Yet you have actually found what you sought."

"Not so," Giovanni replied, "I sought much more than I have found so far, but I should fight my discouragement. Our survey of this coast is far from ended, and there are many leagues yet to sail. The passage may yet appear; the wealth of the land will yet reveal itself."

"The risk," said Berthram, "is that we will not recognize the true value of what we find."

Giovanni answered, "God hears my prayers, and I know that He is there. That is sufficient knowledge for me. I know He will guide me to my goal. "

Berthram knew the conversation was over at that point, and added, "Captain Verrazzano, you are a devoted follower of the Church's teaching and it does you honor. Be proud of your faith."

I know Giovanni thinks that Berthram is somewhat unorthodox in his religion, and perhaps I am beginning to understand why Berthram decided not to continue with his preparations for the priesthood. His tutelage under Erasmus and his studies of Luther's writings have taken root in his mind. He has such an inquiring and probing intellect, I can well imagine that even medicine will not fully occupy him in the future.

March 21, 1524

Made good another fifteen leagues today. Cool wind is blowing from northwest by west. Frequent soundings prompt Giovanni to maintain our course well off-shore. We continue to anchor each night to make certain that we miss nothing important along the coast, or by chance sail onto some unseen shoals in the darkness. The strong pull of the northward current strains at our anchor, but so far it has held firm.

I think it curious that the crewmen are silent about Miguel's disappearance. Christophe has heard no discussion of it—only silence. If no one knows his fate, there should be speculation about it. If, however, they know the fate of the unfortunate Miguel, they would still discuss how it might have happened. But there is only silence. Such absence of talk among sailors is rare and bespeaks a forced silence, I think. If I ask myself who among our crew could enforce such a silence, my only answer is Leclerc. But we must know more before we can accuse and apprehend him. Someone on the crew will eventually break silence, and then we will act.

March 22, 1524

Northwest by west continues to give us fair sailing. However, we all long for the balmy temperatures that prevailed for our first few days.

Today we sailed past a cape similar to the one where we first saw land.

Translator's note: Their location was Cape Lookout, North Carolina.

March 23, 1524

Made good fifteen leagues today with steady offshore winds from northwest by west.

I am beginning to become accustomed to our regular overnight stopping. The ship feels very different when it is not moving. Rocking gently back and forth lacks the sense of motion. But the ship at anchor also loses the creaks and groans of timbers under constant strain of wind pushing against the sail, pulling on the mast, and transferring the strain of every wooden beam all the way down to the mast bed in the keel. This strain takes its toll on a ship causing cracks and leaks to form in the caulk. We are quite dependent on those pumps in the bilge.

March 24, 1524

Grim news today. Christophe, our boatswain, overheard a sailor speaking of Miguel, the young Spanish sailor that was washed overboard. Christophe told us he heard a rumor that the French sailor, Leclerc, grabbed Miguel during the storm and gave him a shove just as a great wave was breaking over the deck. He also verified that Leclerc is also the sailor that has most agitated the crew against "that Italian fisherman" for dismissing Conflans. The fact that Giovanni and I are both completely French men who happen to have strong Italian connections makes no difference. In fact, that probably makes it worse. This break in silence is enough to bring Leclerc to justice.

Poor Miguel's only flaw was that he was Spanish. Logically this bias should include me, as well as the surgeon, Peeters, who is from Flanders. But of course, logic never is a part of such thinking. Somehow, illogically,

Spanish-born Carlito is not an object of this intolerance. What makes him exempt? Is he Leclerc's ally in some way? Giovanni is determined to solve this problem before it gets out of control. So far the crew has shown no manifestation of their biases other than grumbling after Giovanni dismissed Captain Conflans. There is always a risk that a strong leader like Leclerc could stir this unrest among the crew into a dangerous brew.

Chapter 13

October 20, 2010 Rouen

I finally had an exchange of emails with Lorena, hoping to clear the air. Not much progress. I wrote that I would like to accept that we both said some foolish things when our pleasant holiday suddenly turned sour. Her response was terse. "It seems to me the foolish statements all came from you. It's clear," she wrote, "that you are not interested in being burdened by me and the feeling remains mutual."

Email is such a shitty way to break up a relationship. We'll have a major repair job on our hands when I get home. Judging by today's exchange, the relationship may be shipwrecked.

Well, I suppose I could have chosen my words more carefully. Sometimes I just cannot say the appropriate thing and something blurts out that takes on a life of its own. If I had been thinking I might have sensed that it was not the right time to "speak frankly." Calling Lorena stupid was pretty stupid, I'll admit. Nevertheless what I said was how I felt, and she should not have expected me to drop everything when she suddenly had a whim to travel. Mostly I really can't believe she let her imagination…or was it insight…of Nicole work her into such a jealous fit. She's never been that way before. My recent emails to her have not been answered.

Nicole and I still take coffee breaks together. We enjoy talking over lunch, but there have been no more nights of passion. For now it just feels good to have a female friend for conversation with no underlying issues. We took a long walk together during an extended lunch today. Very pleasant.

March 25, 1524 Offshore new land

We continue to sail well offshore in this area of such variable soundings and shoals. Giovanni declared that he named the land in this area Annunciata in recognition of today's celebration of the Annunciation.

Translator's note: Verrazzano's Annuciata included parts of South Carolina and North Carolina.

Giovanni is elated beyond belief today. He burst into the chart room on the quarterdeck with a song on his lips. "I have found the passage, I have found the passage, I have found the passage." He repeated this refrain as he paced back and forth. His hand was shaking as he poured glasses of wine for himself, Berthram, and me and made a toast to our good fortune. "Drink with me to the glory of God for guiding us to this great discovery." He then offered a second toast to his muse Orizontas for her persistent pull to this important spot. Giovanni calmed himself enough to explain, "The lookout had just seen the object of our search, and even now the passage to the Oriental Sea was visible from the quarterdeck and you must step out to see the sight for yourselves."

Berthram and I became excited too when we saw what is certainly a large arm of the sea that will no doubt take us to the Orient. It is separated from us by a narrow isthmus less than half a league wide. From our vantage point we see no passage through the isthmus, but it is clear that the sea, which we have already declared a part of the Oriental Sea, goes beyond the horizon. This is a wonderful discovery even though the newly discovered sea has no connection to our ocean. Giovanni's earlier gloom about making no valuable discoveries on this voyage is now completely gone. I have not seen Giovanni so excited since that first day in Le Marin when he danced around the tables. He named the strip of land Isthmus of Verrazzano.

This is truly an important discovery. We now have evidence of a passage through this great continent. The king will surely consent to another voyage to explore this passage and sail through it to the Orient. Giovanni and I are assured of another voyage such as this one, and all the recognition that goes with a major discovery.

Berthram and I urged Giovanni to anchor in these waters for a few days and send the boat with a few men to cross the isthmus that lies between us and the distant sea. The men with the boat could also continue for a distance on the passage waterway to test the waters for depth, salinity, and tides. These bits of information could help verify that the newly discovered sea is truly the long sought passage.

For reasons I cannot understand, Giovanni decided to push ahead without investigating his new discovery. He said, "Too much time would be wasted, and I am eager to return to France to begin arrangements for another voyage. To be frank, my main concern is anchoring out in the open water. The coast before us lacks the protection of a natural harbor for anchorage. Anchoring in the open water for an extended time carries risks if a storm should arise. I simply refuse to take that risk when we are so isolated from all help. Furthermore, the northward current would cause a steady pull on the anchor and perhaps pull it loose."

Whatever the true reason, Giovanni felt no need to discuss the decision further. When the captain decides, it is inappropriate for anyone on the crew to voice unsolicited opinions. All our questions will be answered upon a return voyage if the king agrees to give his sanction again. Giovanni feels certain the king cannot resist the lure of a passage to be explored. I, for one, cannot see how Giovanni himself can resist the lure to have a closer look.

Translator's note: The Dauphine *was at that time sailing past Cape Hatteras, sometimes called the "graveyard of ships" because so many ships have wrecked in the area over many years. The main problem is the shoals and currents that can complicate navigation. Verrazzano was wise to keep his ship well offshore away from hazards. However, he did make a major error by keeping a wide margin between himself and the shore. Verrazzano mistook Pamlico Sound for an arm of the Pacific Ocean. He also misjudged the long narrow offshore bar that forms Cape Hatteras and the Outer Banks to be an isthmus. River waters entering Pamlico Sound must eventually break through the bar to the ocean, creating gaps in the bar. There are such gaps today and certainly would have been in 1524.*

In his defense we should note that Pamlico Sound is eight to twenty miles wide, and from his distant position offshore, he would have seen nothing but water beyond the bar. Depending on the height of the crow's nest above the water, the horizon would not have been more than six or seven miles away. The low-lying terrain west of Pamlico Sound could not have been visible from his position.

Samuel E. Morison, a well-known hands-on historian, flew offshore of Cape Hatteras and verified that he could not see the far shore of the sound from the low flying plane. I think Verrazzano, having only one ship, was justified in his insistence on staying away from the shore, but he missed some major features of the land in doing so.

March 26, 1524 Offshore new land

Made good sixteen leagues today and we are maintaining a north-northeasterly course following the trend of the coastline. The weather is changing, with light rain settling in for hours at a time. The shore seems more distant with this change, due to the reduced visibility. I estimate that we can see less than a half-league in this mist. The shore is not always visible, but I feel certain we will not miss any major features of the land. We are cold to the bone in this damp sunless weather.

Today Berthram answered my unspoken question about giving up his pursuit of the priesthood. He seemed to sense that our previous conversations have always left that question hanging.

"Gerolamo," he began, "I appreciate that you have been most patient with me and have never pressed me for answers to an obvious, but very personal, question; that is, why in God's name did I stop my studies for the priesthood and turn to medicine?"

I replied, "Berthram, I respect your privacy and felt that as our friendship grew you would eventually want to tell me your reasons."

Berthram took a breath and held it in briefly as he pondered where to start, then began his story. "I was in

Rotterdam and very content with my path toward becoming a priest. I knew this to be an honored profession, and also one which my family expected me to follow. As you may know each family of the faithful is urged to direct at least one of their children into the priesthood, or to a nunnery in the case of female children."

"In Rotterdam I studied under the tutelage of Erasmus for a short time. He saw great promise for my future and urged me to expand my background and my understanding of the faith by a thorough study of the Christian philosophers. I asked him instead to send me on a lengthy retreat in a monastery. At first Erasmus adamantly refused to arrange a monastery visit for me. He holds strong views against withdrawal from the world as the monks have done. He resisted my request saying that Christianity was meant to work within the everyday world not the cloistered life of the monastery. Eventually, though, he relented and arranged for me to be received at the renowned Benedictine Fleury Abbey, the site in France where St. Benedict's bones are kept. If you have ever traveled to Saint Benoît-sur-Loire, you will remember this beautiful abbey."

I interjected that I had not been there but hoped to go sometime as a pilgrim.

Berthram continued, "The monks treated me as a postulant for their order rather than a visitor, although I planned to stay no longer than a year. There I received instruction on the Rule of St. Benedict and how its many aspects are involved in the day-to-day living of our faith. I practiced their rigid life with many periods of prayer through the day, interspersed with work and study. The work assigned to me was in the infirmary where I gave food and medicines to monks suffering from illness. The training in that infirmary, as you may guess, eventually led to my present interest in medicine."

As Berthram talked we shared a piece of Carlito's good ale bread with a cup of wine. I felt a great pleasure that Berthram was willing to tell me his private experience with his profession.

After a short pause to enjoy his wine, Berthram continued, "As I learned their rules and studied their manuscripts, I discovered there is a great difference in the monastic practice of the faith compared with the practice found in parishes. The monks are in touch with ancient manuscripts written by the earliest eastern mystics of the Christian faith. We in Europe think that only one valid version of Christianity exists. But we do not realize that after the resurrection, Christ's apostles dispersed in many directions. Some remained in Palestine, Egypt, and Syria. The main apostle we know about is Paul who came to the west, particularly to Rome. Hence his writings are a primary source of our understanding of Christianity."

"Those who stayed in Palestine or Egypt presented a concept of God that is far different from anything I had learned up to that time. They wrote that God could be found through individual effort. They said nothing about a priest being our intermediary with God. Nor did they devise a complicated seven-step hierarchy like Pico. They saw a unity of all creation in which we are one with all beings and with God. Jesus also taught these ideas, but later Europeans dropped the idea of man's singleness with God and focussed on the importance of order and structure with a hierarchical authority as a means of access to God. This understanding was codified during a council called by Roman Emperor Constantine in the city of Nicaea in 325, and became the law by which the western Christians operated. Much of the discussion at that council focussed on which writings should comprise the New Testament with the result that writings telling of God within each person were rejected as heretical. The monks in the abbey, however, sought the presence of God within and the unity of each person with God. How simple, I thought, but I found it is not easy at all."

"Gerolamo, you are sensing this approach with your interest in Giovanni Pico when he said that we can scale the hierarchy of angels to those Seraphim that reside closest to God. But Pico made the mistake of using the analogy of scaling a ladder with God at the top. He wrote that humans could reach God through their own intellect, through their own effort, and that man determines his own destiny through intellect. Pico saw the seeker moving through seven steps, beginning with moral philosophy and ultimately reaching mystical union with God. This approach was derived from Pico's attempt to devise a single unifying philosophy that would unite all philosophies from Plato and Pythagoras to the early mystics, Judaism, and Christianity. Pico's approach to mystical union with God is quite complicated and accessible only to those with the highest intellect.

At this point I said, "Pico's approach to God is somewhat beyond my grasp. Either I am too slow witted, or Pico is overly complicated."

Berthram continued his explanation with no notice of my comment, "The nub of his approach, however—that man can reach God by his own effort—is the aspect of his writings that brought him under investigation by the Church. Fortunately for Pico he somehow persuaded the bishops and cardinals to let him keep his writings intact."

Berthram stood and walked around the table as he gathered his thoughts. Then taking another sip of his wine, he continued, "Monks today still follow the practice of an indwelling God, a monastic practice brought to France around 415 A. D. by a Christian monk in Egypt, John Cassian. He was invited by Pope Innocent the First to establish an Egyptian style monastery in Marseilles, France. Cassian started a monastery and began creating manuscripts, recording much of what he learned in the East. Those writings so impressed St. Benedict that he included much of Cassian's wisdom in the well-known Rule of St. Benedict. Cassian's monastery, the Abbey of St. Victor, became the model for monasteries over much of Europe, and Benedict's Rule became the guide for living a balanced life between work and prayer."

"Berthram," I interrupted, "I still do not see how this knowledge of the early mystics influenced the decision to change your profession? It appears to me that what you learned might have reinforced your decision for the priesthood."

"Where do my beliefs fit into this story?" Berthram continued, "I became immersed in the life of the Benedictine monastery, along with the Eastern concept of the God-man relationship. I came to realize that my prayers no longer consisted of a list of tasks for God to do in my behalf. They became simply a wordless channel for communication. I came to see myself, not as the center of creation, but as an element that mingles freely with it.

Gerolamo, I soon realized that this is not something for a parish priest to be teaching his flock. Any bishop would brand me as a heretic and send me for retraining or worse. I could not give up what I had learned, and I also could not keep it hidden if I were a priest, so I gave up my profession."

I was in awe at the end of the surgeon's story. "Berthram," I said, "it is most kind of you to tell me your innermost feeling in this way. Be assured that I will not betray your trust, for it could obviously lead to some difficulty for you. In fact though, you have opened my mind to possibilities of which I never dreamed. Your story will certainly affect my thinking about my faith, but I cannot see changing my approach to faith without also having the immersion that surrounded you in the life of the abbey."

It was good that my brother remained on the quarterdeck during this most revealing conversation with Berthram. I think Giovanni would see only heresy in Berthram's thinking.

March 27, 1524 Ashore again

The rain has stopped but low visibility continues. We are progressing along the coast on a northeasterly course. Light wind is blowing from the northwest. Giovanni has decided to name this immense land after our King Francis, and declared that it shall be known as *Francesca*. I have now applied that name to my map, and perhaps someday soon this land will become a large colony for our king. To be sure the king will be pleased to hear this place bears his name.

After sailing only a short distance today we found a place to anchor offshore. It was not a protected inlet as we hoped, but a place with deep water close to shore and a manageable surf through which our ship's boat could safely pass. Giovanni sent twenty-five crewmen ashore in the ship's boat while the rest of us watched from the *Dauphine* anchored beyond the surf. Giovanni sent trading goods and two of the men had muskets with them. The instruction was to refill our water kegs and give some items to the inhabitants.

The men were instructed to keep muskets out of view so as not to alarm the indigenes. It is doubtful that the local inhabitants would recognize a musket as a weapon unless they had been visited by Europeans earlier. Giovanni knew that Portuguese fishermen had been in the Newfoundland waters discovered by the English, and there is a possibility that the Portuguese explorer, Corte Real, might have sailed this far south. With these unknown contacts by Europeans it is wise not to appear hostile.

As it happened the surf was indeed too dangerous for the boat to navigate safely. By this time the indigenes on shore had seen them and began beckoning for the men to come ashore. They appeared excited and very happy to welcome the visitors from the sea. Some of the men were unsure if the natives were beckoning in friendship or if they were setting a trap.

Boatswain Christophe chose Louis to swim ashore through the surf, carrying some bells and mirrors with him. The unfortunate lad swam well but had great difficulty with the surf, which first retarded his progress, then pulled him under, and lastly threw him onto the beach exhausted and half dead. The native people immediately ran up to him and carried him by his arms and legs some distance from the shore. Poor Louis, with Carlito's stories of cannibalism fresh in his mind, felt certain he was about to be killed and eaten and he began to scream in terror. The people spoke to him and seemed to be trying to calm him but the lad remained very agitated.

The people laid him on the ground in the sun and stripped off his wet clothes. This action terrified Louis anew but it appeared the natives simply wanted to dry his clothes. While the lad was stripped the people marveled greatly at the whiteness of his skin, although he was quite brown from the sun on his arms and face. Even more alarming for Louis, the people built a huge fire nearby and placed the sailor and his clothing near the heat to warm him. The look of terror on his face was really quite understandable, for none of us had the least idea what would happen to him.

The men waiting in the boat were equally filled with terror, and wondered if they should go ashore to rescue the unfortunate Louis. But rescue would have been impossible as the twenty-four men left in the boat were far outnumbered. Fortunately no one made the mistake of firing a musket into the midst of the native people. Giovanni's admonition to avoid shooting was well-heeded.

As time passed it became clear that the native people had no ill intent. Their cheerful and friendly manner soon convinced Louis, and all of us, that he was quite safe and well-tended. Louis's courage was now beginning to return.

He spent a short time regaining his strength, donned his clothing, and indicated to the people that he wanted to return to the boat. The group responded with the greatest kindness. They embraced him and held him close in something of an emotional farewell. They walked with him to the edge of the sea and stood watching him until the lad was safely in the boat.

Once back on board ship Louis retold his tale many times to a willing audience that included us all. He managed to enhance each repetition of his story with new embellishments of his courage and bravery. He accurately told us what he observed about the people: they are of dark color with smooth, almost glossy, skin. They are of medium height, slender build, and possess quick wit, suggesting a high intelligence. All in all we learned nothing different from our first encounter with indigenes. There was no sign of precious metals nor any kind of wealth that would excite the interest of the king.

March 28, 1524 Offshore new land

Most nights while at anchor we see firelights, sometimes quite distant from the shore. Certainly all this land is inhabited, and probably by the same kind of people we encountered when first we landed.

Today is the Friday before Easter, and Giovanni has ordered an additional prayer service with readings pertaining to the Stations of the Cross. This day commemorates the crucifixion of Christ and, at sea as on land, we make faithful observance.

The misty rain stopped in the night and during my watch on deck the gibbous moon shone a delicate light on the crest of each wave. The nighttime land breeze carried aromas of pines and earth moist from the recent rain. We also sense another sweet fragrance emitted like an aromatic oil from plants. It truly was enchanting to feel the immense presence of this mysterious land in the stillness of the night. Giovanni is right. The land is beckoning. "Come and see," it says.

The beauty of this night made me pause to think of the immensity of the sky that one sees from a ship...the morning dawn, the setting sun...each gives a new view of the heavens. I wrote a few lines to remind me of those sights.

Ocean mornings break with
dawning from dark to gold.

Evening mirrors ocean morning
with a rich glow on cloud pillars.

Night at sea brings a penetrating
view into the starry cosmos.

If this improved weather continues, we will begin searching for a safe haven to anchor and go ashore again. Giovanni is eager to assess the potential of this land for precious metals or any other resources. Berthram is hoping to spend enough time with the people to learn something of their way of living and their language. He also wants time with them to learn what they think of us. During our previous landing our greatest difficulty was communicating. It was easy enough to indicate our need for water and wood. The indigenes warmed to us quickly when we gave them pieces of cloth, fishing hooks, or items that they could use as ornaments, particularly little bells. These gestures of friendliness removed any fear they may have of us. I can scarcely imagine how fearful they were on first seeing us. We must appear other-worldly to them, arriving suddenly in a huge ship with our pale skin, beards, heavy clothing, and strange speech.

March 29, 1524 Offshore new land

Made good fourteen leagues on a northeasterly course that follows the coastline. We continue to notice the pull of the north-flowing current, but we observe that the effect of the current diminishes as we sail closer to the shore. Today is fair although we can see ominous cloud banks on the northwestern horizon. Perhaps more rain is coming to make us cold and wet again. When the rains come sailors who are not on watch have difficulty finding a dry place to sleep. They have no sleeping quarters and must find an out of the way place for a little rest before their next watch. Most of them crowd into the sheltered area under the forecastle.

March 30, 1524 Offshore new land

Rain has returned as before, and there is no relief in sight as I peer toward the western horizon.

This is Easter Sunday, and we are holding two extra prayer services today to be certain that all watches have an opportunity to participate in celebration of the Resurrection.

Giovanni said, "Each man on this ship will join in our services of praise and thanksgiving. I only regret that we have no priest on board to provide the Eucharist to us all. Nevertheless we will do our best to revere the occasion."

Everyone is truly thankful to our merciful God for the protection and safety He has provided for us. Our prayers pled that His goodness continues to be with us for the remainder of the voyage. The misty rain cast a somber tone over the day but all hands responded dutifully to the captain's order.

March 31, 1524   Offshore new land

Made good twelve leagues. Weather continues foul with very poor visibility. I asked the question, "Giovanni, do you think it is possible that we are missing a passage during this terrible weather when we can barely see beyond a stone's throw?"

"There is nothing to be concerned about," Giovanni answered. "I am taking the precaution of slowing our progress to be certain we do not overlook important features. The weather will soon clear again, and we can inquire of the indigenes if a big waterway exists in the nearby area. I am sure they will know if such a thing exists."

"But Giovanni, we can only communicate enough to express our basic needs. I doubt if we could make the indigenes understand the idea of a big waterway."

"This is why I brought the surgeon," Giovanni said. "His job is to solve this riddle of communication. I feel confident that he will rise to the occasion because he is an intelligent and thoughtful man well-versed in languages. We have already seen a waterway that promises to be the passage we seek. There is little problem if we fail to find another."

I thought it interesting that this was Giovanni's first mention of the arm of the Oriental Sea that we saw just beyond an isthmus a short time ago. He was so elated at that time and began making plans for another presentation to the king. Strange, I think, that he has never mentioned it again.

Translator's note: By then the Dauphine had already passed Chesapeake Bay, which Verrazzano missed entirely. If he had seen that large opening in the shoreline, he certainly would have investigated what appeared to be a possible passage; also he was searching for a suitable anchorage for landing, and Chesapeake Bay would have provided good anchorage. Low visibility and his distance offshore were no doubt the reasons for missing such an obvious feature.

April 1, 1524 Offshore new land

Made thirteen leagues on northerly course following coastline. Weather is clearing, and wind has shifted to southwest by south. The temperature is pleasantly warm again and we are once more sailing with a following sea.

Chapter 14

April 2, 1524 Offshore new land

Weather remains fair with a southwesterly wind. Everyone is somewhat cheered by the return of warmer temperatures.

I asked Giovanni if his delight at finding the passage to the Oriental Sea had changed. He seemed surprised that I asked.

"Even though I have not said much since its discovery," he told me, "I assure you I am still in high spirits over this wonderful discovery."

I rolled out my parchment chart with plotted coastlines of our discoveries during this voyage. Giovanni looked with great admiration at the lines I had sketched it on my gradually emerging map of the New World. He especially liked the sight of the Oriental Sea on my chart.

He said, "You must know Gerolamo that I am considering renaming this branch of the Oriental Sea. I want to call it the Sea of Verrazzano."

I immediately agreed and penned that name below the words Oriental Sea. Perhaps that will be our final name for such an important feature. Giovanni will be long remembered for this discovery. He told me with careful detail about the plan he has prepared to present to the king, the bankers in Lyon, and to Viscount Ango. In this plan he proposes a city, the first one in France's new possession, to be on the shore near the isthmus. Its primary purpose will be a port city serving as an entrepôt for transferring goods from ships arriving from the Orient and loading them onto ships bound for France.

"Gerolamo," he said, "I want you to read my plan for exploiting our great discovery. I think you will be impressed, and I want to know what you think."

Translator's note: The non-existent Sea of Verrazzano, with variations in the name, was actually included on maps by various cartographers for the next 200 years, all based on two maps resulting from this voyage.

Giovanni has plans for establishing a shipyard for building ships on the west side of the isthmus using the abundant timber from forests in the area. He proposes that this entrepôt would also receive minerals, timber, and precious metals from the nearby region for shipment to France. A city established at this port would eventually become one of the important cities of the world! I must agree with Giovanni, it will take a grand plan to entice the king to sanction such a venture, and this truly is a grand plan in the making. I have no doubt the bankers of Lyon will see great amounts of money when they see the plan.

Giovanni deserves credit for being a man of vision. He visualized this opportunity for France to compete with Spain and Portugal in the new world. And he brought it to fruition with great effort and a helpful boost from Viscount Ango. Now Giovanni is working on another vision of even greater magnitude. This vision will establish a permanent link between France and the Orient, making China and India easily accessible. The keystone in his vision is the port city at the isthmus. Such a place would give France total control of transport goods through the passage. Uncooperative realms could be denied access altogether and port fees could be collected from all ships. The latter would produce a healthy income for the king and all the bankers. Perhaps Giovanni's muse, Orizontas, has bestowed her ample blessings upon him after all. He has found his horizon and will transform it into an empire for France.

Additionally, Giovanni has drawn up plans for a fortification to be manned by French soldiers. This addition is needed to ward off usurpers who are certain to come. Spain, for one, has the backing of the pope giving Spain the right to all lands west of an arbitrary line. This bit of foolery has not stopped England, nor has it stopped the king of France. Nevertheless, any establishment in the New World is sure to be challenged, hence the need for fortification.

Giovanni's plan includes yet another vision for the future of the port. The greatest venture, after the port is operating smoothly, would be a canal dug through the isthmus. This neck of land appears to be less than one-quarter of a league wide in places, and it barely rises above sea level. It would be one of the greatest feats of our time. Although it would still be a huge project requiring hundreds of workers, Giovanni cannot resist showing the king his vision of what could lie in the future for a king of great imagination and enterprise.

Immediately after reading Giovanni's plan, I hurried up to the quarterdeck. "Giovanni," I said, "this is truly a master plan. Your proposal is the most exciting idea I have ever seen. I can easily see you as the governor overseeing this grand enterprise and realizing wealth and fame beyond your dreams."

Giovanni grinned with obvious pleasure at my acceptance of his idea and put his hand on my shoulder. "Thank you, Gerolamo, I value your opinion," he replied, "but I see you as the minister who makes it all happen. A dream wants an executor. Plans are nothing without an able administrator to implement them. These are your skills, dear brother, and I want you with me throughout this endeavor."

"Naturally I am pleased at the prospect of managing such a venture, Giovanni, but I think you have been overly generous in your regard for my management skills."

"Nonsense." he said, "It is settled."

Giovanni often ends a conversation with such a statement, and I know the discussion is truly ended. Also I know that Giovanni will never fully relinquish control of anything that was his own idea. His treatment of Conflans is sufficient proof of that. Therefore I conclude that much of our conversation was intended to flatter me a bit and to reassure me that I will be included in some way.

April 3, 1524 Ashore again

Made good only five leagues today when Giovanni decided abruptly to go ashore. He wanted to make contact with the people again and learn more about the land. We anchored offshore and Giovanni, Berthram, and I went ashore with twenty men. The coast was beautiful, with great forests and wide, sandy beaches. We saw signs of inhabitants before we left the ship, but they apparently fled when they realized we were sending a landing party. We searched, but as soon as we discovered some of them, they fled again.

When we finally managed to gain their confidence and approach them in their village, we saw that these people have lighter skin than the previous group we met. Their clothing consists of grasses woven with threads of wild hemp. Their food includes some most delicious pulses, similar to our lentils and beans, but of a different color. They also hunt birds, small animals, and fish. They are skilled with bows, which are made of a very hard wood, and arrows made from reeds; we can see that they devise clever snares for capturing small game.

They are also skilled in making boats from a huge single tree. The marvel is that they fashion these boats without metal tools. We saw no use of any metal among this group. The method for making the boat is to use fire to hollow out a tree trunk, and they do the same to shape a prow at the front of the boat. The homes built by the people were farther inland and we could not visit them. I would guess their homes are also made of grass and wood, similar to those of the previous people we met.

This land is more beautiful and fertile than the previous landing point. The trees are rather sparse, and would be easy to clear for agriculture. I feel sure this would be a most productive place for grain, fruits, and beans. We saw many wild climbing vines. Many had sweet tasting fruit, which could doubtless produce good wine if properly cultivated.

Wild roses, violets, and lilies, along with many types of fragrant herbs which we could not identify, grew in abundance. Giovanni has named the area Arcadia for its comparison with the idyllic pastoral paradise described by the ancient Greeks.

Partly we wanted to meet the native people in order to bring one of them aboard the ship to take to France. We finally apprehended an old woman hidden in some tall grass along with a young girl of about eighteen or twenty years. The old one had two little girls on her shoulders and a boy clinging to her. These three small ones appeared to be about eight years of age. The younger woman had three small girls clinging to her. When we first met them they began to shout and create a big disturbance trying, I suppose, to frighten us away. They made signs toward the woods, indicating that the men had fled into the trees. As a gesture of friendship we offered them our food, which the old woman readily accepted and ate. The young woman, however, wanted nothing to do with us or our food, and she threw it angrily to the ground.

We grabbed the boy from the older woman and tried to capture the younger woman, who was very tall and attractive, but she was physically strong and determined not to be captured. She set up such a noise and fight that no one could contain her, so we had to leave her and take only the boy. Considering that we were far from the ship and had to pass through several sections of forest, it was impossible to bring her.

Translator's note: Explorers in the sixteenth century commonly kidnapped native people for two reasons. First, they wanted to display unusual things they found in the strange lands. This helped make investors and the public aware of the successful expedition. To this end they might return with plants, animal hides, rocks, and people. Second, part of the ritual of claiming a new land was to return with physical evidence of the place, even if only a bag of soil. Indigenous people were ideal for this purpose.

The name Arcadia appears on Gerolamo's map in approximately the area of the Delmarva Peninsula that includes parts of Virginia, Maryland, and Delaware. Their landing site was possibly to the north of Assateague Island. Today a span named the Verrazano Bridge connects Assateague Island to the mainland of Maryland.

April 7, 1524 Offshore new land

Made good nine leagues following the coast in a northeasterly direction. The weather continues fair and warm. After three days ashore during daytime and sleeping aboard at night, we are all well rested and glad to be back at sea. Our supply of food and fresh water is well replenished.

The young native lad we brought aboard is faring well and, after a short period of adjusting to our food, he is eating heartily. He seems to be very afraid of us now but as we have done nothing to harm him, he will soon accept our hospitality. When he sees how well people in France live compared to his own people, I am certain he will be content that we have changed his life so favorably. At present we are keeping him confined below deck so he will not be tempted to jump overboard and possibly drown. I presume the young woman we tried to bring aboard was his mother and for now he probably misses her. But with time he will recover from this separation. In France he will become the center of attention wherever he goes. The king may even grant him a living stipend.

In the meantime, Berthram is working with the lad, trying to teach him French and at the same time learn some of his native language. Although the lad is only eight or nine years of age, he has enough command of his language to be of great help if Berthram can learn some key words and signs to be used in future contacts with native people. Berthram has not yet elicited any verbal responses from him but is hopeful that the boy will soon begin to speak. So far the lad is silent and appears to be in a dark mood. I am confident Berthram will soon gain the boy's trust.

April 8, 1524 Offshore new land

Made good ten leagues sailing northeast along the coast. Wind is from northwest by west. The land visible from the ship has changed little since our landing in the place Giovanni called Arcadia. We see no inlets for possible harbors, hence we continue sailing well away from the shore, anchoring each night.

On this particular evening while anchored for the night, Carlito was finished with his cooking chores and began telling a story to two sailors standing nearby. When others, including me, heard a story beginning there was soon a gathering around the fire hearth. The story was a fascinating tale suggesting that this strange land we discovered was actually a reappearance of a continent that sank into the ocean in antiquity. Carlito said the lost continent was named Lemuria because of a strange animal that inhabited it. This animal supposedly had a ghostlike face and was believed to be the spirit of the dead. Along with this ghostly animal there were brown-skinned people living on this continent who were far different from those we had encountered so far. He made it clear that we may yet encounter these unusual inhabitants on shores yet to be seen.

Carlito went to some length to describe the distinctive nature of the people of Lemuria. They are known to be more than twice the height of us ordinary men. And if that were not startling enough, they also have an eye in the back of the head while the front eyes are moved to the side so that these people can see in all directions at once.

By this time every listener was expecting Carlito to tell how fearsome the inhabitants of this ghostly continent could be. But he ended his monologue with the reassurance that the Lemurians are of a happy disposition and free of all sickness, so they pose no threat to outsiders. I wondered if Carlito's story was intended to put some fear into the gullible sailors. But it has enough plausibility to be true.

I told Berthram about the Lemurians and he recognized the story as an ancient legend about a sunken island, or continent, in some unknown part of the world. He said the location of the lost island changes through time. One cannot help wondering if such a persistent story must have some truth. Also I wonder how Carlito happens to know so many exotic tales.

April 9, 1524 Offshore new land

We continue on our northeasterly course. A warmer wind has veered to west-southwest, two points south of west, making for more favorable sailing. Matthieu has ordered the foresail to be furled to hold our speed down a bit. Giovanni is concerned that we maintain a slow pace to allow for thorough observation and mapping of the coast.

April 10, 1524 Offshore new land

Made a distance of eight leagues today. Weather and wind direction holding steady.

April 11, 1524 Offshore new land

Made good ten leagues. Wind has veered back to northwesterly and dark clouds are moving in from the northwest. A change from the bright spring weather appears headed our way.

Berthram is in a bad mood today over his lack of progress with the native lad we captured. The boy is not eating well now and he still refuses to attempt any communication. He eats a few bites then throws the remainder to the deck. Afterward he sits and glowers at Berthram. Our surgeon is almost convinced that it was a big mistake to capture the boy. He may be of no help and in fact may become weakened and ill if he continues to fast.

Berthram said, "I know it is believed that the native people of the world lack the feeling and emotion that we more advanced people have, but the more I am with this lad, I feel that he is in a state of deep sorrow. He is less afraid now that he knows me a little, but he continues his dark and mournful mood."

"Take heart," I told him, "the boy will soon come around. Just remember that the best minds of our day tell us that the primitive people are much closer to the animals than are we. Therefore their behavior is more like that of the animals. So far as we know the animals have little emotion; therefore, we may assume the same is true of the primitive people."

I can see that Berthram is unconvinced, but the deed is done and perhaps a necessary part of our expedition. What better way to show the king and the people of France what sort of inhabitants live in the areas we discovered?

April 12, 1524 Offshore new land

Made good nine leagues following the coast. The weather has turned cool again with steady northwesterly winds and fine misty rain. Visibility has reduced to one quarter of a league. Much of the time we cannot see the shore but, as before, I think we can see enough that we are not missing any major land feature.

The ship's master, Matthieu Ango, reported the results of his investigation into the disappearance of the unfortunate sailor, Miguel. Carlito finally revealed to Matthieu that while he was standing alone under the forecastle during the second storm, other crewmen were preoccupied with furling the foresail, reducing the mainsail, and tying down anything on deck. It seems that although many were present on the deck during the storm, they were all too busy to notice Miguel was missing until later.

Carlito's story places a shroud of guilt on Leclerc, the sailor who was often heard criticizing any foreign-born sailor. We knew that Leclerc had started a rumor that something very bad would happen to the *Dauphine* because Captain Verrazzano had dismissed Captain Conflans. Giovanni was the villain, according to Leclerc, because he was not a true Frenchman. In Leclerc's eyes, this made Giovanni inferior to Captain Conflans. Carlito tells that Leclerc had gone far in stirring up discontent among other sailors.

Carlito told Matthieu that on the night of the storm, our decks were awash with waves breaking against the sides of the *Dauphine*. Sailors put their lives at risk merely by moving about on deck. As usual during a storm the sailors strung ropes between the masts and along the rails. When a wave washed over the deck everyone grabbed for a rope or any object that was tightly secured. This was common practice and experienced sailors staked their lives on those ropes.

Carlito claims he saw Miguel swept off his feet and completely engulfed by a wave. He slid across the deck with arms flailing to grab anything within reach. He came to the gunwale right at the feet of Leclerc, who was holding tightly to the rail. Leclerc reached as if to help Miguel to his feet and in one quick motion hoisted the poor lad over the side. Leclerc then looked about quickly to see if his deed had been noticed and went about his work as though nothing had happened.

As the storm began to abate Leclerc, in an act of deceptive chicanery, was the first to make notice of Miguel's absence. At first he showed great concern for the fate of Miguel. As time passed it was accepted that Miguel was lost at sea.

That might have been the end of the matter if not for Leclerc's earlier complaints about Miguel being a "lazy Spaniard." Both the boatswain and the master had suspected foul play and together began quietly asking questions among the crew. For several days Matthieu and Christophe held their findings to themselves until they felt certain that Carlito had not given false testimony. After all, Carlito had close ties to Miguel going back to their common history at the Spanish monastery. The master was concerned that perhaps Carlito was also an object of Leclerc's hatred of foreign-born shipmates. If so Carlito would also have reason to indict Leclerc from fear of him. After questioning other sailors Matthieu determined that Carlito had been exempt from Leclerc's venomous and seditious talk. No one knew why Carlito should have some exemption, but all agreed on its existence. The best guess was that Carlito curried favor with Leclerc by giving him some extra rations. All this suggests that Carlito, like the rest of the crew, feared Leclerc.

Carlito confirmed this notion. "When Leclerc finished his villainy, he looked about and noticed that I was the only witness to his evil work. Leclerc immediately came to me and warned that the same fate awaited me if I told anyone what I had seen. I knew he was a vicious man and issued no idle threats."

Giovanni has no choice but to punish Leclerc for several reasons, primarily inciting mutiny and committing murder. Giovanni ordered Leclerc brought to the quarterdeck and questioned him on all the points against him, but Leclerc gave no response to any questions. Leclerc's refusal to answer the captain's questions is itself deemed insubordination and worthy of the lash. But more importantly Leclerc must be punished for the murder of Miguel and kept in confinement until we return to Dieppe.

There he will be given over to the local magistrate for trial and probable execution.

Giovanni immediately ordered one hundred lashes as punishment. At the noon change of watch Giovanni ordered all hands present, and they gathered amidship as Leclerc was brought forward and tied to the mainmast. Only the helmsman and the lookout remained at their posts. The gray, bleak, overcast sky added to the somber feeling of the occasion. Christophe was ordered to administer the lashes across Leclerc's back. Christophe brought out the short-handled whip with its nine knotted leather strands. The very sight of this instrument sent a chill through my body, but I think no one else dreaded the thought of seeing this scoundrel suffer. In truth, I know people find pleasure in public punishments and executions. Nevertheless the punishment itself had an intensely sobering effect on all the crew. No one could deny the horror of seeing so many bright red welts and gashes on a man's back. Many must have realized how close they came to allying themselves with Leclerc and could well imagine themselves in his place.

Watching a man under the lash is not a pleasant sight for anyone, even if the man is a villain. It is shocking how long such a punishment seems to last. On and on it went with Christophe leaning into each swing of the lash. Even Christophe began to show signs of fatigue before the last lash finally fell. The poor boatswain had no appetite for his task, but the captain and the master both corrected him if he began to lighten the force of his blows. "Lay into it, Christophe. You are weakening," Matthieu shouted at one point.

Finally Leclerc was released from the mast and fell to the deck as his knees buckled. Two crewmen walked Leclerc to a place under the forecastle and gently laid him face down on a bundle of canvas with his red-striped back oozing fluids. Berthram took his box of herbs and potions, and went to tend Leclerc's wounds. He washed them with salty water, which normally would have been painful in open wounds, but Leclerc seemed to be in a state of numbness and apparently felt no pain at the moment. Berthram told me later that he had often seen the sensation of pain mysteriously disappear for a person in such a severe state of distress. Apparently Leclerc was blessed with this gift today. Later the pain will appear according to Berthram. Leclerc was taken below and put in chains.

April 13, 1524 Offshore new land

Made good ten leagues today. The rain has stopped and clouds are not so heavy, probably some clear weather ahead. Wind has veered to the west. Our course continues to follow the coastline in a northeasterly direction.

All is quiet following Leclerc's lashing yesterday. Giovanni and Matthieu are keeping a keen eye on the mood of the sailors. Usually everything returns to normal within a day or two after a severe punishment. We shall see how this one goes. If Leclerc is as popular with the crew as he thinks, they may harbor their solemn mood much longer, but Matthieu feels certain there will be no further mention of Leclerc.

Matthieu reported that Carlito told him, "I am thankful to be relieved from the fear of Leclerc. He maintained a power over this ship through his constant threats." Other crewmen standing nearby had voiced agreement. If that is so then he deserved to be in chains long ago.

The man is now below deck where few of the crew are allowed to go. The only persons with authorization to see Leclerc are our young steward, who takes him food and drink twice a day, and Berthram, who inspects the wounds daily.

April 14, 1524 Offshore new land

Made good eight leagues with a light and variable wind. The sky is clear again. No change in course nor sighting of possible inlets for anchorage.

This beautiful coastline is not offering us enough opportunity to stop and visit her. Surely there will be a sizable river flowing from the land someplace but we certainly have not yet seen any evidence.

April 15, 1524 Offshore new land

Made good nine leagues, wind varies from west to northwest. Weather is fair with clouds scattered about.

Berthram told me the native boy ate a small amount of food today but remains in a dark and somber mood. I am sure he will eventually warm to Berthram's gentle manner. As Berthram spends more time with the boy, he is developing great feeling for the shock the boy has experienced.

"I feel almost fatherly toward this unlucky lad," Berthram said. "I find myself imagining what I would feel if I were in his place or if he were my child. I never imagined feeling empathy for such a primitive person. I always accepted that primitive people have little or no emotion.

But now my mind is changing. I am beginning to see him as not only one of God's creatures, but a human created by God, the same as you or me. I have doubts that our capture is of any benefit to him."

I pondered Berthram's predicament a few moments and replied, "Berthram, your year with the monks must have made a radical change in your thinking about God's creation. We are told to go over the earth converting these unenlightened people to the salvation of Christ. Now you suggest that the Church may be wrong to push this command that came directly from Christ. Your faith appears to be weak when you express such heresy."

"On the contrary, Gerolamo, I think my faith is made stronger by my doubts. The Gospel of Mark tells us of the man who told Jesus, 'I believe, help my unbelief.' My mentors in the Fleury Abbey constantly struggle with their doubts. This is a great surprise to outsiders who think that monks have unshakable faith with no shadows of doubt. It is they who taught me to face my doubts directly and think about them. Acknowledging doubt and accepting it is essential to a stronger faith. That explains why the monks appear to have such unshakable faith. Each time they think through a new doubt they emerge with renewed faith. Yet new doubts never cease to creep into their minds. Monks are human in every way; they seem different because they have seen the enlightenment described by early Christian mystics. They have a different understanding of the teachings of Christ. We will talk some more on this if you are interested, but now I need to go tend to Leclerc's wounds."

"Berthram." I asked, "how is the prisoner faring?"

"Leclerc is at times angry and striking out when I come near. At such times I cannot safely tend his wounds, and the steward boy can only push food and drink within reach of the chained man. Most of the time, however, he seems adapted to his confinement. He never speaks more than a few words, but will allow me to see his wounds. Fortunately the pain of his lashes has subsided considerably."

Each time I talk with Berthram, I see a new depth to the man. I can only think he learned something from the monks that the rest of us are never taught. As I know him more I sense a peace and compassion within him that most men do not have. For example, although most ships I have sailed with have at some time meted out severe lashes to some miscreant sailor, in no case has anyone aboard tended to the resulting wounds with such a show of concern. Giovanni thinks that Berthram's compassion is a weak trait that should be overcome and sometimes chides Berthram about it. But Berthram never defends his feeling and I regard that as a sign of strength more than weakness. He obviously learned something different in that monastery and I intend to hear more about it.

April 16, 1524 Offshore new land

Made good ten leagues under ideal sailing conditions; fair sky, steady northwesterly wind.

The mood of the crew has lightened considerably since Leclerc's lashing. Matthieu feels certain that most of them suspect that Leclerc murdered an innocent man and deserved punishment. Some still have lingering doubts about Giovanni's action against Conflans, but without Leclerc around to agitate this doubt it may soon disappear.

Chapter 15

April 17, 1524 Failed landing

Made five leagues before we came upon an inlet which appears to be the mouth of a great river, the largest we have seen on this voyage. The embayment on the ocean came to a narrow neck situated between two small prominent hills, then opened beyond into a large bay of the most beautiful and inviting land we have seen. Giovanni immediately declared the name of this enchanting place, *Angoulême*, for the principality and family name of King Francis I.

We sailed only as close as the neck through which the river flowed deep and wide from the inner bay. A laden ship could easily pass through the opening into the inner bay, but as we knew nothing about the water depth or locations of rocks within the inner bay, we anchored at the narrows and took the ship's boat to shore. About twenty of us went in the boat, including Giovanni, Berthram, Matthieu, and a group of sailors. When Giovanni saw the beauty of this inner bay, he named it Sainte Marguerite, for the king's talented and well-loved sister, Marguerite d'Angoulême, the Pearl of Princesses.

Translator's note: The Dauphine *probably anchored near what is today the Brooklyn end of the immense double-deck suspension bridge that spans the Narrows between Staten Island and Brooklyn. It is appropriately named the Verrazano-Narrows Bridge. From there they took the ship's boat into the inner bay, now called Upper New York Bay.*

We found the place densely populated by people that seemed to be essentially the same sort we had seen before, being mostly naked with animal skins covering their loins and colorful bird feathers decorating their bodies. To our surprise they showed no fear of us. Rather they came directly toward us shouting with joy and wonder, and guided us to the best spot for beaching our boat.

The inner bay is quite large, about three leagues in circumference. Soon thirty of the native boats appeared on the bay coming toward us from various directions. Apparently our arrival has been noticed far and wide around this bay.

Just as we were intending to disembark from our boat, a sudden thunderstorm arose with a terrific wind. The wind was such that the *Dauphine*, now some distance from us, was in danger of dragging anchor and drifting toward shore. With the safety of the entire expedition in mind, Giovanni ordered an immediate return to the ship. Our oarsmen pulled heartily and we covered the quarter league back to the ship in a short time. Immediately we weighed anchor and moved the *Dauphine* out to sea with wind-filled sails. Blustery winds continued the rest of the day and we made little headway, but at least we were all safe aboard and out to sea.

It is truly a disappointment that we could not investigate this almost perfect spot as it has every indication of a land of great value and high fertility. Giovanni is certain the surrounding hills contain minerals of value and best of all is its outstanding potential for safe anchorage. Many ships could traffic in that beautiful bay. Although we were there but a few hours, we left the land and the bay with names that are certain to please the king. But now we have set our course eastward because the coastline makes a sharp eastward bend at this location. Our direction varies from east to one point north of east, that is, east by north.

Translator's note: Disappointment indeed! One has to wonder why Verrazzano did not secure the safety of the ship until the end of the storm, then return to this inviting site. The potential for settlement and exploration up the Hudson River would have provided a wealth of attractive information for the king. Eighty-five years later Henry Hudson, sailing for the Dutch, made a thorough investigation of the area and the river, leading to Dutch settlement soon afterward.

April 18, 1524 Offshore new land

Made good twenty leagues today on an east by northeast course. Giovanni hastened our pace during the day, partly because of the eastward turn in the coast. He feels the possibility of a useful passage extending toward the north is low. If any passage emerges with a northward trend, it probably would not lead toward the Orient. Therefore he has ordered full sail on foremast and mainmast during the day. We continue to anchor at night mainly for security reasons. The storminess continues but we have frequent breaks during which we can see the nature of the coastline. It is lined with mounds of sand blown from the beach by the wind. Scattered clusters of trees and lagoons can be seen beyond the sand banks. Giovanni named this area Flora in honor of the Roman goddess of spring.

Translator's note: The name Flora applied to the south coast of Long Island.

Giovanni questioned Berthram about the status and health of our two prisoners. He is very concerned that the boy stay in good condition. Giovanni said, "We have little to show for the voyage up to now. There are no signs of gold or other precious metals. We have found no valuable trees comparable to those found in Brazil and the islands of the Caribs. For what it may be worth, the boy is of value for his similarity to people from India or Cathay. That native boy with his eastern appearance and the discovery of the opening to a passage behind the narrow isthmus are the main arguments for our returning for another exploratory voyage."

Giovanni shows no interest in Leclerc other than returning him to France alive and healthy enough to be tried before the magistrate for the murder of Miguel. Leclerc's past agitation of the crew elicits little sympathy for his well-being from Giovanni, who would readily hang him today. He will not go that far lest he reignite sentiment against himself. Letting the law deal with Leclerc gives Giovanni the result he wants without blood on his own hands.

Berthram gave his analysis of the situation. "Leclerc's wounds are not festering and it appears they will be fully healed by the time we reach Dieppe. Other than his wounds Leclerc is in good health. I am afraid the boy is a different matter. He is eating small amounts and his health remains good, but he still shows a sullen and gloomy character. I would like to bring him on the main deck for short periods to let him see the sun. Perhaps that would brighten his feelings."

Giovanni refused, "I will not take the chance that the boy might try to escape leading to his death. He is too important for our needs."

As usual Giovanni made his feelings known with few words and ended the conversation, leaving no opportunity for further discussion.

April 19, 1524 Offshore new land

Made good twenty-three leagues. Our course follows the coastline in an east-northeast and east by north direction. The sudden storminess that erupted while we were in the large bay two days ago has diminished, but there continue to be heavy black clouds with short periods of gusty wind and rain. Steady wind continues from west-northwest and with this following wind we keep the mainsail furled, relying on the foresail completely. It is such a pleasure to see the sails filled with the wind of a following sea. I never tire of looking at their taut perfection as they become pregnant with the wind and deliver our *Dauphine* through the sea.

Giovanni is in a foul mood today. Despite his early finding of the link to the Oriental Sea, he has decided the voyage is not going well. This morning he told me, "Gerolamo, unless we can discover the promise of precious metals soon, I fear this will be our final voyage to this area. I sense that we have already covered most of the coastline of this great mass of land, and our latitude of forty-one degrees tells me that we have only five or six more degrees of northward travel before reaching the point where we must turn back toward France. From that point northward the English and Portuguese have sailed and found neither passage nor gold."

"Take heart, Giovanni," I replied, "your discovery of the Oriental Sea beyond the isthmus and your inspired plan for development will be enough to entice the king and all investors for another voyage to this land. I am sure of it."

Giovanni was unconvinced and could not be shaken from his gloom. He spent the rest of the day on his bed without speaking, nor did he eat more than a few bites. He has neglected his usual practice of measuring our speed and bearing, leaving that task in the hands of Matthieu and me. Normally Giovanni insists on verifying all our measurements. It has been several years since he experienced one of these dark periods. As always the darkness appears when he feels failure lurking on his shoulder. The perplexing thing is that Giovanni has never really failed at anything important, but he sometimes feels the opposite is true. He is for the most part a compatible and positive sort of man, but a dark negative spirit occasionally takes control of him. I fear this may be one of those times.

April 20, 1524 Offshore new land

Made good twenty-two leagues with a following sea. Giovanni ordered that the mainsail remain furled to better control our speed in this variable wind. Course remains at east by northeast staying with the trend of the coastline. Weather continues overcast with dark clouds. Rain occurs intermittently, sometimes heavy with strong wind.

Today as I walked the main deck to stretch my legs near the forecastle I heard Carlito spinning another story to a captive audience. As a cluster of sailors ate their cold meal Carlito filled them with yet another possible disaster story that surely awaits a ship in unknown lands.

As I approached I heard Carlito say, "Magnetic islands made entirely of lodestone can completely destroy any ship that sails too near, and these islands are known to exists at several places in the world."

One sailor expressed a hesitant skepticism, and asked, "How can a lodestone's power possibly destroy a ship?" Carlito obviously hoped someone would ask such a question and he quickly answered, "If the island has a powerful concentration of lodestone and if the ship has iron nails or any other iron, the ship will be drawn toward the island and eventually be grounded. In a few cases the lodestone is so pure that the nails are pulled out of hulls and decks and the ship disintegrates in a few minutes."

This shocking idea stilled the skeptic, but Carlito had more, "Make no mistake," he said, "this very ship has more than 500 weight of forged nails in its hull and decks. We would be gone in a minute." He closed with, "Beware when our compass goes crazy. That's the first sign." Most of Carlito's rapt audience nodded in understanding, although I doubt if they understood anything about it—nor do I.

Carlito is old and has traveled to every place in the world so sailors tend to believe his stories. Some even said they had heard of lodestone mountains from other old sailors. The disturbing thing in their minds is that they all know the compass is not constant and must be adjusted occasionally. This in itself is somewhat troubling to them. No one has an answer for this mystery which lends belief to Carlito's story. Frankly I feel somewhat anxious about such things myself. On the other hand, Carlito is a born exaggerator. No one aboard this ship knows the total weight of all its nails, least of all Carlito. I think he sometimes fabricates facts to enhance his fiction. But that still does not negate the possibility that he is right about the dangers of lodestone mountains.

We discovered a triangular-shaped island which we judged to be about fifteen leagues from the mainland. Giovanni, whose disposition has brightened somewhat, named the island for the king's well-known and accomplished mother, Louise. He declared the island reminded him of the island of Rhodes in Greece, both in its shape and its tree-covered hills. Judging from the fires visible along the shore, the island is well populated. We found no suitable harbor and sailed toward the mainland.

Translator's note: The name, Louise, was applied to Block Island off the coast of Rhode Island.

April 21, 1524 Landed at *Refugio*

After a short sail from the island and a night of anchorage we arrived under fair skies at a most wondrous place: a broad bay inviting us to come and anchor. The wide opening to the bay was about one-half league wide with deep water at its entrance. This haven became irresistible when we smelled the sweet scent of forests on the land breezes. Giovanni commented on the perfection of the bay, having ideal locations at its mouth for fortifications to protect the harbor. He was delighted when he saw it and immediately named it Refugio, for certainly it appeared to be a much needed refuge from the days of storminess we had just endured. He vowed to stay in this excellent place for a period of much needed rest and to resupply our wood and water. Although Giovanni is somewhat brightened today, surely an extended rest will remove the dark spirit that held him for the past few days.

As we entered the bay indigenes on shore began shouting in excitement, and loading into twenty canoes they paddled out to meet us. They stopped short when they came within about fifty paces of us. We copied their gestures of excitement and friendliness and tried to reassure them that we came in peace. Two of the natives appeared to be very important among the group, chiefs or kings I would say, judging by their dress and head feathers. One was perhaps forty years of age and the other only twenty-three or twenty-four. They wore stag skins hanging from their waists that had been skillfully worked with various embroideries. Chains decorated with many vary-colored stones hung around their necks. Both men carried themselves with dignity and confidence, neither of them showing the least sign of fear or anxiety. The two chiefs came forward and boarded the *Dauphine* with great dignity and commanding presence. Soon many of the other men came aboard as well. These impressive men conveyed a sense of purpose and confidence which we had not seen among our prior contacts with indigenes. Perhaps their stately bearing was a display to intimidate strangers and it surely would work with men lesser than ourselves. Nevertheless I immediately liked and felt drawn to them. I think this is going to be a most interesting place.

After coming ashore we learned more about them. The people in this almost perfect bay are the most handsome and civilized in their customs of any we have so far found. They are somewhat taller than most of us, with well-formed bodies and bronze-colored skin. They have sharply defined facial features, with long, smooth, black hair arranged in various ways with knots or braids. Their black eyes express alertness and intelligence, while their manner of moving and speaking shows a kindly and gentle demeanor. These are altogether an extremely handsome and engaging group of people.

The women are no less attractive in their beauty and charm. They move with grace and poise. They all wear some sort of adornment, such as rich fur strips from lynx or other animals attached to their arms. Women also wear their hair in braids which hang on either side of their breasts. Some women have their hair in arrangements like the women of Egypt or Syria. We surmised that this hair arrangement indicated the women were married. Both men and women are nude except for an embroidered deer skin covering their private parts. We are in agreement that the pendants and trinkets they wear as adornment are similar to those we would expect to see on Orientals. The metal we found in abundance was copper. We observed that they use copper exclusively for their trinkets and items of adornment. When we showed them examples of gold they showed no interest in them; their only interest was for items of copper. Neither did they show interest in our iron weapons and tools. They discarded those items in favor of their stone implements.

We gave them gifts of little bells, crystals, and other trinkets that they could wear on their ears and hang from their necks. When we gave them mirrors they laughed uproariously as they looked at themselves. We were surprised to see that these people had a great generosity. When we gave an object to one of them, he would enjoy it for a while, then give it to one of the others. We all found them attractive and most welcoming and pleasant.

Giovanni rightly decided that the crew needed an extended cessation of sailing duty. This wonderful bay is truly the only place we have found that fits our needs so well: deep water harbor, protected from the ocean, and a congenial people. The recent short stop at Angoulême would also have worked well, but we are all thankful to have arrived to this haven safely. Giovanni immediately ordered a special evening prayer service of thanksgiving for reaching this Refugio.

Translator's note: Again these explorers compare the people they encounter to Orientals although most Europeans at that time had never actually seen an Asian person. This can be explained partly by the fact that they fervently hoped they were close to Asia and interpreted their observations accordingly.

This location, which the crew of the Dauphine *welcomed so gratefully, is today known as Narragansett Bay, Rhode Island. Although historians are uncertain of the exact landing site, Gerolamo's journal suggests it was on the east shore, perhaps near the present site of Newport.*

Here there is now a third bridge commemorating this voyage, the attractively arched Jamestown-Verrazzano bridge connecting the west shore of Narragansett Bay with Conanicut Island.

April 23, 1524   Refugio

These charming natives at Refugio enjoy demonstrating their games, which, though different, bear some similarity to the types of games we play with a racquet and ball. They have a stick with a small basket on the end which they use to throw the ball at a target placed atop a pole. The racquets are also used to throw a ball to each other. Among their various games, foot racing appears to be one of their favorites. An aspect different for us is that both women and men play these games, sometimes separately and sometimes competing men against the women. They generously invited our sailors to join their men's games, and the sailors happily accepted although none were so skilled as the natives. Nevertheless the sailors had a wonderful time engaging in something other than ship duty.

After playing games the native people brought food to our sailors which they found quite tasty. There are apples, plums, various nuts, and some other foods that we could not identify. These native people eat a variety of foods such as various peas and beans. They also grow a grain which they call mahiz, that is like nothing we have seen in Europe. It grows on a tall stalk and the grain is not a head, as in our barley, but grows on a small cylinder that appears on the side of the stalk. It has a very good flavor and they grind the grain to make a tasty bread or porridge.

The native men will not let us near their women. Whenever the people boarded our ship, the men came but the women stayed in the canoes. We tried various ways to invite the women to come aboard, but neither trinkets, cloth, nor bells would persuade them to leave the canoes. I am sure the women were wise to avoid contact with us. Our sailors have been at sea for nearly four months now and most of them are used to reckless lives when ashore. If any Frenchman took one of the native women, it would cause a great rift between us and the people and their hospitality would end abruptly. When Giovanni saw the care with which the native men protected their women, he ordered that any sailor guilty of bad conduct with one of these women would be severely punished. After witnessing the punishment meted out to the unfortunate Leclerc, any crewman will think carefully before letting his sexual impulses take control.

April 25, 1524 Refugio

Berthram has discovered some interesting things during his effort to communicate with the people. By learning a few basic words of their language he discovered that they call themselves Wampanoag, and that their tribe extends for many leagues to the east. Immediately to the west is another group, called the Narragansett, with whom the Wampanoags are not on friendly terms. It seems the Wampanoag now occupy an island that they took by force and there is an uneasy peace that the Wampanoag chiefs fear will end when the Narragansetts try to reclaim their land. Berthram has the definite impression that the Wampanoags see us as very strong potential allies against the Narragansetts. He tried his best to assure them that we would be leaving soon and our return is uncertain. How strange to find ourselves in the midst of a tribal feud of which we have no understanding.

Of course we all understand the nature of conflict between neighboring countries only too well. King Francis I is constantly at odds with the kings of England, Spain, Portugal, the emperor of the Holy Roman Empire, and the pope. I suppose that is no different from the conflict between the Wampanoags and the Narragansetts except that we are more familiar with the combatants in Europe. Humans are a race inclined toward conflict despite the church's constant prayer for peace on earth and goodwill among men. In truth, past popes have instigated more than a few conflicts themselves.

April 30, 1524 Refugio

I have lapsed in my journal entries. The spirit of rest prevails during this period at Refugio. Everyone is active but the routine of sailing has stopped, giving a holiday atmosphere to all the crew. The men have daily work on the ship: repairing sail, manning pumps, and the constant caulking, scraping, and tarring the outside of the hull. There are many such tasks but the men also have much more idle time than usual. Any captain knows that too much idleness is not good for a crew, and can cause unrest. Therefore Giovanni has arranged exploration parties to survey all the surrounding lands within three leagues. These surveys have proved to be a great source of information about the land and all that grows and roams therein. Berthram has made it a point to accompany these surveys to compile a collection and description of plants and rocks around this area. Many excellent building stones are present here with which our French builders and masons could erect fine buildings. Also the forests offer trees for building, including large oaks and many others. We see many fruit-bearing trees with apples, plums, filberts, and many other nuts.

Another benefit from the survey parties is the occasional stag brought back to the ship. Fresh meat is most welcome after months of dried pork and fish. There is a great abundance of deer, lynx, and other wildlife unfamiliar to us. The indigenes who accompany these parties are greatly impressed by the effectiveness of our muskets for hunting. Strangely they show little interest in having one of our weapons. They obviously feel more comfortable with their bows and arrows.

The survey parties had good opportunities to visit the houses of the indigenes. These houses are circular in form and fifteen paces in diameter. The frames are the shape of hemispheres made by arching saplings in the form of an arbor. Mats of expertly woven grasses or straw cover the frame to protect the inhabitants from rain. When the people move to a new location, they take the mats with them and leave the wood frame behind. About thirty family-related people live in each one of these houses. Their diet consists mainly of grain, beans, and lentils, while the meat is mainly fish. The bean, lentils, and mahiz are grown in nearby fields with careful notice of the phases of the moon and the rising of Pleiades to determine the proper planting time. I was very curious to know how they came to follow the same customs concerning planting as do many Europeans, but none of them knew from whence this knowledge came…except that it is ancient.

These people appear to be in very good health with an adequate supply of food. We see a number of elderly people among their group, suggesting longevity, and we seldom see anyone with an illness. Their treatment for wounds involves cauterization with a firebrand during which time the patient does not cry out. They make great lamentations with mournful howls and lengthy songs when a relative dies. In our short time with these people we have come to admire them in many ways.

One day I accompanied one of these survey parties and we walked for a long distance along the beach before going inland. All along the beach I noticed the smooth sticks and twigs that had formerly been parts of trees, but now were worn, sand-polished, and washed up on the beach. The thought that these twigs had been brought to this beach from some far place, just as I have come here from a faraway land, inspired a few lines:

> Beaches' sticks lie buffed by sand and surf.
> Blanched by sun and salt.
> Ceaseless movement subdues cedar trees to twigs.
> Carried by wave and surf, relics from
> a distant place found this lonely beach.
> By chance concurrence of time and space,
> I arrived where they lay,
> and felt their essence merge with mine.

As our survey party began to move inland we came upon a brackish lagoon surrounded by dense forest where we saw many geese and other familiar birds. But one bird was unlike any I had ever seen. It was standing in water on long legs like a stork but was quite different in other ways. It was a beautiful blue-gray color with a black streak on its head and fringe-like feathers on its neck and its beak was smaller than a stork's. As we came near, this great bird spread its enormous wings and gave us a wonderful display of effortless flight. I shall never forget the sight of this unusual bird. Again I wrote a few lines which I dedicate to this lovely creature:

Stony slate statue in perfect stillness.
Poised on stilts with doubled neck
A spread of great wings lifts her
with slow strokes, silently gliding.

Translator's note: Gerolamo apparently saw a Great Blue Heron, which was unfamiliar to him because it is not present in Europe.

May 2, 1524 Refugio

Our captured native boy has shown no improvement in his attitude toward Berthram despite every effort to show him kindness. The boy is eating more but his silence persists. Berthram has tried speaking to the boy using words learned from the Wampanoag people but he shows no sign of recognition. I wonder if he truly does not understand the words or simply refuses to reply. I fear it is the latter and that we may have made an enemy of him. We continue to keep him below deck while we are so near shore. We do not want him to see the local people nor do we want them to see him. I fear they would become suspicious if they found we had captured him even though from a different people. Giovanni has ordered the boy to be kept from sight until we leave this place.

May 4, 1524 Refugio

Giovanni alerted the crew to begin preparations for embarkation in two days. They must complete our resupply of wood and water sufficient perhaps for the remainder of the voyage as we are uncertain how soon we will turn east for the crossing to our port in Dieppe. The men are continuing to join in with the activities of the native people and relations have remained good for the entire time. One frustration the men have voiced is the impossibility of going near the women, even the young unmarried ones. The native men are very careful in this detail and Giovanni's promise of severe punishment is also a great deterrent. I suppose if the men had greater access to alcoholic beverages they might not be so obedient. To that end Giovanni has kept the allocation of cider to normal amounts that are not sufficient for drunkenness. This precaution is not only for the benefit of good relations with the natives, but is the continued practice of leading a Christian and temperate life at sea for the sake of holding onto God's mercy in times of danger.

One of the chiefs wanted to bring his woman, with her many attendants, to see the ship. As they approached the ship they stopped at a distance and sent a courier ahead to announce their intention and we sent word back that we would be pleased to receive them. I am not certain if this procedure was an important formality for them or if they were merely using caution for their own safety. As they approached the ship our sailors began shouting with great enthusiasm at the sight of this group of women. The chief became so disturbed by this sudden display of interest in the women that he sent them back to the shore. Giovanni was astonished by the outburst of his men and quickly told them to be quiet, but it was to no avail. The chief was convinced the men were a danger to his women.

The chief then came aboard alone and remained with us for a long while, showing much interest in the ship's equipment; we gave demonstrations of unfurling the sails and working the tiller and rudder apparatus. He went up on the quarterdeck, making a gesture of great pleasure at the view from there. Afterward he ate some of our food and tasted our cider and wine, none of which seemed to interest his palate in the least. When his curiosity was fully satisfied, he very politely took his leave.

At other times the chief and his retinue of men approached our crewmen during their work ashore gathering wood or water. The chief offered his men to help with these tasks, joining in with great enthusiasm. Later he entertained us with demonstrations of their skill with bows and arrows and in several games or races. They gave us the opportunity to examine their bows which we found very strong and expertly made. The arrows are a thing of pride and beauty for the men who made them. The arrow tips are made of handworked jasper, hard marble, or other hard sharpened stones, but we saw no items made of iron. The only metal we saw was copper for adornments.

When the native chiefs discovered we planned to leave soon, they invited the officers of our group to join them in a ritual. We entered one of their shelters and sat in a circle with their chiefs and a man we assumed to be something like a priest.

The priest began a ritual of facing each of the four cardinal directions. In each position he would stop and raise a basket above his head and chant some words which we could not understand, nor did we yet know the meaning of this ritual. When he put the basket on the ground we saw that it contained food they had grown, along with an elongated roll of a dried plant leaves. The priest then repeated his movements with a long, thin wooden pipe that had a small red stone bowl attached to one end. He held the pipe before him in a vertical position and again uttered a chant as he slowly faced each of the four directions. In his incantations he repeatedly spoke the word "tabago" that I assume referred to the pipe, but may have been the name for the dried plant.

At this point the priest tore off a piece of the dried plant and inserted it into the bowl at the end of the pipe. He then took an ember from the fire in the center of our circle and held it to the dried plant. He sucked on the end of the hollow tube and drew smoke into his mouth and exhaled it. This was repeated as he again faced four directions in turn. As he stopped at each of the cardinal directions, he drew a mouthful of smoke through the pipe and exhaled it into the air. As the smoke left his mouth he again chanted. Having completed this, the priest then handed the pipe to the elder chief who took one mouthful of smoke and exhaled it. The pipe was passed to the younger chief who also took a mouthful of smoke. The pipe was then passed to each of the village elders present.

Among our group Giovanni was first given the pipe with indication that he should mimic the others. He coughed rather then exhaled the smoke and passed the pipe to me. I nearly choked on the smoke, but managed to recover. The smoke had a very strong, although somewhat pleasant, taste. The pipe was passed around a second time during which our men managed without choking and coughing. After the second draw on the pipe I felt a slight lightheadedness and hoped there would not be another round on the pipe. Berthram later commented that this unknown plant apparently was some strong narcotic. The natives obviously held the plant in high value for ceremonial uses.

The purpose of this ritual soon became clear to us. The indigenes were showing us a lasting bond of friendship which was to last until we meet again. They indicated to us that the smoke carried their thoughts and prayers to a greater spirit to whom we had all communicated. Each of us were strongly moved by this experience and sensed that we had indeed become attached to these men.

Chapter 16

May 6, 1524 departing Refugio

We weighed anchor at high tide very early this morning just at the beginning of the second watch. How sad we are to leave this idyllic place and these congenial, friendly people! This land we are leaving is on the parallel, 41° 40' North, approximately the same as Rome.

Made good ten leagues on an easterly course following the trend of the coast. Wind is from northwest to west, with unsettled and cloudy weather. As we moved a distance away from the coast we no longer felt the push of the warm current that had been with us previously. The current must have veered to the east at some time before we arrived at Angoulême.

Translator's note: The Verrazzano brothers once again proved their excellent skills with celestial measurement. Newport, R. I. *is located at latitude 41° 30' North. Verrazzano certainly had ready access to the latitude of* Rome *(41° 54') and many other major places in Europe in a rutter, the mariner's handbook in print at the time. His measurement of 41° 40' was off by only ten minutes of latitude, 11.5 miles, which is very good for the instruments, cross-staff, and astrolabe, available to them. They would have sighted the sun or Polaris a number of times and averaged the results.*

May 7, 1524 Offshore new land

Made good nine leagues during daylight today. We continue to anchor during the night. Our course is following the coast in a northeasterly direction.

Berthram brought the native boy up on deck today for some fresh air, as he has become concerned for the boy's health. He coughs frequently and shows great fatigue, perhaps from the bad air below deck. Berthram fears the boy may be under some bad influence of the stars for which there is no treatment. Despite all our advances in medical treatment, we still do not understand many illnesses. When Berthram encounters such a blank spot in his knowledge of treatments, he resorts to the wisdom of astrologers which has prevailed for many centuries.

May 8, 1524 Offshore new land

Made good eight leagues. Wind continues from the northwest. Today our short distance was through the most treacherous passage of sailing we have experienced in our entire voyage. Giovanni guided the *Dauphine* through the most difficult array of shoals and currents imaginable. In places the water was barely deep enough for our keel to pass safely. On both sides nearby we could see visible signs of very shallow shoals. We crept through this area working constantly with sounding lines. Once we had to stop and resort to sweeps to make a sharp change of direction through a shallow pass. Near the east end of the shallowest water we encountered currents that further impeded our progress.

We made this dangerous passage while sailing among islands set close together, and we were surprised to find ourselves caught in such a hazardous situation. Giovanni had usually stayed farther away from land. Unfortunately, as we approached that it was not obvious that shoals lay ahead. Giovanni amused himself by naming this terrible area Armellini, for a most dreaded papal tax collector of great renown, Francesco Cardinal Armellini. My guess is that if Cardinal Armellini hears of this place bearing his name he will deem it a well-deserved honor in happy ignorance of its true nature. We all had a good laugh that Giovanni was in such good humor after passing through this perilous place. He was doubtless greatly relieved that we had again been guided by Divine Hands four days after our special Ascension Day service.

Translator's note: Verrazzano encountered treacherous shoals on the day he sailed through Vineyard Sound, Nantucket Sound, and the Pollock Rips at the south end of Cape Cod. As Gerolamo points out, this route was not in keeping with Giovanni's usual practice of staying far offshore. Water in some areas is only three feet deep, and Verrazzano and his crew did a masterful job of finding the channels through these shoals. No doubt they relied heavily on men in the ship's boat going ahead and making soundings before advancing the Dauphine. *Verrazzano might well have gone around the south side of Martha's Vineyard and Nantucket Island, but once into the hazardous area there was no turning back.*

May 9, 1524 Offshore new land

Made good ten leagues on a northerly course following an abrupt change in the direction of the coastline. Weather continues fair with westerly winds. Giovanni named the point of land at this turn of the coast, Pallavisino, after one of the king's prominent generals who, like Giovanni and me, comes from among the Florentines living in France.

May 10, 1524 Offshore new land

Made good ten leagues today on a west by northwest course. The northerly trend of the coast ended abruptly, and proved to be a long spit of land enclosing a very large bay. We sailed across the opening of the bay to reach the main coast again and resumed a northerly course.

Translator's note: They were sailing past Cape Cod and Cape Cod Bay.

May 11, 1524 Offshore new land

Made good twelve leagues on a northerly course following the coast.

Giovanni conducted a special prayer service today in recognition of Pentecost, the coming of the Holy Spirit to Christ's apostles. On this holy day the captain ordered an extra ration of meat and cider for all the crew. This caused much good feeling, and the men brought out instruments for music and dancing in the evening after vespers.

Berthram announced that the native boy's health has shown a slight improvement, but the unhappy lad still refuses to talk. His cough has diminished and he shows signs of increased energy. Carlito, who sometimes takes the boy his meals, wants to perform an exorcism on the boy. Not surprisingly Carlito claims to know the procedure for exorcisms. Giovanni rightly forbade Carlito to risk the safety of our ship with such potentially satanic rituals. Only a priest of the Church can be trusted to exorcise a demon without possibly incurring the power of Satan, and thereby inviting the extreme disfavor of God. Giovanni made it clear that Carlito would face severe punishment if he were to disobey the ban on exorcisms, which would certainly endanger the ship and the success of the expedition.

May 12, 1524 Offshore new land

Made good nine leagues on a north-by-east course along the coast. Wind varies from the west and northwest-by-west. Weather has turned misty and cool.

Giovanni and I had a conversation with Berthram with various questions concerning the health of the native boy. Although the boy is somewhat improved, he remains in poor health. He is now eating less, has great fatigue and weakness, and feels feverish to the touch. Also he still refuses to attempt any communication. Berthram suggested that the boy was in mourning at the separation from his mother and his home.

Giovanni said, "Mourning seems unlikely among these primitive people. Surely this boy's feelings are not fully developed."

"I think otherwise Captain Verrazzano, if you will forgive my saying so," replied Berthram, "but I watched the great lamentations for dead relatives among the people we met at Refugio. Their moaning and wailing was not dissimilar to the mourning I have seen in many places in

Europe, particularly among the women. Also I think the boy is of an age of great dependence on his mother. So perhaps fear is controlling him more than mourning. In either case his mood has taken his appetite and may be making him ill."

Giovanni dismissed Berthram's concern. "Mr. Peeters," he began, "the boy is young and youth has great resilience for adversity. I concede he may miss his mother but he will get over it in time. I suggest that you do your best to bring him back to good health. The boy is very important for me. I must show them how much this boy and his people resemble the orientals that we have seen in paintings done by other travelers. Therefore it is most imperative that you do your best with the boy." Changing the subject, Giovanni inquired, "Now as for the murderer Leclerc. Tell me how he fares."

Berthram responded, "Leclerc is a rock. Nothing seems to bother him; not confinement, not chains and irons, nor the decreased food allowance due to his not working strenuously. He now talks incessantly whenever anyone comes near. He brags that the law will never convict him because there is no evidence against him. On top of it all, he is in excellent health. His wounds have healed leaving horrible scars but he has been completely unperturbed through it all. I think he is enjoying his freedom from work."

"I will soon correct that oversight." said Giovanni, "Leclerc will become permanent pumper and man the bilge pumps as needed around the clock. As this voyage progresses the leaks have increased despite our constant caulking and tarring. Therefore more pumping is required while Master Matthieu Ango and his assistant, Christophe, are hard pressed for men to do the work. Perhaps this will take some of the cockiness out of him. I will speak to the master about it immediately."

As Giovanni went up to the quarterdeck I realized that all of us, except Berthram, had forgotten about Leclerc chained below, free of any work assignments. Fortunately Giovanni made the appropriate change.

May 13, 1524 Offshore new land

Made good ten leagues on a north-by-east course. Weather is clearing again, and wind is from the northwest. We are sailing five points off the wind…about as close to the wind as possible without considerable tacking. Matthieu has ordered the main sail furled, and we are using only the foresail in a half-furled position in order to keep our speed low.

During a quiet moment in the afternoon I finished my meal of bread, fish, and wine, and Bertram joined me. At last I had another chance to ask Berthram more about his experience in the monastery.

"Berthram," I began, "I do not want to pry into your private life, but could you indulge me by allowing one question? Tell me more about the life-changing situation you found in the monastery?"

"I am glad to tell you more about my experience Gerolamo," he answered as he sipped his wine, "for I have seen that you have an open mind that can absorb diverse ideas. This is a good trait I think and one which makes you a most engaging man. You have a great curiosity which is a wonderful gift to be nurtured throughout your life. You are right to ask questions without coming to judgement against a person having new ideas."

After a few moments to chew his bread he continued, "What I found in the monastery goes to the very core of Christianity as we know it. In our daily lives in this world we hear from our priests that God is a distant Being that can only be reached through the sacraments which, in turn, can only be administered by a duly authorized person, namely a priest. Thus the priests effectively control your life, your death, and only by their intercession will you know salvation. This approach places God out of reach to ordinary people without the help of the church. The church has prospered for centuries under this feudal system. They collect revenue from everyone, rich and poor, and they own vast tracts of income producing land. But the important thing, from the point of view of the church, is to maintain the condition in which an individual cannot experience God without the church."

"The monastery is a community of monks who are actually ordinary people that have devoted their lives to a search for God. I found in each of the monks a vital presence of God much like the presence described by the early Christian mystics from Egypt and Syria. This presence is the result of a monk's search for a total connection with God, and the exciting thing is that they find God within themselves, not far out in some unreachable place."

Giovanni had returned by this time and entered the conversation. "Mr. Peeters," he began, "you imply that monks are ignoring the church and doing something entirely different but that cannot be. Many monks are priests and they perform the Eucharist and other sacraments daily in the monasteries. The monks fully accept the authority of the pope. So what is the difference? In my opinion those monks would serve better if they lived among the daily problems faced by ordinary people striving and hoping for salvation."

"Well said, Captain," Berthram replied, "monks indeed conform to church dogma. In that they are no different. There are also many monks who are not totally cloistered but work in the world in universities, infirmaries, and caring for the poor. My mentor, Erasmus, fully agrees with you on that point. He believes it is completely wrong for monks to become cloistered where they cannot do the good works that he believes necessary for salvation. In fact it was with great reluctance that Erasmus agreed to arrange my year-long retreat in a monastery."

"Where the monk's practice differs is in his view that God is around us and within us. The monk devotes his life to seeking an awareness of His Presence and to the practice of seeing the sacred presence shining everywhere. All God's creation contains this presence and the monk aspires to see it constantly. Early Christian teachings, including those of Jesus, support this perception of God."

"The monks do not feel that they have become deities but are, in fact, more fully aware than most of us of their distance from real godliness. The monk comes to realize his own shortcomings and is guided by a spiritual mentor on how to deal honestly with them. Attaining this level of self-discipline is perhaps the most difficult and painful accomplishment any human being can make. Few people outside the monastery can focus so intently on their spiritual discipline. However one of the sayings of monks is that they strive to be like angels on earth. They hope thereby to let the light of angels shine in their lives."

"To this end a monk practices the presence of God in everything he does: his work, his prayers, and his study. One of the earliest aids to this practice of the presence of God is the Prayer of the Heart, which is first mentioned in a text called the *Philokalia* by the ascetic fathers of Christianity beginning in the fourth century. The Prayer of the Heart is a meditation that empties the mind of its mental pictures and concepts in an effort to reach an intense consciousness of God's presence. Ideally they will be able to carry this consciousness into the world no matter where they happen to be."

After Berthram finished this discourse of the life and purpose of a monk, Giovanni and I were both silent. Giovanni broke the silence first.

"Yes, Mr. Peeters, I can see how a monk who attains such spiritual consciousness will be a force for good in the world and he may have an immense influence. However I remain unconvinced of the value of a cloistered monastic. He becomes a better person with his enlightenment, but I can see no good beyond himself."

At that moment we heard a bell signaling the change of watch, and we each went about other duties. I continued reflecting on Berthram's words about his experience with monasteries. It occurred to me that the sea is my monastery. The sea is the place where I am able to feel God's presence more than any other. These thoughts inspired these few words:

A ship at sea is the union of two worlds:
Sea and sky; man and God.
Open to the horizon and serenely peaceful.
The sea is a haven for my soul.

May 14, 1524 Offshore new land

Eleven leagues made good on a northerly course, following the line of the coast. Weather is fair with a steady northwest-by-west wind. We have little need for tacking with present course and wind direction.

Giovanni is in a foul state today. For what reason I do not know, but I think he is agitated again from not finding more positive signs of rich mineral wealth among the native people we have met. He complained, "My muse, Orizontas, is a deceiver and a whore who lured me with promises of great gratification. Now she has cast me aside with nothing but a new map and a sick captive boy."

"There are voyages that seem to challenge your very existence," Giovanni continued. "You work, sweat, and nearly kill yourself trying to accomplish something—and you can't. Not from any fault of yours. You simply can do nothing, neither great nor small. What you seek is simply not there, and forces greater than yourself thwart every effort. This voyage, the dream of my life, was one of those voyages."

I tried to soothe his anguish, "Dear brother, you will be remembered in the future for a great contribution. You alone will have been the first to prove the continuity of the new continent from the Spanish Florida to Cabot's Newfoundland. You have collected a great amount of information about the landscape and its people. And lest you forget, you have seen the Oriental Sea just beyond the narrow isthmus. Have you forgotten how excited you were at its discovery? That will yet become the foundation of your presentation to the king for the need of another voyage. You have seen lands of great potential for settlement at Angoulême and Refugio. Giovanni, what is missing that has disappointed you?"

He answered with bitterness, "The one thing missing, which would be of great advantage for you as much as for me, is gold! The Spanish and the Portuguese found it in abundance. It disturbs me to the very soul of my being that they should have what I cannot. I know the king is only interested in immediate wealth. A promising future is of little interest to him. He wants wealth above all else. In that regard he will see this venture as a failure."

I had no idea Giovanni's feeling of failure had become so strong and nothing I said could mollify his disappointment. No matter how much I tried to point out the real achievements that certainly will be associated with his name for a long time to come, he could not be shaken from his ill humor. My hope is that this darkness in him will have a short life and he will soon return to his optimism. We shall see.

May 15, 1524 Offshore new land

Another ten leagues made good during daylight while sailing along this beautiful coast. The land has become a continuous forest of the type seen in the northern lands of Europe. The coast is very rocky and offers many small inlets that could be possible anchoring sites. We are in need of resupplying wood and water at the earliest opportunity. Giovanni wants to go ashore at a place inhabited by native people so we can exchange our trade goods for food from the natives. He realizes that we are entering waters uncharted but possibly frequented by European fishermen from England, France, or Portugal. Fishermen wander in search of fish but create no written record or map. When Giovanni is certain that we have reached charted waters we will return to France.

October 25, 2010 Rouen

Monday morning in the library. Here I am with the project to die for and I'm losing my steam. I don't know why I'm feeling so aimless at the moment. I think the Lorena disruption took all the wind out of my sails. Damn her! Why did she have to show up right in the middle of this. I had a pace, a momentum to my work. It's like I stumbled and can't get up again. Yeah, I'm still making progress, but now it seems like hard work.

October 26, 2010 Rouen

Nicole stopped by my basement workroom for a chat this morning. I hadn't seen her for several days.

"How is your work going," she said.

"The work is okay, but I'm having trouble concentrating."

"Aaah, of course you miss your Lorena and can't think about your work. I know just the answer for such problems. I am taking some days vacation from the library at the end of the week and I think you should join me for a few days of relaxation and being a tourist."

After a little balking on my part and claiming that I already had too much interruption, her steady persuasion changed my mind. How could I resist such an invitation anyway. "Okay," I said, with more enthusiasm than I expected, "where are you going on this little vacation?

"Good," Nicole said. "You are interested in early sixteenth century France, so you should know more about the king and how he lived. I have visited the king's palace at Fontainebleau several times and yet have seen very little of it. I want to go there, eat some good

food, see the palace, and walk in the gardens. I think it will be much more interesting with a good companion. This will be an easy trip and you will feel rejuvenated when we return."

Actually I feel somewhat rejuvenated just thinking about some time with Nicole, and I should really see the palace built by this self-aggrandizing man, King Francis the First.

October 28, 2010 Fontainebleau

I met Nicole at the station for an early train to Paris, then a thirty-mile bus ride to Fontainebleau.The bright sunny morning gave me a lift and my mood already improved. We got a room at the Hôtel le Richelieu, dropped our bags and headed across the street for the palace. Nicole told me to notice likely restaurants where we might come for lunch later. She's always thinking ahead when it comes to eating.

We walked a short distance to an entrance into a large courtyard where I had my first glimpse of Francis's Fontainebleau. This old palace overwhelms the mind. The size, the opulence, the art treasures, the expansive gardens all fill every view. Nicole was familiar enough to give me a quick orientation.

She began her brief intro as we stood by the Fountain of Diana, with the goddess of the hunt at the top and sculpted hunting dogs pissing arcing streams into the water. "From the twelfth century to the sixteenth century this site was a royal hunting lodge for kings in the middle of a 110 acre forest of oak, beech, and pines" she explained.

"Would Verrazzano have visited this palace," I asked.

"No, Francis began this ambitious project three or four years after your Verrazzano sailed. When Francis the First decided to expand the hunting lodge into a palace he brought in Italian architects to design it, Italian artists to adorn it, Italian landscapers to build the gardens, and an Italian fountain designer to build this fountain.

Francis was determined to bring the Renaissance to France and he succeeded. Various kings after Francis expanded the palace even more until they had this monster you see before you, but it will always be considered Francis's palace. Even Napoleon made this his home and chose the White Horse Courtyard, where we first entered the grounds, to bid his troops a final farewell at the end of his reign. Now they call it the Courtyard of Goodbyes."

I commented, "The most noticeable consistency in this building is the ubiquitous letter 'F' emblazoned as part of the decoration of friezes and cornices everywhere. Francis could never be described as a self-effacing man."

"Well of course it's good to be the king," she laughed.

I laughed too at the Mel Brooks reference and realized I was already having a good time.

We had a flawless dinner at the Richelieu, and retired to our room for an evening of rest and love. Nicole was right, I am rejuvenated. Not only that, I sense a deepening of my relationship with her.

October 29, 2010 Fontainebleau

Coffee and brioche didn't quite satisfy for breakfast this morning so I ordered a soft-boiled egg and felt ready to start the day. We returned to the palace and saw some of the grand ball rooms, apartments, and throne room in an endless progression of spectacular opulence. My senses quickly became oversaturated with the ornate adornments of every wall and ceiling. Soon I was begging Nicole for a change of pace with a stroll through the gardens. They are also extravagantly done but much easier to assimilate, I think.

Around one o'clock we went back to town and found a nice bistro where we sat at an outside table in the October sun. Over our pizza lunch (yeah, I know why would you eat pizza in France?)

Nicole asked about Lorena's visit. "Did you and Lorena have a good time in Dieppe?" she asked.

I thought for a few moments as the traffic rushed by and the comfort of the warm October day sank in. Suddenly all my feelings, frustration, anger, embarrassment, and hurt came together and I told Nicole the whole debacle. I expressed feelings I didn't even know I had. Anger that Lorena came. Frustration that it got out of hand so quickly with so little discussion. Embarrassment over some of the dumb things I said that only added fuel to the fire. How the whole mess got out of control.

Nicole quietly listened to all this with no comment. Then said, "Ross, what you tell me explains a lot. When you first told me Lorena was coming, I sensed no enthusiasm. When I offered to be your tour guide, you turned pale and killed the idea immediately. I was surprised when you told me she had gone home sooner than expected. Ever since she left I see you closed up in your library work room, seemingly a very glum boy. If I may offer my opinion, Ross, you may have been in a relationship that was looking for a way to end, and unfortunately both of you were hurt."

"Maybe you're right, Nicole. I had never consciously thought my relationship with Lorena needed to end and I'm not sure it actually has ended. She wrote one irate note then quit answering my emails, so I won't know until I get home how the situation stands. What I do know, Nicole, is this: you're having a terrific effect on me. I feel good when I'm with you, and I'm very grateful for your caring. This little trip with you is wonderful—fun, relaxing, and no drama."

October 30, 2010 Fontainebleau

This morning after breakfast we took a stroll through the town of Fontainebleau. Everything about this town is geared to tourists, which makes it seem a bit unnatural, but the result is having many choice eating spots for any food, from finest French to Japanese and Italian.

In mid-afternoon we boarded a bus back to Paris and trained home to Rouen. I needed this three day break much more than I realized.

Chapter 17

May 16, 1524 Trading with native people

Made nine leagues on a northerly course. Weather fair with westerly wind. The breeze from the land continually refreshes us with the smell of pine forests.

Our lookout saw native people gathered on the shore waving to us and Giovanni decided to take advantage of the opportunity for another session of trading our goods, replenishing wood and water, and perhaps hunting for fresh meat.

As our group approached in the ship's boat, the people gestured for us to stop and not come ashore. They began making signs of unfriendliness, but not actual hostility. It was difficult to understand just what it was they desired of us.

At that point, the natives directed our boat to the base of a low escarpment that rose vertically from the shore. Then we could see that they brought baskets of items for trading but signaled to us not to come ashore. They began lowering their goods in baskets, and in return we put in our trade items: trinkets for adornment along with some mirrors. This operation was repeated several times until the natives indicated they were finished. Then they made signals for us to leave immediately which we did. As we rowed away they began making derisive-sounding calls to us. Although we could not understand their words there was no mistaking their tone and intent. Many of them began making vulgar gestures such as baring their backsides to us and yelling in most derisive tones.

No one among us had ever seen such outrageous behavior. Although some were amused by the display of the natives, it was clearly intended as an insult. One man aboard our boat suggested we give them a taste of lead from a musket to humble them a bit. Giovanni, though insulted, refused to allow anyone to fire upon the natives. As we boarded the *Dauphine*, Giovanni declared that he would name this place "Land of the Bad People."

After vespers we discussed the unusual behavior of these unfriendly people and wondered what could have induced such hostility toward us when all other encounters had been at least cautiously friendly. I think Berthram came nearest the answer with his idea that their unfriendliness stemmed from previous unpleasant encounters with Europeans arriving in ships. They obviously wanted to have the items that we brought for trading even before they saw what we brought. Fishing vessels from England or Portugal possibly sailed this far south from their usual fishing waters of Newfoundland. If so, the fishermen must have had little concern for the local inhabitants and may have stolen the natives' trade goods, or perhaps one of the natives was killed. Whatever the cause, we agreed that we had done nothing to incite their disdain.

Translator's note: The Abenaki tribe occupied the coast of Maine where Verrazzano was sailing at the time. As Berthram Peeters suggested, their unfriendly behavior was probably an indication that the expedition had reached waters already known by European fishermen.

A brief research of the subject shows that "mooning" is an ancient and cross-cultural means of expressing scorn or derision.

May 17, 1524 Offshore new land

Made good twelve leagues today. No change in the weather or winds. The temperatures are pleasant. Giovanni alerted the lookouts to seek another possible landing place. We were unable to obtain the wood and water at our last site because of the "Bad People."

May 18, 1524 Offshore new land

Made only eight leagues today when the lookout spied another cove for anchorage. Giovanni ordered Matthieu to move the ship into the attractive harbor and anchor.

About twenty-five men went ashore with water kegs, axes, and muskets. As they stepped from the boat, a barrage of arrows came at them from the edge of the nearby forest. The indigenes then turned and fled in fear. None of our men had a chance to fire a shot and fortunately no one was injured by the arrows. The natives had disappeared so completely that we went about our tasks of gathering wood and water as though nothing had happened. The harbor was good and the land looked appealing, so Giovanni decided this was a good place to explore.

In the distance we saw mountain peaks glistening in the sun. Giovanni opined optimistically that the mountains offer a hint of possible mineral deposits worthy of further investigation. Berthram suggested to Giovanni that we stay for a day or two to explore the immediate area. Two parties of men were ordered to push two or three leagues into the interior and report on the presence of human habitation, minerals, and other resources.

At the end of their work the men returned with little of interest. The party encountered more native people but met no further hostility. Unlike the people at Refugio, the inhabitants here have no cultivated food crops—neither beans, peas, mahiz, nor squash. They appear to be living entirely by gathering roots and fruits that happen to be growing naturally in the area. The main part of their diet is fish. We concluded however that the nearby hills must contain mineral deposits, judging from the copper earrings on a few people we happened to see more closely.

After two days at anchor Giovanni decided we had spent enough time in this unproductive place. At the next high tide we weighed anchor and departed.

May 21, 1524 Offshore new land

Made good twelve leagues during daylight, on a north-easterly course. Weather continues fair with a steady northwest-by-west breeze.

Our recent fruitless exploration of the land reaffirmed Giovanni's conviction that this voyage was ending in naught. His gloomy mood has returned as he feels his ambitions thwarted by fate. He spoke with me again about his disappointment, which now verges on bitterness. "Gerolamo," he said, "I denounce this faithless muse, Orizontas. I followed her call and promise and she has failed me miserably."

Fearful of agitating his mind further, I answered very carefully. "Dear brother, perhaps you have misunderstood the call of your muse. She did not actually make you a promise. Fame and wealth are not hers to give. She has not deceived you. Orizontas merely called you to come and see what lies beyond the horizon. She was your inspiration to move beyond the known limits and expand your world. That is all. She did not say, 'Come and take the gold.' She only said, 'Come and see.' It is your hopeful expectations that have caused your disappointment. Nothing was promised. You answered her call to come and see and, in so doing, you changed the perception of the world for everyone. This is an achievement that few men have ever made, or ever will make. This makes you one of the few men in all history to change how we view the world. This is no small thing and you will be long remembered and commemorated. I feel sure the king will see opportunity in your Oriental Sea suggestions, and in your Refugio settlement ideas."

Giovanni had become somewhat subdued when next he spoke, "My brother, I see wisdom in what you say regarding my expectations. But knowing that disappointment comes from unfounded expectations does not lessen its effect on me. I can see that the solution is to change my expectations, to adapt to what is rather than what I expected."

"To be truthful, Gerolamo, I am not confident that the so-called Oriental Sea is actually a passage to China and India. That is part of my despair. I know not how much to emphasize its possibilities to the king. Some cosmographers already suspect that the new continent is much bigger than shown on the first maps. There are some who think the new continent is as big as Africa, or perhaps even Asia. If that is the case then I would be foolish to suggest a water passage of such length. Although no one could actually refute the idea, it would seem implausible to many.

This dilemma combined with my disappointment about the lack of precious metals has led to my agitation. I feel that I have fallen short, and I see no way to ameliorate the situation. I see no way to make it look like a success."

He continued, "As always, dear brother, you have proven a reliable companion on a voyage. Your thoughts are welcome. I know that I am often churlish to you and others but I truly have great fondness for you."

Giovanni left after that last statement, which I took to be a blanket apology for everything, past or present. My brother requires a certain amount of patience from anyone who works with him but he seldom sees fit to make an apology, especially one in which the reason for the apology is so uncertain.

May 22, 1524 Offshore new land

Made good twelve leagues during daylight. Weather is cooling as we sail northeastward. The rocky and forested coast is well supplied with coves for possible anchorage if needed. We see some signs of habitation in this area.

Matthieu came in as we were eating a quick midday meal and addressed Giovanni.

"Sir, Leclerc's assistant rigger, the seaman named Paul, has ably taken over Leclerc's duties and now requests to bring some information of interest to you."

"Tell him to come in," Giovanni answered.

Paul was visibly uneasy standing before Giovanni. He doffed his cap, and stood silent until Giovanni motioned for him to speak.

"Captain, my mentor Leclerc, warned me to remain silent on this subject but as he is in chains, my conscience urges me to speak. I received my gunnery training under him during our time in the navy, but for this voyage we were assigned as gunners aboard the *Normande*. I thought it surprising to assign gunners on a voyage of exploration until I saw cannon being loaded aboard her in the night. Leclerc threatened me with great harm if I told anyone of this, and the secrecy made me realize they were operating without your authorization. I never heard who ordered cannon for only one ship but the secrecy made me certain it was not you, Sir."

"You are right to tell me these things," said Giovanni, "but please continue your story. Did you hear of any reason for loading cannons onto the *Normande*?"

"Yes, Captain. Whoever ordered cannon on board the *Normande* intended for Captain Conflans to seek out a Spanish ship returning from the New World and confiscate its treasure. The intent, according to Leclerc, was to pay for this expedition and make a handsome profit as well. Leclerc told me he suspected one of the investors wanted to enhance his return and that each of the seamen aboard the *Normande* would receive a share."

"A few days before we left port two other gunners came aboard the *Normande* and Leclerc and I were reassigned to the *Dauphine*. Leclerc was greatly upset about this but I think the reassignment was ordered by Captain Conflans because of past conflicts with Leclerc. I am sure

Leclerc felt cheated out of his small portion of any treasure."

Giovanni asked if Paul had any additional information, then ended the report with a reassurance to Paul that he was correct to come in and that he should have no fear of Leclerc. When Paul was gone, Giovanni turned red and exploded in a rage. "I have been betrayed by the one I trusted most. Conflans claimed he ordered the cannon on his own authority but now it appears he was hiding the real villain. I feel sure Viscount Ango is behind this double dealing. He has his own history as a corsair in the name of France. Who else would have reason for this, and the authority to order it?"

"Indeed you have been wronged, Giovanni," I countered, "but I can imagine another who had incentive and authority for this action. Viscount Ango, if he were involved, could not have made such an order without the knowledge of Admiral Bonnivet. We will surely find the answer when we see Dieppe again."

Giovanni was not so easily calmed. When he spoke there was bitterness in his voice. "I swear this was all done because of Conflans. He alone would not have the authority, but this concession would have been given in compensation for losing command of the *Dauphine*. Something had to be promised in exchange to make Conflans so compliant. If you recall, Conflans seemed in extremely good spirits the morning we left Dieppe. He even had the audacity to suggest finding Spanish gold and I thought he spoke in jest. How brazen he is!"

May 23, 1524 Offshore new land

Made good fifteen leagues today under an increased spread of sail. Giovanni indicated that the coast is showing no change or items of great interest, so he has begun to increase our speed. I think he is now eager to return to France and feels that our survey of the continental coast is ended. Nevertheless he is still unwilling to sail at night lest we hit unseen shoals or rocks.

His mood has never brightened since hearing Paul's account of the cannon. He often mutters the question, "Why was my trust betrayed? I am severely mistreated."

May 24, 1524 Offshore new land

Made good another fifteen leagues today. After vespers Giovanni unexpectedly told Berthram and me to give him our logs of the voyage by tomorrow morning. He believes that we are entering water already explored by the Genoese, Cabot, or the Portuguese brothers Corte-Real. Within two or three more degrees of latitude, up to about forty-six degrees north, he will be certain that there is no need to continue our survey of the coast or our search for a passage to the west.

He explained that he wants to use our logs in preparing his report for the king. He said the report will include an abundance of information on events of the voyage: the results of our coastal survey, details of habitation, landscape, and potential of the land for cultivation and minerals. Berthram's journal contains much of this information while mine records many events, with details on courses sailed, weather, landings, and shipboard activities. Of course Giovanni is keeping a log as well, which will confirm and add to information in the others.

I can fully understand Giovanni's wanting our logs which form a detailed account of the voyage. I will happily give him my daily log that I made in accordance with my duties. It provides a record of distances, courses, storms and other pertinent information. However, I have kept this personal journal separate from my log of the voyage. This journal is my private record and I confess I have written some of my thoughts and records of conversations that I would not care for Giovanni to read. I will not give this one to him but perhaps I should discontinue writing in this journal until we reach France.

November 2, 2010 Rouen

Translator's note: Gerolamo's journal ends at this point with a multitude of unanswered questions. What happened when they arrived in France? Was the king disposed to sanction another voyage? If so, were the bankers interested in funding it? I soon found that Gerolamo had indeed continued writing after they disembarked in Dieppe.

I had a pleasant surprise today when Nicole Duval told me she had opened another chest of papers from their recent bequest, and found in it another hand-bound book with fragile leather covers, written by Gerolamo. When I had a look I realized that this book contains a journal revealing events subsequent to their return to France and accounts of other voyages. The dates indicate that Gerolamo waited until he returned to France to continue writing. Whatever the timing of his work, it nevertheless answers many questions. Fortunately I still have enough funds to finish it.

Chapter 18

Translators Note: The second journal of Girolamo Verrazzano begins here.

July 9, 1524 At sea and arriving in Dieppe

After Giovanni collected our log books I did not write a daily account for the rest of the voyage, although I made a few scribbled notations regarding events to serve as reminders. My intent was to compile a narrative at the end of the voyage to complete the record. I suppose I had some concern that Giovanni might also demand to see anything I wrote during our expedition. There was probably no reason to be so careful but I was still disturbed by the sudden loss of my log. I expect Giovanni will return it in due course.

The coastal survey of the new continent continued up to 49 degrees latitude. At that time Giovanni declared that we had definitely entered the waters explored by John Cabot when he sailed for the English. Cabot's description of his survey of the land he called Newfoundland is well-known by all navigators in western Europe. We made no more landings until the last day of our coastal survey. We went ashore one last time for water and wood then on Sunday, the first day of June, we turned the *Dauphine* on an eastward course. Oh, how good it seemed to turn the prow of our faithful ship toward home!

Giovanni said special prayers of thanksgiving during our matins prayers. Most sailors by now could recite the Salve Regina along with Giovanni and this pleased him very much. He feels his regular observance of prayer has perhaps changed some of the men and made them more aware of the constant protection we sailors receive from God. Perhaps he helped them become men of greater faith. Giovanni feels certain that his insistence on strict observance of pious behavior at all times is the main reason for the safety we have enjoyed throughout this expedition. There has been no serious damage to the ship beyond that normal to sailing: leakage of the hull resulting from the constant twisting motion the ship endures from the battering of waves and strain of the sails on the hull. Nor has anyone had serious injury that could not be mended by our skilled surgeon. The one blot on our voyage was the murder of the poor Spanish boy, Miguel, and the villain in that deed, Leclerc, is in chains with hard labor at the pump. The native boy's condition has not improved. He has fever and little appetite.

The voyage went smoothly with only routine sailing along 49 degrees north latitude. We had fair northwesterly winds every day driving us on a straight course toward our beloved Dieppe. We encountered four days of storminess that were exhausting for the crew, but not dangerous, though it assailed us with heavy rain almost constantly. The only bad consequence of this storm was that no one had dry clothing for those four days. To a sailor, constant wetness is grounds for the most heartfelt grumbling. They must sleep in wet clothing and eat cold food because Carlito cannot keep a fire going under such conditions. Even those who have a change of clothing in their seabags, eventually have both sets of clothes soaked. Dispositions become very sour and everyone falls into a dark mood.

This storm passed eventually and the bright sun changed everything. Wet clothing was hung everywhere and spirits lightened as the men anticipated a cooked meal for a change. Carlito did not disappoint them. Fortunately he had made certain that wood was stored below deck where it was kept dry. Carlito prepared a hot beef and pork stew made from his supply of dried meat and Giovanni ordered an extra ration of cider for each man. Everything changes with sunshine and a full belly. I should mention that Giovanni's generosity with the cider throughout the voyage is partly responsible for the disappearance of grumbling about having an "Italian" captain. Also confining Leclerc, the primary source of the grumbling, below deck in chains quieted all discontent. It proved worthwhile to have Leclerc out of sight for that reason alone.

I had many more satisfying and enlightening conversations with my friend Berthram, for now we had indeed become friends. We discussed more about the life and spirituality of the monks and the amazing changes taking place in our time regarding Luther's challenge to the Church. What impresses me most about the work of men like Luther and Zwingli is that they are promoting the idea that individuals can have a direct contact with God. This is truly new thinking for people outside a monastery. I cannot imagine where this idea will lead, but I feel certain that, once begun, it will never disappear.

When we were still three leagues from Dieppe, we were spotted by fishermen who recognized our flag. They soon alerted the harbor neighborhood announcing our return. On a Tuesday morning in July we approached the harbor with the rising tide and by the time we reached the quay a thousand people had gathered to welcome us! The church bell was tolling, harbor flags were flying, and the crowd was shouting "hurrahs." I am sure many people in the crowd suspected that we would not return when they learned last January that we were sailing alone. Even our great benefactor Viscount Ango was there to greet us. The Viscount was visibly proud of his nephew, who had performed flawlessly as second in command. I am certain that Matthieu will soon be assigned as a captain on his uncle's ships.

Upon our return to Dieppe Berthram saw his wife, Alaina, waiting on the quay. He was nearly dumbstruck at the sight of her. He had no expectation that she would be in Dieppe or that anyone could possibly be expecting the *Dauphine* at this exact time. As it happened she had come to Dieppe for the summer to stay with an uncle who lives there. She waited daily for the *Dauphine* to return so she could see Berthram immediately. This is another uniqueness about my friend Berthram Peeters—he has a marriage based on love, not family arrangements. I know of no other like it. Giovanni, for example, certainly is married to Beatriz for convenience, but Marie is his real mate. All this convinces me that Berthram lives a life like no other man I know. Marie was also at the quay dressed in her finest gown and kirtle and beaming at the prospect of being with Giovanni again. The sight of her put Giovanni in high spirits.

During the last weeks of our voyage he wrote a lengthy letter to our king and signed it on the date of our arrival in Dieppe, July 8, 1524. This is a momentous time for Giovanni and the act of writing the letter to the king has stimulated him sufficiently to drive away his feelings of failure. He is now convinced that he has completed a great triumph and that soon he will be duly rewarded for his effort. He is certain the king will want another voyage to bring people to develop the new lands and explore the passage to the Oriental Sea found in the early days of our voyage. Giovanni sees himself as the overseer of a grand enterprise in the near future. He repeatedly reassures me that I will also reap the benefits of this enterprise but, to tell the truth, the idea does not appeal to me so much. I greatly enjoy my voyages with Giovanni and I hope to continue them in the future, but my heart lies in completing my map of the New World right here in Dieppe. There is ample income from our family fortunes for me to continue living comfortably. I am content with the way things are right now and I hope to continue as long as possible. Giovanni is the adventurer, the dreamer, and the trader who seeks fame as much as fortune, and I wish him well. I am the one who steadily plods through without great notice. The occasional voyage with Giovanni is ample diversion for me and is far more than most men ever experience.

Giovanni immediately sent his long letter to the king along with a request for an audience in the near future. Now he is beside himself with anticipation while he waits for a response from the king. The murderer, Leclerc, was quickly given to the King's Magistrate of Normandy with a statement describing the charges against him. Viscount Ango, as Governor of Dieppe, will have a great influence on the fate of Leclerc.

Alas, the poor native boy we brought to France is ailing and losing strength. Although he eats, it is very little, and I fear he will not recover in time for Giovanni's audience with the king. Berthram tried everything known to men of medicine regarding the proper use of herbs and minerals but the boy has not improved. In fact he has developed a fever and coughs up a dark sputum. Berthram says that is a very bad sign. Perhaps it was a mistake to capture such a youngster who still pines for his mother. A mature man or woman would probably have survived.

Translator's note: Unfortunately, the captives that explorers brought home seldom survived long and many could not even survive the voyage. Most met their demise from disease and infection, particularly pneumonia.

July 12, 1524 Dieppe

This evening Giovanni and I had a fine roasted pork dinner with Berthram, Alaina, and Marie at Le Marin. The atmosphere of the evening was most convivial, with everyone in high spirits over a happy reunion combined with farewells. Giovanni was full of eloquent toasts to his immediate friends, to the benefactors of our trip, and to Viscount Ango and King Francis. And finally, to my great surprise, he raised his cup in tribute to me.

"To my faithful brother, without whom I would not have the fortitude nor the courage to face the unknown. He supports me when I am low and praises me when I meet success. Gerolamo is the one who is always there to make certain everything works properly and he never asks for credit. I am the one who craves recognition but my brother Gerolamo, although he has accomplished much, avoids glory and fame. He is truly a humble man who enjoys helping in the success of others. I think there is no other like him and I admire him immensely. Let us drink to his good health."

I had never heard Giovanni speak publicly of his feeling toward me before and it left me speech-less...almost. I recovered from my embarrassment enough to offer a response honoring my brother.

"Thank you, dear brother, for your kind words and now I will speak a few of my own. Occasionally there is a man brought to this earth who has the imagination to dream of great deeds, and who also has the determination to make them happen. Giovanni is one of those rare men who has both the desire to follow the lure of the unknown and the skills to succeed. My brother has his Orizontas, who recently beckoned him to the distant, ever-retreating horizon until he eventually saw a land never before seen by any civilized men. We can only admire a man who makes a lasting achievement like this and I ask you now to drink to such a man, my brother, Giovanni da Verrazzano."

The warm glow of camaraderie, along with generous quantities of food and wine, gave us an evening that we felt would never end. But alas these happy moments do end and good friends part. I bade a sad farewell to Berthram, who had become a very close friend indeed. I must travel to Rouen soon to see my friend, Felice, and I hope to visit Berthram and Alaina as well.

July 19, 1524 Dieppe

Viscount Ango invited Giovanni and me to his home in the afternoon for dinner and a personal account of our voyage. As usual Ango was hosting guests from many parts of Europe. To my surprise he had persuaded my friend Berthram to stay longer in Dieppe and to attend this dinner. This promised to be another enlightening evening at the Ango table.

We arrived at Ango's quay-side home in the late afternoon and were ushered up a stairway into the great hall that viewed in one direction toward the sea and the other looking down on the harbor of Dieppe. These are the very leaded windows from which the Viscount waved farewell as we set sail last January. Other guests had begun to assemble in the room. To my surprise and Giovanni's dismay, one of the guests was none other than the infamous Captain Antoine de Conflans. Giovanni obviously felt uneasy at having Conflans in the room but, as he is wont to do, he faced the situation directly and greeted Conflans in a polite, but delicate manner.

"Captain Conflans, how good to see you again," Giovanni began, "I trust you had no serious problem with your damaged rudder during your return voyage from the Madeira Islands."

Conflans, being equally gracious, responded, "Oh, no, Captain Verrazzano, the voyage was slow because of the *Normande's* poor maneuverability but we arrived safely in about three weeks. Your letter of explanation, which I carried, was most helpful in explaining what happened and in authorizing my receipt of 100 *livres*, which I finally received on the day of your return. I only regret that I could not participate in the great adventure you just completed."

Giovanni and I both knew this was a lie. Conflans had no interest in being sent on a voyage of exploration, and he had blatantly disobeyed orders. As Conflans moved away, Giovanni stunned me with news concerning the contents of the letter carried by Conflans back to Admiral Bonnivet. "Gerolamo," he said, "I was so eager to dismiss Conflans that I wrote blatant lies in the letter I sent with him to the admiral. In explaining his return with a damaged ship, I saved Conflans from embarrassment, or worse, by claiming that he had to return only because of storm damage to the *Normande* and I made no mention of insubordination or the resulting damage by cannon fire."

Conflans's apparent cordiality suggests that he knew he had been spared by Giovanni's generosity. My brother never ceases to surprise. I have often seen his generosity, but forgiveness for such a grave affront to his authority is astonishing. Giovanni confided that his generosity was motivated only by a selfish desire to prevent Conflans from damaging his chances for a second voyage. A humiliated Conflans could inflict untold harm to Giovanni's reputation with blatant lies.

In truth I cannot help but wonder if the admiral would soon have learned that the damage was obviously caused by cannon balls smashing wood and not by storm driven waves. I am certain that carpenters repairing the *Normande* could see that the damage was more characteristic of shell fire than wind and wave. Furthermore both Giovanni and I suspect the admiral gave authorization for the insubordination that led to the damage, so must have realized the plan to plunder a Spanish ship had gone amiss. Nevertheless Captain Conflans was saved from public disgrace and had no further cause to malign Giovanni.

Further proof of the success of Giovanni's letter was apparent from the Viscount who was full of praise for Giovanni's courage in sailing an unescorted ship into unknown seas. I suspect another motive for Giovanni's leniency with Conflans: that he may have felt insubordination by a junior officer might reflect on his own ability to command a fleet of ships.

Eventually we all gathered around the massive table in the center of the room and servants began bringing great roasts of beef and pork with delicious sauces. A wonderful aroma of roasted meat immediately filled the room. We were especially pleased to see beef on the table. This was truly a special occasion and only someone of the Viscount's stature could acquire such quantities of beef. Among the guests were other ships' captains from Ango's fleet of merchantmen and fishermen. I was pleased to see the elderly scholar, Doctor Professor Fortier of Caen University, was again present. I remembered his interesting discussion of Giovanni Pico last autumn. I hoped to get Berthram engaged in a conversation with the professor.

The dinner had barely begun when Viscount Ango addressed Giovanni. "Captain Verrazzano, we are awaiting an account of your voyage. The guests are eager to hear your story."

Giovanni paused a moment to find a starting point then answered, "My dear Viscount, I hardly know where to begin, but I think the account of our survey of the coast of the new continent will be of great interest to you and your guests."

Giovanni continued for about an hour telling the high points of our wonderful experience—the Oriental Sea, the great embayment at Angoulême, the welcoming people of Refugio, and by sharp contrast, the repugnant people to the north. All this continued with occasional questions from the guests. Giovanni concluded with a full description of his grand plan for a return voyage, with additional ships and people for developing the resources of the new lands and exploring the Oriental Sea. Giovanni deftly described two important aspects of the new lands: first, their economic potential for valuable minerals, timber, agriculture, and defensible ports; and second, the people and their potential for conversion to Christianity, and their potential as slave labor. On the topic of religion he reported that the people show no sign of having a proper religious practice of any kind, therefore missionaries will find an open and fertile field for conversion.

At the end Ango inquired into the well-being of the native boy and wondered aloud if such a capture was the right thing to do. No one else at the table felt disturbed by the fate of the boy, except for Berthram, who responded to Ango's question.

"Viscount Ango," Berthram began, "if I may, I will respond to your question concerning the native boy. I think you have remarked on a practice that has been followed without question by many explorers. Captain Verrazzano ordered his crew to treat the native people kindly and that was done throughout our voyage, nor does the taking of captives seem to violate such an order. But I feel the suitability of this practice has recently come into question. Until now there has been no uncertainty of the appropriateness, because the native people are generally regarded as having little sensibility beyond ordinary animals. There is an undercurrent of a new perception on this subject, especially among a few intellectuals who see humans everywhere as thinking, rational beings."

"Some philosophers are beginning to think that even primitive men have more awareness and intelligence than previously thought. I can imagine a future time when explorers will persuade native people to return to Europe with them rather than capture them by force. Until that day comes we continue the practice with little thought about its consequences. As for the fate of the boy in question, I fear he has fallen very ill and may not recover."

After Berthram's words there was some mumbling among several guests, but no one spoke in opposition to anything Berthram said. Giovanni looked a little uncomfortable with the thought that the capture and likely death of the young boy may put himself in a bad light. He quickly changed the subject back to his grand plan and wanted to know what the Viscount thought about it.

"Captain Verrazzano," Ango began, "your plan is magnificent, and any king with an ambition for empire should be quick to approve it. I applaud the thought you have put into this idea and I expect that the king will be interested. I must warn you, however, that the king is currently under attack by an army of Italians led by none other than one of our king's own generals, Charles, the Duke of Bourbon. This traitorous villain has gone over to the side of the emperor and the pope, and at this time is fighting with an army of 80,000 men against the king's army in northern Italy. Captain, I say this to alert you to a dire situation that could possibly divert the king's attention from his dreams of empire. In short, the king is extremely occupied by these endless conflicts with Emperor Charles V and the pope. Furthermore the king is extended almost beyond his means by the acquisition of ships, weapons, and supplies needed for an army. Adding to the king's woes is the grave illness of his beloved wife, Queen Claude. The king himself is now hastening to the field of battle."

Poor Giovanni fell silent for a few moments at this gloomy news then blurted out his feelings. "I love this king, but I despair his constant, damnable fighting with the pope. Think how many opportunities he misses for making France stronger in the world. He could expand his horizons much farther if he spent more time with alliances and less time with battles."

"But Captain Verrazzano," the Viscount explained, "I think you do not realize the extreme threat these forces make to the very existence of France. These forces against us are hoping to partition France among themselves and this would mean the end of France as a viable power in the world."

"Forgive me, Sir," said Giovanni, "for I know nothing of the emperor's ambitions, nor do I pretend to know the king's business. I certainly have no intention of pretending to tell the king what to do. I should not have spoken so rashly."

As the sated guests were departing at the end of the evening, Viscount Ango drew Giovanni aside and had a private conversation, which I could not hear. I could tell however from the look on Giovanni's face that he was hearing something very unpleasant. His jaw sagged and his head drooped in a manner that I seldom see in him and his erect stature began to slump. He looked as though he had been hit by a falling spar.

When Giovanni joined me for the walk to Le Marin, he was silent for some time then it all began to come out.

"There is serious doubt that the king will grant me an audience to hear my proposal in person. His Highness sent a letter to Viscount Ango directing him to tell me the news. My report was forwarded to the king, who was then traveling toward the battlefield. He is interested in my report and wants to hear of my plans for empire but he will probably not sanction another voyage of exploration for the next year or more. It is that simple. The king is in a state of distraction and cannot be concerned with other affairs. Also he needs all the funds and ships that French bankers can provide to conduct these damnable wars and will not allow any money to be diverted to exploration. Hell and damnation!"

"And to add to my torment," Giovanni continued, "that louse of a man, Conflans, waited until our return to collect his 100 *livres* retainer. Now it will always appear that he accompanied us throughout the voyage, and received his pay at the end like everyone else."

"The brighter news is that Viscount Ango assured me, when I confronted him, that the order for cannon on the *Normande* indeed came directly from Admiral Bonnivet, and the Admiral wanted to make it appear that Conflans acted alone. The Admiral is away fighting the king's war and I could never confront him with my complaint. I feel vindicated to have returned safely from a long voyage despite the deceptions which undermined my efforts. I now know I was right to think that this trickery was done to mollify Conflans for his loss of command of the *Dauphine*."

I told Giovanni to take comfort in the fact that Viscount Jean Ango was not a party to the deception although he learned about it. "Captain Conflans' credibility was diminished in the eyes of many while yours has risen immeasurably," I told him, "Do not let this little chicanery blind you to the value of your accomplishment in the eyes of everyone. Anyone can see what Conflans has done in attempting to restore his own legacy."

Giovanni brightened and said, "There was however one positive note attached to the bad news. The viscount wants me to return to his service as a mariner trader. He will provide a provisioned ship with crew and take a share of the profits. I will command a ship, find, and purchase the trade goods for a one-sixth part of the profit. My contribution, in addition to my navigation skills, will be to purchase and sell the merchandise. This one-sixth will make a princely income and I hope you will again share it with me, both by your presence and by your monetary investment. The viscount wants to enter the brazilwood market, which is yielding great profits for the red dye made from the wood of this tropical tree. So my ambition is thwarted and I am to return to the life of a trader."

When we reached Le Marin, we found Berthram there already. He had come to say farewell again. Marie was also at the table. All of us but Marie had eaten heavily that day, so we spent the rest of the evening in a quiet conversation with too much wine. Giovanni said almost nothing the entire evening and Marie, although she obviously noticed his unusual quiet, knew him too well to question his mood in the presence of others. Most of the conversation was light banter with no focussed subject. Each of us seemed to be thinking about what lay ahead for our separate lives more than about the great news of our recent success. Marie ended the evening by saying that Giovanni was obviously very tired and should get some rest in her bed. Berthram left with the expressed hope that our paths would soon cross again and I went to my rooms.

I pondered at length what my response would be to Giovanni about joining him on his next voyage. This will be a good opportunity for more voyages to the new lands which intrigues me greatly. But I am eager to begin work on my map of our recent discoveries in the new continent. Of course I will be glad to invest funds in Giovanni's venture as merchant mariner but to join him will certainly delay the completion of my map.

Chapter 19

July 28, 1524 Dieppe

As it happened Giovanni had an unexpected opportunity to see the king. Our monarch interrupted his journey to the battlefields when he heard of the death of his wife Claude, Duchess of Brittany, and stayed for a time in Lyon. While there he agreed to listen to Giovanni's report of the voyage of discovery. Giovanni was ecstatic over the opportunity to face the king directly with his proposal for future exploration. Needless to say Giovanni left immediately for Lyon.

The king's interest in the New World is obviously still alive, as it must be if he is to vie with his great rivals Spain and Portugal, and of course the emperor. The emperor has schemed for years to humiliate our king in any way he could. King Francis, for his part, has been equally avid to contain the emperor's ambitions. So France has been subjected to war after war since the anointing of this Spanish Holy Roman Emperor a few years ago. Although most of the battles occur in Italy, the cost to France has been enormous. Not only the cost but the diversion of our king's attention and fortune from other pursuits has hurt France. This dilemma has been a great source of frustration and anger for Giovanni because it impedes his own objectives.

August 20, 1524 Dieppe

Giovanni returned from his audience with the king greatly subdued. The king showed great interest in everything Giovanni told him and listened attentively to the entire account of the voyage. The king was full of questions and suggestions for the future, and Giovanni felt that another voyage was well within reach. Then at the end the king's tone changed. He responded to Giovanni's presentation at some length. The king was greatly pleased that his name had been given to the new land, and that the name of his family duchy, Angoulême, had been applied to the land surrounding a potential harbor at the mouth of a great river.

The king was however not impressed with the report of possible riches. Giovanni had found no gold, silver, or precious stones. There were no wealthy cities with silks or other produce of great value. Giovanni had offered only the vague hope of aromatic trees of possible medicinal value, possible metals in nearby hills, and of fertile soils. Above all, no strait had been found to the Indies. The king questioned Giovanni closely about the supposed Oriental Sea. But when he learned that Giovanni had not actually investigated the validity of the sea, he expressed his dismay.

"In short," Giovanni quoted the king, "you have found little of real immediate interest. No wealth nor any strait."

Giovanni knew enough of the affairs of state to see that the sudden negative tone was the result of the king's preoccupation with the war. The king's mind was focussed on obtaining more money and more ships. This long-lasting conflict was rapidly draining his resources. To make matters worse for the king, the bankers of Lyon were becoming reluctant to continue pouring money into the king's unprofitable ventures. Bankers must, after all, expect a return on their money. Giovanni also learned from bankers in our family that the king has been putting immense pressure on them to continue funding his wars, and has even threatened to banish them as undesirable aliens if they fail to comply. We have been faithful citizens of France since our birth yet we are considered to be "undesirable aliens" at the least sign of disfavor. What must we do to be accepted?

Translator's note: Francis I banished Florentine bankers and some merchants from Lyon with an edict on September 16, 1524. The bankers and merchants mostly stayed in France, merely moving to other major cities, particularly Troyes, Rouen, and Paris.

August 25, 1524 Dieppe

Giovanni has entered another of his dark moods. This negative meeting with the king was worse than having no audience. He now has to face the reality that there will be no realization of his dream for wealth in the New World. Nor is the viscount's offer to help Giovanni return to his role as merchant mariner any consolation. He will eventually begin that venture but merchanting lacks the excitement of exploration with its potential for fame and sudden wealth.

At this moment of despair Giovanni announced that the king's secretary told him to submit all log books of the voyage, The king's chosen Italian cartographer, Maggiolo, will use both our log books to create a map of our discovery. This was devastating news of the direst nature. It had never occurred to me that I might lose my record of the voyage by which I intended to make the first complete map of the lands they now call America. Now I am ruined and cannot possibly finish the most important work of my life.

The cartographer Vesconte Maggiolo is from Genoa, and is another example of the king's fascination with all things Italian. To his credit Francis 1st brought to court the great sculptor and silversmith, Cellini, with the stipulation that he produce beautiful art on commission. The king has also brought numerous others to France, including the great da Vinci. Now he has made his own choice of a Genoese cartographer who knows little of our voyage, and the king has at the same time confiscated my own means of producing the map. I have great respect for Maggiolo's skills, but I detest losing my means of making my map. As a cartographer who participated in the voyage I expected the honor of creating the map under the auspices of the king. Now I must join Giovanni in his disgust with the king. Fie on him, I say, fie! Am I now to be regarded as French rather than Florentine? At other times I am considered not French enough. Damnation upon these bigots!

Giovanni tried to console me in my anguish but he was feeling no better due to his own disappointment. "Gerolamo, we are both in a state of despair. Our dreams have crumbled. Our futures seem uncertain and bleak. The worst is that we have been outmaneuvered by a king and there is no recourse. There is no avenue for protest. Our only solace is in returning to the things we know well and try to reshape our lives. You gave me a valuable lesson on the power of expectations to cause disappointment when I lamented that Orizontas had failed me, now you must digest your own words of wisdom."

Of course Giovanni is right but I am uninterested in hearing words of comfort and advice at this time. I must first enjoy my misery to its fullest.

September 1, 1524 Dieppe

Giovanni brightened considerably today with the news that Beatriz had safely borne a son in July, the month of our return. The news was doubly surprising because he was unaware that she was expecting. This is exactly the right antidote for his gloom as he often despaired that he might leave this world without an heir. Beatriz had not conceived after several years of marriage and Giovanni feared she might be barren. I suspect part of the problem may be that he was too often away. But now he is off to Lyon for the christening of his son. I hope he stays in Lyon long enough to overcome his darkness. I think the birth of an heir is sure to do it.

October 30, 1524 Dieppe

Giovanni has remained in Lyon. I think he has not been with his wife for this much time since their marriage. In a recent letter he writes that the mood among our Florentines in Lyon is very hostile toward the king at the present time. Giovanni explained in a letter as follows:

> Not only has the king seen fit to banish many prominent Florentine families from Lyon, he has also taken arms against the principalities of northern Italy. His actions in the latter may, in fact, have led to the former. The Florentine bankers in Lyon denied further funds to the king not only because he was overextended, but also because he was fighting against Italian armies drawn from the northern principalities, including our homeland of Tuscany. This put the bankers in the unpleasant position of making questionable loans to a king who was fighting against their families in the north of Italy. The fact that the king was doing this to protect France from the grasp of Holy Roman Emperor Charles V did not sway the Florentine bankers and merchants in his favor. The king regarded them as traitors and told them to consider themselves fortunate to escape arrest and imprisonment. Such a move would have allowed the king to declare his debts invalid, and many here in Lyon marvel that the king has not made such a declaration.

November 15, 1524 Dieppe

My spirit has been morose since the news of the loss of my log book and the means for making my map. This gloom has left me in a state of lethargy for nearly three months. I have not studied. I have written little in my journal. I have not even associated with friends who could possibly dispel my melancholy. I fear I have come to feel comfort in my misery, and am attempting to keep it healthy. To that end I recently began reading my journal of the voyage thinking that reminiscence would nourish my anguish.

To my surprise I found that I included many bits of information on courses and distances within the journal and I began to feel a surge of enthusiasm. I had of course kept the sketchy plots I made of our positions along the way. After examining the journal and reviewing my sketches, I found I have enough information to assemble a complete map. Good fortune! My map can be completed, and I am again in good spirits. Maggiolo now is months ahead. My map may not precede his but it will be completed in due course.

February 28, 1525 Dieppe

The situation with our king became even more dire while he was in the field with his army on the plains south of Milan near the town of Pavia. The emperor's forces overwhelmed them and even though the king's forces fought bravely, they were sorely defeated. Three of our leading generals lay dead in the field, including our own supporter, Admiral Bonnivet. The king himself was taken prisoner. Many of us think it was extremely unwise for the king to expose himself by going to the battlefield in the first place. Now France has lost her leader, and his mother, Louise of Savoy, has taken the role of regent in his absence. She is an experienced and wise woman accustomed to power and judicious rule. We pray that she will carry on with France's best interest at heart until the king is returned to us.

Tomorrow I plan to visit my priestly friend, Felice, in Rouen. We have not been together for more than a year now, and I fear he may have been moved to another diocese. Surely he would not go without leaving me a word of his whereabouts. If he is gone, I will try to find Berthram.

Chapter 20

May 15, 1528 Dieppe

This gap of more than three years in my journal has occurred for two reasons. First, I have had an almost daily focus on producing the map of our voyage of 1524. This has required a long and tedious process of recalculating and plotting our daily distances and bearings that were taken continuously along the coast. It was also necessary to sort out the names that had been given to places along the way. In some cases, Giovanni designated more than one name to a place, or perhaps it had become unclear which name went with which location. In truth, my journal and notes are somewhat unclear in places and I needed to sort out ambiguities. This will be a part of my new Mappa Mundi, which will ultimately show the most accurate representation of the coast of Francesca we surveyed from Florida to Labrador in relation to the rest of the world.

As I expected, a map of our Francesca was printed last year by Vesconte Maggiolo of Genoa. I am still irked that the task of making the king's map was not assigned to me. Alas, such are the vagaries of events, especially when kings are involved. I am firmly determined; I will finish my map.

The second interruption to my map was another voyage with Giovanni in 1526 to the low latitudes of New

World for a load of brazilwood. Supposedly Giovanni was to continue searching for a passage through the continent but the real purpose was simply commercial. He was to bring back three ship loads of brazilwood. In the spring and summer of that year we completed the voyage and made a handsome profit. The result was outstanding. All investors realized ten times their investment and plans began almost immediately for another voyage, which is now set for summer of this year.

The textile makers and merchants in Lyon are particularly interested in the valuable heartwood of the brazilwood tree for its excellent red color which can be extracted for dying cloth. This new resource has excited the textile industry by the sudden availability of a reliable, high-quality, red dye. With past sources red and purple dyes have been so expensive that only the nobility could afford to wear garments of these colors.

Translator's note: Laws governing the consumption of food and other goods, called sumptuary laws, were used in Europe during the thirteenth through the eighteenth centuries to control public access to items pertinent to social status. As the merchant class grew more affluent, it became necessary to establish a code to maintain a distinct visible identity for the nobility. These laws included such detail as the allowable length of long-toed shoes and which colors might be worn. Reds and purples were particularly reserved for people of noble birth.

Red dye, derived from relatively rare plants and insects in India and Turkey, was very expensive. The discovery of brazilwood in the New World led to an important new source of red dye from the heartwood of the tree, hence an excellent high-value cargo for the Verrazzano brothers.

As before, the investors led by none other than Admiral Philippe de Chabot himself, have eagerly invested and provided four ships, and put Giovanni in command again. Chabot replaced poor Bonnivet as Admiral of France upon Bonnivet's death in battle. Giovanni has long forgotten his gloomy days after the 1524 voyage, when the king showed no interest in another voyage. After a year, the king was released from imprisonment by the emperor but Giovanni had moved on to the idea of getting rich as a merchant mariner.

"Gerolamo," he said recently, "there is nothing wrong with being a merchant mariner again. In truth it now looks quite good. After my failed quest for glory and empire, I have come to see the merchant life in a different light. I see that I can accrue a little wealth, and have some adventure added to the mixture. I think this style is better for me after all. I often remind myself that matters could be worse; I could be constantly quarreling with Conflans again." Giovanni laughed heartily as he considered the joy of having Conflans out of his life.

This voyage will explore the area crossed by the Spanish explorer, Balboa in 1513. Balboa learned from local natives that the land narrowed to an isthmus there and perhaps there is a water passage in the area that has been missed by others. Again the primary reason is commercial but exploration for the passage must continue until it is found. Giovanni also plans to sail the coast of Francesca again, just to make sure he did not miss the elusive passage on that voyage of 1524. This will be an excellent voyage and I will certainly be aboard. I only regret that my traveling companion of 1524 will not be along. Berthram is now well established as a surgeon in Rouen.

May 30, 1528 Dieppe

Giovanni's third voyage to the New World began today with little fanfare. We are now just one of many ships departing daily from the busy port of Dieppe as our project has been pared to one ship. So now we again sail unaccompanied through the empty seas of the great Atlantic and along the coasts of the New World. Giovanni's plan is to sail from north to south past Francesca and Florida, then head southwest toward the isthmus crossed by Balboa, thence to Brazil for more wood. There is an element of risk in this venture, as the Portuguese feel they have a monopoly on all commerce in Brazil. Despite this it is always possible to find suppliers willing to trade for a good price. On our previous voyage we often anchored along a deserted length of shore and harvested a few trees on our own. This had the advantage of lower costs by excluding local cutters and suppliers.

May 31, 1528 At sea

We sailed out of La Manche as before but as we exited that channel, we headed due west along latitude forty-nine degrees north. This route required considerable tacking as we constantly faced northwesterly winds. We sailed for about forty days, backing and forthing, until the familiar northerly coast of the New World came into view. On this voyage there is no intent to record details of the land, the people, or the resources. We only want to have a second look for the passage. This seems a little peculiar to me. I have no sense that we might have missed any major features during our previous visit here but Giovanni wants to be certain. I think he is so convinced that such a passage exists that he must look again in the place he was so certain it would be. This means he wants another look at the Oriental Sea he saw separated from us by a narrow strip of land. He has expressed to me many times his doubts about the validity of that sighting, even though he made expansive plans around its existence. He feels he was too far from the shore to make a true assessment and wants to look again. The advantage for me was that I could fill some gaps in my information on bearings and distances caused by the loss of my logs.

July 8, 1528 At sea

Our voyage has now retraced our survey of 1524 by sailing from Newfoundland south to Florida. We have made no landings except for water and wood. Never have we attempted to look farther inland nor to encounter the native people for trading.

Our route took us again past Refugio, Angoulême, and other familiar places from our previous voyage. Giovanni and I often talked of the congenial people we found at those places, but stopping again was out of the question. This was, after all, a commercial voyage that was merely making a little detour before heading toward the sources of wood.

July 20, 1528 At sea

Fortunately we have not encountered a single Spanish ship as we sail in these Florida waters. During our previous voyage in this area, we were extremely cautious to avoid any possibility of seeing one of Spain's well armed ships. It now seems our fears were groundless. There are no Spanish ships here.

July 21, 1528 At sea

These tropical seas are the most beautiful I have ever sailed. They are dotted with small islands surrounded by white beaches and the clearest water I can imagine. Many of them also have dangerous reefs, sometimes near shore and sometimes offshore. In either case these reefs can easily ground a ship and tear a gaping hole in her hull. Of course we will need to stop for fresh water and wood from time to time but always we will need to take great care not to become careless in our approach.

July 22, 1528 At sea

The crewmen love this warm water for bathing. Each time we anchor, we immediately find several men in the water…bathing and washing clothing. We have lately been anchoring each night just for the pleasure of enjoying the water. Once Giovanni sent a crew ashore in the ship's boat for water and wood. No inhabitants of the island were encountered and we wondered if the islands might be deserted.

Our old cook, Carlito, from the 1524 voyage, is with us again. He assures us these islands are inhabited with very hostile people, some of whom are cannibals. We have long since learned that Carlito loves to scare young seamen with his tales of lands occupied by giants and man eaters. He says he was in these waters with Columbus and knows them well.

July 23, 1528 At sea

Giovanni is eager to be off to the mainland coast to look for a passage through Balboa's isthmus. Tomorrow we will weigh anchor and end this leisurely pace through the islands.

July 24, 1528 Offshore an island

This day started like most others during our sail through these stunningly beautiful tropical islands. The sun shone brightly and the breezes filled the sails.

As we neared an island, Giovanni saw plumes of smoke, a canoe on the beach, and other signs of habitation. He decided for the first time on this voyage it would be prudent to make contact with these people for possible trading and to determine if they possessed any valuable metals, or perhaps this would even be another source of trees for our cargo.

The island, like many others, had offshore reefs in many places around the island. Giovanni did not care to look for a spot where reefs might be absent. The inland plume of smoke was nearest to this side of the island so this was where we should anchor. We anchored the ship and lowered the boat into the water. Giovanni directed me to stay with the ship as next in command while he and six crewmen rowed toward a deserted beach.

The offshore reef presented a minor barrier even for the small boat, because the surf broke along the reef. But the wide lagoon beyond the beach was like water on a pond. As the boat reached the beach, Giovanni and the six men stepped ashore and pulled the boat out of the water, then turned and began to walk across the beach.

Like a sudden explosion, a hundred native men ran out of the trees and immediately attacked our seven shipmates with stone weapons and spears. The scene that followed was the most horrifying I have ever seen, and I think I shall never recover from it. Giovanni and the six crewmen were simultaneously killed by screaming natives striking, cutting, and stabbing. The lifeless bodies were then stripped of all clothing, after which the natives began cutting off large pieces of flesh. The white sands of the beach became red, soaked with the blood of my poor brother and his six crewmen. As fast as the natives stripped off a piece of flesh, they ate some of it on the spot with great shouts and jumping about in a frenzy of excitement. As they reached the interior of the bodies, they began eating inner parts as well. When one of them would cut out a heart, he would hold it above like a trophy and then cut it to bits for distribution to the others. The natives themselves became covered with blood and gore beyond description. The entire spectacle appeared to be a ritualistic orgy of mutilation and flesh eating.

To those of us left on the ship this was a most horrifying and shocking experience. We had no boat to go to the rescue nor would there have been time even if we had one. As a merchant ship we had no arms capable of stopping the carnage. The whole disaster erupted in an instant and ended in minutes. There was nothing to be done.

When the murderous hoard left the beach they carried away all remnants down to the last bone, including all items of clothing and the boat. They left behind a ghastly scene with unimaginable gore amidst the bloody sand.

Although we were distant from the shore we were close enough during the melee to see and hear the entire scene. Some of our crewmen screamed obscenities at the horde, and not one of us was without tears on his face at seeing our mates slaughtered and eaten before our eyes. As the natives disappeared into the forest we all continued standing at the rail as though in a trance. It was some time before anyone moved or talked. Even Carlito was silent. I am sure he will never again speak of cannibals to this crew. I stood for a long time before I realized that we must come to our senses and tend to our own well-being.

The first business was to protect the ship by moving her away from this dreadful place. We now had no boat with which to go ashore for future replenishment of wood and water. After watching this scene I am uncertain if anyone on our crew could ever again be induced to go ashore in an unknown place.

The lack of a boat also became a part of the next major decision. Should we seek a Spanish or Portuguese settlement in the hope of finding a replacement for our boat? If we acquired a boat, should we then proceed to our original destination for a load of brazilwood? Or should we return immediately to France empty handed? This last choice held the least risk for the safety of the boat and crew, and considering that the crew was now six hands fewer than before, I opted for a direct return to France. This option will cause certain loss for all investors and will surely end my future prospects for command of a merchant ship. Nevertheless it is the most prudent choice and I will simply have to live with the consequences, whatever they may be. How could I possibly continue to Brazil as though nothing had happened? To that end I commanded the pilot to set a course that would return this ill-fated boat with its forlorn crew back to Dieppe.

I hate to leave whatever remains of my brother on this damnable island. He will never receive a proper burial with an appropriate monument. I must do my best to see that he is remembered for his great accomplishments. Poor Giovanni enjoyed many successes, but could see only his disappointments. Now it has all come to naught for him…and for me too. I am beset with indescribable grief until my dying day.

Translator's note: Gerolamo finished his map the next year, 1529, a reproduction of which I found in the box of Verrazzano papers in the Rouen library. His journal ended, and he was never heard of again after completion of the map.

January 20, 2011 Rouen

I've finally finished the basic translation and booked a flight home. Now I have a few weeks worth of annotation and notes to complete. The main thing facing me is wondering if there is anything left of a relationship with Lorena. My work here has gone well but at a great unexpected cost.

I took Nicole to a nice restaurant for dinner and told her how much I appreciated all the help she had given me. During dinner I decided to risk having my hopes dashed and raised the question of a future with her. "Nicole, I'm growing a strong love for you and I want to be with you. I want our relationship to continue and I must ask you to come to New York as soon as possible. You have valuable skills and I'm sure you could quickly find work in New York. Would you consider coming?

"Ross, I am very fond of you and have enjoyed being with you too. But I can't give you an immediate answer. I have many ties in France and love my job. I am well respected among the library staff and it would pain me to leave. If you want in immediate answer, then it must be 'no.' For that reason I must ask you to wait and give me time to think. Believe me, I am so happy you asked me."

We finished the dinner with coffee at her apartment and I ended up in her bed for the night again. She went with me to the train station for a fond farewell and hopeful promises to keep in touch with genuine expectations of meeting again. Unfortunately I have no idea how long she wants to wait before answering my plea to come to New York.

January 24, 2011   New York

When I returned home, Lorena had moved out of our apartment and left a terse note saying, "Don't bother calling." Suddenly I miss Nicole more than I ever imagined.

February 16, 2011   New York

I sent a query letter to six big name publishers with a description of my work and a suggestion that I send them a full book proposal. They each returned letters in short order saying, "While your work has obvious merit, it does not fit our needs at the present time." So this is it? My great manuscript discovery will simply founder and sink like a ship in an indifferent sea. I know I'll eventually find a way to publish Gerolamo's journal, but this news deflates my hopes for quick acceptance.

Perhaps the Verrazzano brothers felt the same twist in the gut when their ambitions were thwarted by others. Both those gallant gentlemen felt bitterness. Even though each achieved his goal, they despaired when the result differed from their expectations. They must have felt the agony that comes from watching a cherished dream slip through their fingers. Gerolamo tried to put a positive light on it when he told Giovanni that his expectations had blinded him to his real achievements, but Giovanni could only see failure.

Author's notes

Gerolamo Verrazzano's supposed journal found by Professor Ross Turner is a document that does not, but certainly could, exist. Most of this account of Verrazzano's voyage is adapted from Giovanni's letter to the king of France in 1524. The events described, the first contacts with Native Americans, most of their behavior, dress, and foods; the storms in the Atlantic; the boy taken prisoner; the landing sites and place names are all derived from the report. The description of the final disaster on a beach in the Caribbean Sea is from other documented sources.

Verrazzano's conflict with Conflans is fiction, and many historians accept that Conflans actually made the voyage with Verrazzano based on his receipt of 100 livre on the date of their return. Samuel Morison wrote that 100 livre was far too small an amount to pay to a man of Conflans' stature for a six month voyage, and suggested that the 100 livre was only a retainer. Also, ex-naval officer Morison maintained that two men of captain status on the *Dauphine* would simply be unworkable.

As thorough as it is, Verrazzano's report left many unanswered questions. For example, there is no mention by name of any other person who went on the voyage. Even his brother Gerolamo, who is known from other sources to have sailed with him, is never mentioned in Verrazzano's report. Therefore all characters on board the *Dauphine*, except the Verrazzano brothers, are fictitious. Real life characters actually present in the story include: Giovanni da Verrazzano, Gerolamo da Verrazzano, Viscount Jean Ango, Captain Antoine Conflans, and Admiral Bonnivet, The reader will also recognize many other familiar historical figures and events, such as the kings of France and England and their meeting at the Field of the Cloth of Gold. The names of bankers and wealthy merchants in Lyon, including relatives of Verrazzano, are part of the known record. Both Vesconte de Maggiolo and Gerolamo da Verrazzano finally produced maps based on the voyage of 1524.

Much is known about Viscount Ango. The appearance of his home, Pensée, in Dieppe is documented although the house no longer exists. The Chateau de Ango still exists a few miles outside Dieppe, but had not been built at the time of this story. Also documented are the names a few of Ango's ships including: *Dauphine* (leased to the navy), *Normande*, and *Pensée*. Ango is, in fact, the subject of several books.

I depended heavily on some other excellent sources. The most exhaustive book on Verrazzano is by Lawrence C. Wroth, *The Voyages of Giovanni da Verrazzano, 1524-1528*, (Yale University Press, 1979). Wroth left no stone unturned and produced the most authoritative investigation of Verrazzano. Another was Jacques Hebert, a French historian who wrote an engaging and readable account of the voyage, *When New York was called Angoulême*, (Trans-ocean Press, 1949). For pure readability Samuel E. Morison is excellent, *The European discovery of America*, (Oxford University Press, 1974). This prolific historian and former admiral lends authenticity to the story by his thorough knowledge of sailors and sailing ships, and his visits and over-flights to historic places armed with maps and aerial photographs.

Other useful sources included: *Jean Ango, Vicomte de Dieppe*, by Gabriel Gravier, 1903; T. Calderon, *Etude biographique sur Ango et son Epoque: Précedée de recherches sur le commerce et la navigation au moyen-age*, 1891; Eugène Chapus, *Dieppe et ses environs*, 1853.

Cartographer Dennis Fitzsimmons provided a valuable critique of my maps. His sharp eye for error caught numerous glitches. I am especially grateful for help from two people in Dieppe. Marie-Christine Hugot, with the Chateau de Ango in Dieppe, provided invaluable help and an abundance of material on Viscount Ango and Dieppe in the sixteenth century. Also Christine Bert of the Hotel Aguado in Dieppe provided some interesting information on Dieppe in modern times.

Most of all I am grateful to my wife, Sue, for her insightful comments, suggestions, and perceptive editing along with big doses of encouragement.

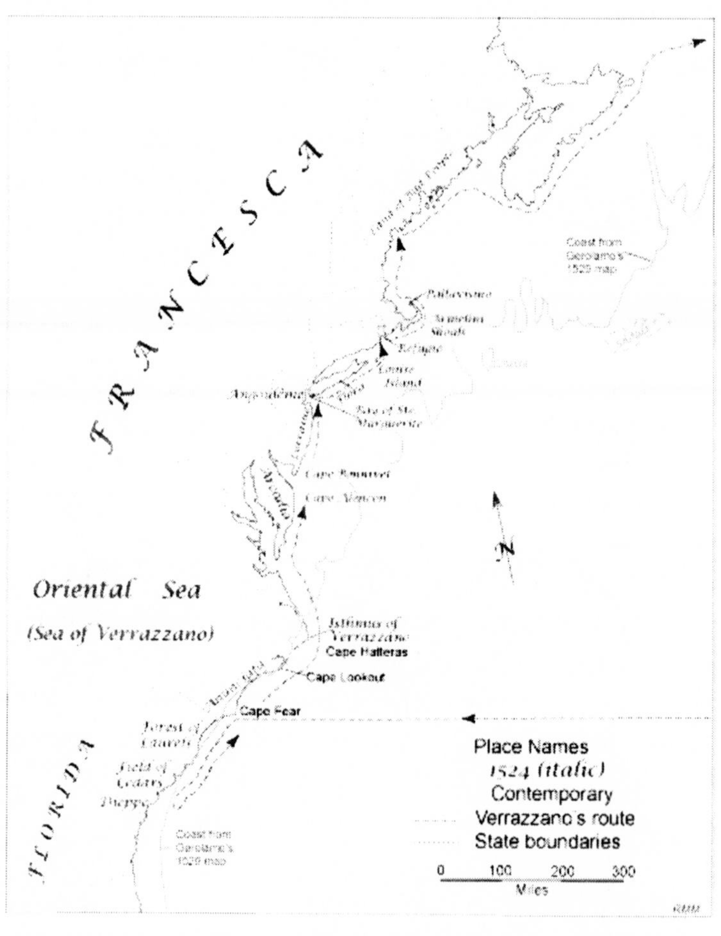

Verrazzano's route along the east coast of North America. Outline of Gerolamo's 1529 map is shown as light gray line. Map by author.

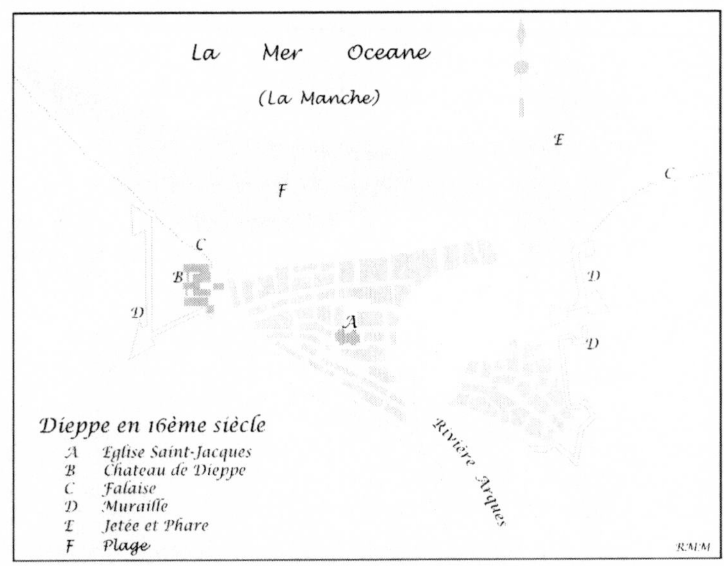

City of Dieppe in Verrazzano's time. A-Church of Saint Jacques; B-Dieppe Castle; C-Sea cliff; D-Walls; E-Lighthouse at end of jetty; F-Beach. Adapted from *Dieppe et ses environs* by Eugène Chapus, 1853.